MW01244813

Mabel,
Murder,
&
Muffins

A Mabel Wickles Cozy Mystery

By

Sharon Mierke

Other works by Sharon Mierke

Mabel Wickles Mystery Series

Deception By Design
Calamity by the Car Wash
Cold Case Conundrum
Frozen Identity

Beryl Swallows Mystery Series

Virtual Enemies
Case Closed.not

Historical Fiction

Sarah's Valley
Return to Sarah's Valley
The Widow's Walk
Old House

Copyright   2019   Sharon Mierke

Sharon Mierke

The twinkling lights of Parson's Cove grew smaller and smaller in the distance. In less than an hour, the dark late model car merged with the other traffic on the Interstate. One vehicle blending in with hundreds, unnoticed and unmemorable. The driver's hand relaxed and dropped down. It touched the cold object on the seat. The gun. Quickly both hands gripped the steering wheel again.

But, there was no blood. Didn't everyone bleed all over the place when they were shot? That, in itself, felt like good omen. How could a person explain blood stains in the trunk of a car?

If there were any truth to what Mabel Wickles said; that young new sheriff and his incompetent deputy would never solve the case anyway. And all that nonsense about her and some old retired sheriff working together? How ridiculous was that!

It was the perfect place to dump a body. It would have been better deeper into the woods but that woman showed up. Why would an old woman like that be walking down the path in the woods in the night anyway? Crazy. Maybe the whole town was crazy.

Didn't matter now anyway, did it?

Chapter One

"Who's the creep in this picture?"

"Creep? What creep?"

Flori handed the camera to me. "The guy who's giving you that menacing look."

"How can you see if someone's giving me a menacing look?" I held the back of the camera up to my face and squinted.

"No, Mabel, hold it out about a foot. You know your eyes don't work close up."

She was right, as usual. My eyes saw only a vague impression. I moved it gradually away until the picture came into focus.

"What creep?" I repeated.

She pointed to the corner of the screen. "*That* creep."

I looked at her. "You've got to be kidding me. You know that man is giving me a dirty look and I can't even tell if it's a man or a woman?"

She shrugged. "I don't know how many times I've told you, you need glasses but do you ever listen to me?"

Before I could, for the umpteenth time, explain how

glasses bothered my ears and hurt my nose, and how I can't think when I'm wearing them, she continued, "Doesn't look to me like he's too happy about getting his picture taken; that's for sure."

"Well, if he's the one who ruined my photo, I'm the one who should be upset. Why would a person walk right out in front of someone who's obviously taking a picture?"

Flori sighed. "I suppose you could cut his face out and fill it in with something when you put it in your scrapbook. It will take something away from it though." She sighed again, this time with a bit more drama.

"Of course, it will take something away from it. There will be a big hole in the corner filled with a silly sticker. And, how many times do I have to tell you that I'm *not* going to do scrap booking?"

"Well, we'll talk about it later, dear. I would help you, you know. Besides, there is no wrong way to scrapbook. I've told you that a million times." She gave me a sympathetic smile, which transformed instantly into a brilliant beam. "I still can't believe you won a trip to Las Vegas. Imagine! You're the first person in Parson's Cove to win a trip. All because you sent in a top off a cereal box. I never thought that ever happened in real life. You know what I mean, Mabel? I thought those contests were all bogus."

"Well, you now have your trust in humanity redeemed. And, it wasn't a cereal box. It was an ad in the paper from some cereal company I'd never heard of before. Besides, I don't know why everyone keeps saying that I'm the first person from Parson's Cove to win a trip. Surely, in the past hundred years or so, someone must have won one. People forget, that's all. Of course, I did have to answer a skill-testing question. You tend to not mention that."

"Right, and the answer was 'ten.' You could've answered that just counting your fingers."

"How do you think I got it?" I crossed my eyes and held up both hands, pretending to count.

Flori's orange hair bounced and her body shook as she settled in for a good laugh. When she was finished and I'd given her the last of the tissues from the box, I said, "You might think that sounds like nothing but trust me, when you're under the gun like that, I couldn't have told you my mother's name. It's extremely stressful."

Flori held my camera up again and moved to another picture. I'd told her to wait and look at them when they were all printed but she didn't have the patience for that.

"These are amazing, Mabel. I can't believe you took these beautiful pictures." Flori's eyes welled up with tears as she clicked from one picture to the next.

"Don't get all sentimental on me. It's no big deal. All you do is set it on 'auto' and shoot, you know. It doesn't exactly take a rocket scientist to figure it out."

"But, a digital camera? Who would've thought you'd be so …" She searched for the right word. "Impulsive? … I mean, it took years for you to get rid of your dial-up phone. And, remember how you fought with me over getting the one with the answering machine?" She raised her eyebrows until they disappeared under her curly orange bangs.

That was a rhetorical question because she knew I wouldn't be answering it. Besides, she didn't give me time to say anything anyway. She took one breath and continued, "Your next investment has to be a couple of good coffee makers."

"What's wrong with the ones I have?"

"They're not coffee makers. You have old glass

8

percolators. They're antiques, if you must know. I don't think they even make them anymore. One of these days, they're going to get too hot on the stove and burst into a million pieces. That little wire thingy you put underneath doesn't do a thing." She shook her finger at me and once again, her eyebrows disappeared from view. "Don't say I didn't warn you."

"Huh! I might be an antique and my percolators might be antiques but don't say that together we don't make the best coffee in the Northern Hemisphere."

Her eyes screwed shut, her lips quivered, and her upper body shook. "Now it's the Northern Hemisphere? You used to say the world," she gasped in between shakes. "You mean your coffee isn't what it used to be?"

"It's my muffins, Flori. My muffins are the best in the world." It looked like my friend was ready to burst into something. "For goodness sake, Flori, are you laughing or crying?"

She grabbed a handful of tissues from the second box on the counter and wiped her eyes. "Oh, you know I'm laughing, you silly old thing." She groaned and sniffed. "I haven't had a good laugh in days." She looked at me through red-rimmed eyes. "Well, ever since you left for your trip, that is."

I couldn't help grinning. Flori and I have been friends since we were in Kindergarten. We know what each other is thinking before we even speak. Well, maybe not word for word but we usually know in which direction the other is going. This sometimes isn't too good. I'm more than likely heading in the wrong direction and Flori is following me, trying to either catch up or head me off at the pass.

Actually, if someone were to take a close look at us, he

or she would be astonished that we're friends at all. Two people couldn't be more like chalk and cheese. Flori is this larger than life woman (I mean this in a literal sense), married for almost half a century to the same infuriating man, Jake, and is blessed with multiple kids and grandkids.

I, on the other hand, weigh about as much as one of her legs, have never married, and have multiple cats, with no grand-cats. She lives in a two-story house with five bedrooms and a wrap-around veranda, three blocks from mine where Jake, who is now unfortunately retired, grows enough vegetables to feed the entire population of Parson's Cove. In the winter, he ice fishes and keeps warm by secretly slipping Southern Comfort into his thermos of coffee. That's Jake's life all rolled up into a nutshell.

(Speaking of Jake's garden: if one more person comes into my shop, complaining about all the zucchini he's given them, I'll have to speak to Flori. I procrastinate because I know it will mean a big upset and no one wants to be around for that. Flori gives everything she has when she laughs but she does likewise when she cries. Every body part gets involved. It's not for the faint of heart.)

She wiped the tears away again, put the camera about two inches from her eyes and squinted at my three-inch LCD screen. This time, she flicked through the last fifty-two pictures in silence. After all, even Flori can 'oooo' and 'awww' only so many times.

She pulled herself up off the chair. "Everyone in town is so proud of you. It's hard for me to believe you really went. And, all by yourself." She reached over and proceeded to crush me to her bosom.

"Okay, let me up for air now." I smiled at my dear friend. "I have to admit it was an adventure, even at my age. But if I'd known you couldn't come, I never would've gone.

You know that.

"Don't even say that, Mabel. How could I help it? It's not every day that I get a new granddaughter. Especially when it was Jakie's firstborn. You know I had no choice."

"I know, but to tell you the truth, it seems those girls of yours are popping out babies almost every month or so. But I suppose this one was different. After all, who could ever imagine Jake Junior becoming a responsible father? Not me, that's for sure."

"You're so silly, Mabel. You know I always believed in my oldest son. Even when he was getting into trouble all the time." She moved towards the door. "Well, guess I'd better go and start supper. Jake will be starving. He went fishing with Scully and Jim this afternoon. All that sun and fresh air makes a man hungry, you know."

"All that sun and beer is what you mean, right? No wonder the lake water has a yellowy tinge with all those men out there drinking beer all day."

She went out the door and I could hear her still giggling half way down the block.

It was hard to get back into the swing of things. Not that there's much 'swing' to my life. I have a little shop called *Mabel's Fables and Things*. Originally, my father sold groceries in it (and, of course, it had a different name). I live in the same house in which I was born. Since I was an only child, there was no battle over property with siblings when my father died at age ninety. He'd been a widower for over ten years. I often think he kept living after Mother died so he could finally enjoy unwholesome food and stay up late to watch old movies on television. He died in his sleep with a smile on his face. I'm hoping to be blessed with the same genes.

The transition after his death was, I suppose, as painless as one could expect. My routine never changed much; it's just that the old house became a bit quieter. My father's downstairs bedroom became my pantry (the biggest in Parson's Cove) and when my cats arrived, they claimed his old recliner as their own. That was fine with me as I'd always found it to be lumpy. My mother's chair was too straight and hard so I moved that upstairs into the sewing room and I bought myself one that was 'just right.' I would've taken my mother's chair out of the living-room sooner but for some reason, my father enjoyed sitting across from it and gazing at it with what I thought was a smug look.

It was almost five and I was quite certain no more customers would be coming in so I decided to close up shop. Although my arches ached from standing all day and I'd gone through a can of coffee, I don't think anyone actually bought anything. Folks started dropping in at nine to see if I'd survived my trip, if I had any exciting stories to tell, and to have a free cup of coffee. At one point, about noon, there was a line-up waiting outside to get in and I had to yell, "Okay, everybody, I know you're happy to see me but if you aren't planning on buying anything, could you come back tomorrow?" I turned to pour someone a cup of coffee and when I looked up, everyone was gone. Except the 'someone' who wanted her free cup of coffee.

Our drugstore stays open until eight (although they will fill prescription drugs at any time of day or night. All you have to do is ring the buzzer and someone emerges from the upstairs apartment.) I locked the front door and headed across the street. Like my father, I lock the front door and leave the back one unlocked. For the first time, I was going to print pictures from a kiosk. At last, no more waiting for my film to be developed, printed, and mailed back from the city. Well, I had to see it to believe it!

"Hey, Mabel," Merlin Cowel boomed from behind the counter before I'd even shut the door. "Welcome home. Saw that big crowd over at your store today. Guess everybody thought you might not want to come back to Parson's Cove. Thought we'd be too boring for you now." He held back his head and roared. If there's one thing Merlin can do, it's roar. I try to be as nice as I can to the man because he sometimes sends customers my way but if he pops over for a cup of coffee (and he does quite often), I give it to him in a paper cup and try to convince him that he's needed in his own establishment. My place is too small for his big voice.

"No, Merlin, I decided I'd come back. Not enough excitement in Las Vegas. Too quiet for my taste."

"Ha! That's a good one, Mabel," he bellowed and slapped his hand on the counter so hard that two pens flew to the floor. He didn't notice. "Now, what can I do for you, little lady?"

"First of all, you don't have to yell, Merlin. I'm not deaf, okay?"

He grinned and yelled, "Sure thing, little lady."

"Secondly, you can stop calling me 'little lady.'"

"Sure thing, little lady."

Does he do this to irritate me or does he have cotton balls for brains? I'm just grateful his wife fills out the prescriptions.

I held up my tiny memory card. "I'd like to get my pictures from the trip printed." I looked over at the intimidating kiosk. "I'm not sure I know how to work this contraption. Could you help?" I held up my hand. "And if

13

you say 'sure thing, little lady,' I'll never give you another cup of coffee again. Got that?"

Before he could answer, I said, "Just nod."

He nodded.

It was after seven by the time I got out of there and my eardrums were still buzzing when I walked into my house. In my hand, however, I had my precious pictures and memories of my great adventure. Now Flori could hold each photo in her hand and admire them all over again.

The cats swarmed me as soon as I stuck my foot in the door. I don't know if they were concerned that I might disappear for five days again or if they were just plain hungry. It's hard to tell with cats. I never planned to have any cats at all. In fact, I'm not what you would call an old cat lady. There are such people, you know, but I'm not one of them. I don't go gaga over kittens or have pictures and ornaments of cats all over the house. My original desire was to have one cat to keep me company during the lonely winter evenings and to catch the occasional field mouse that sneaks into my house each fall. Actually, it wasn't my idea at all; it was Flori's inspiration and she spread the word.

About a week later, a customer brought a small male kitten into the store. I named him Phil. *Him* turned out to be *Her* and *Her* had five kittens. The father of this brood, a mangy stray that hung around Main Street Café, joined his family. That made seven and I made darn sure that none of them ever procreated again. That was several years ago. Now, some have found homes elsewhere and are happy. I would like to say I never miss them but that would be lying. Sammy was one of my favorites but he's found happiness out in the country. He was the only one that seemed to enjoy solving crimes. Maybe that's why I miss that cat.

The moment their dishes were full, they scattered in

different directions and forgot who had fed them. Cats, it seems, have no idea what good manners entail. With a sigh, I picked up the teakettle and filled it with water. After bingeing at 'all you can eat' buffets during my trip, I hadn't returned to my usual cooking routine. Nothing seemed to taste good anymore. My taste buds were too accustomed to grease and gravy. I'm sure I ate at least twenty thousand calories a day while I was away but I hadn't gained an ounce. Flori says it's disgusting. Sometimes I'm convinced she thinks I have some sort of eating disorder.

"I can't help it," I tell her. "It's my metabolism. The scale is stuck at a hundred and two and there's nothing I can do about it."

"But it's not fair," she wails. "I look at food and get fat."

To make her feel better, I always say, "Don't say fat, Flori. You are voluptuous; that's what you are."

"Oh, thank you, Mabel." And, she wipes away the tears.

I opened the fridge door to see if anything looked appealing and all the cats rushed over to join me.

"All right, you heathens, you've eaten. Get out of here." Three of them already had half their bodies inside. I yanked them out and shut the door, hoping no heads were still in the way. It was then that I noticed the answering machine light blinking.

I obtained the touchtone phone and answering machine to appease Flori. It seems that's one of my many purposes in life. If there were any way I could get away with it, I would get rid of that contraption. Unfortunately, it's part of the phone and I don't even know how to shut the stupid thing off. Besides, Flori would never speak to me again if I did. Since she now has a cell phone, all she does is dangle it in front of me but knows better than to ever suggest I invest in one too. It's enough that I have a touchtone phone, a digital camera, and a laptop.

I figure if someone phones and there's no answer, that person knows I'm not home or I'm in the bathroom or I don't want to talk to anyone and she or he can try again. With this idiotic machine, they leave a message and then the onus is on me; now *I'm* under obligation to return the call. Something isn't right with that. If I don't call, everyone gets in an uproar: "Mabel, you didn't return my call." "Mabel, didn't you get my message?" "Mabel, how come you didn't call back?" "Don't you ever check your messages, Mabel?"

No matter how long I stood and glared, the light kept right on blinking - three messages and probably all from Flori. She'd be wondering why I wasn't home yet. I told her I was getting my pictures printed right after work but she probably forgot. If I called her back now, she could easily take up an hour or more of my time. Not that I didn't enjoy her calls, it's just that I was so looking forward to savoring my pictures over a quiet cup of tea. I left the light blinking and sat down at the table. Before I could pull the pictures out of the first envelope, the kettle whistled. I grabbed the teapot, a cup, a spoon, and the little jug of honey and sat down again.

I still couldn't get over the fact that I, Mabel Wickles, from little Parson's Cove had won a five day trip to Las Vegas. Sin city. Of course, what happens in Las Vegas, stays in Las Vegas, right? Since in my case absolutely nothing had happened there, I guess I could bring it all home with me. In fact, I would never think of telling anyone here (well, perhaps Flori someday) but after about three hours, I was homesick. I will admit, Hoover Dam lived up to its name - it was 'dam' interesting. Other than that, if you've see one slot machine, you've seen them all. Of course, there was the food. I suppose that in itself could be worth the trip. Overall, however, there was too much noise, too many people, and too many lights - too much hustle and bustle. Did I say too many lights? I still get flashes in my eyes occasionally.

Four other people had also won the trip: three women and one man. I was the oldest, the shortest, and the lightest. The one and only man, Ralph Murphy, was probably in his fifties. He had a nasty habit of scratching his scalp every five minutes or so, thus leaving behind a layer of white flakes on all his shirts. Other than that, I liked him better than I liked any of the women.

Sally Goodrich sat beside me on the plane. It was hard to guess her age because she'd had so many surgeries on her face and probably other areas of her body too. Her swollen lips formed a puffy straight line and she had to talk through her teeth. She reminded me of Flori's kids when they were small and made scary faces. Her long blond hair was in desperate need of a retouch and she must have weighed close to two hundred pounds. All the fat was in the right places; it's just that there was an over abundance of it. You always had the feeling that she might explode out of her clothes. Since she was so honest about all her face-lifts (at times, going into gory details), I thought I'd ask another obvious question and one that everyone was talking about behind her back:

"Have you ever thought of liposuction for your derriere?" I asked, one morning as we were waiting in the hotel lobby to leave for a tour.

Her eyes got big and she said, "Are you serious? It cost enough to get it looking like this." With that, she tried to lift her chin but I think the skin was too tight. She did manage, however, to swing her hips as she walked to the bus. If a person watched them for too long, I imagine one could almost get seasick.

Grace Hobbs and Andrea Williams were the other two women. We used to have a Mr. Hobbs living in Parson's Cove but Grace said she was sure he wasn't a relative. Of course, after I learned she was married, I realized he wouldn't have been her relative anyways - he would've been her husband's relative.

I didn't see too much of Grace and Andrea after the second day because, I discovered, they would rather gamble than tour. Gamble and eat. Preferably at the same time. I didn't see much of Sally or Ralph anymore either because they, I discovered, liked each other. I was happy to have my camera and a good pair of walking shoes.

Of course, there was Mr. Hatcher. He was the cereal company's representative. He sort of drifted in and out of our lives while we were there. He was always in the background, making sure we were looked after, making sure we didn't get lost, making sure we didn't get too bored or get into trouble, I guess. At least, that's what we were told. It was hard to form an opinion about him because it seemed to me that he wasn't very interested in his job. I asked him how many times he'd been to Vegas with a group of winners but his answer was very vague.

On the last day, all of us grand prizewinners met in the lobby of our hotel. It's hard to believe but I think I was the only one who looked like I'd had a fairly enjoyable time; therefore, that wasn't saying much for the others. I assumed Grace and Andrea were going home much poorer because they were very sullen. It appeared that Sally and Ralph must have had a tiff because they weren't talking to each other. Or, perhaps it was just Sally not communicating with Ralph.

He still seemed to be walking around, looking like a sick dog. It made me feel much better; at least, I would have pictures of Hoover Dam and the desert to take home. In my opinion, all of them had wasted what could've been a perfectly good free vacation.

Moreover, I did have some excellent pictures. I slowly examined each of the one hundred and twenty three pictures that I'd taken. How could so many photos fit on that small memory card? Of course, I now realized that no matter how many you took of the dam, you could never really get the depth of it all. Forty-four pictures taken at different angles and each one looked the same. I might have been carried away with the shots of my bedroom too. Five pictures of my whirlpool tub were a bit much. I thought Flori might find those interesting though. Also, my bed with the canopy. I took four different angles of that.

Flori had been right about that one picture. I had snapped it outside one of those hotels where a twenty-foot tall mechanical cowboy kept lifting his hat off and then putting it back on. I took that one for Jake. I, obviously, hadn't noticed the man walking right in front of me. All my attention was on the cowboy and his hat. It took some concentration to catch it at the right moment with the hat in midair. Now I not only had the cowboy holding his hat up in the air, I had a gangster staring at me from the corner of the picture. At least, that was my first impression. Well, no need for me to worry. After all, this was Vegas. He was probably someone's doting father or husband.

I realized after examining it more carefully, he wasn't looking at me at all; he was looking at someone or something either behind me or beside me. For some reason, that seemed to ease the tension in my shoulders.

The phone rang. I jumped and the pictures flew to the floor. The cats raced over, thinking it was a treat for them, sniffed, gave me a disdainful look, and walked away in all different directions. Meanwhile, the phone continued to ring. I left the pictures where they lay and stood up. I got up slowly because both knees were bothering me. I figured it was from walking on cement all day, every day, during my vacation.

"Where, on earth, have you been? I've been calling and calling," Flori yelled in my ear.

"Well, you haven't been calling and calling, Flori. I'm sure I told you that after work, I was getting my pictures printed. You can get instant pictures now, you know. My goodness, how did you manage when I was gone? You must've been up half the night worrying about me."

"If you must know, I was. All I could do was imagine you alone in that huge city with all those gamblers. You have no idea how relieved I am that you're home, safe and sound."

"I phoned you every night. You knew very well that I was safe."

"If you're home now, why haven't you returned my call? It's after eight. I left two messages for you."

"Or did you leave three? My machine is saying there are three messages."

"I phoned twice. Good Heavens! You have messages and you haven't checked them? You'd better listen to the other one, Mabel. Who knows? Maybe you won another trip!"

"One is enough for me, thanks very much. By the way, why don't you come to the shop in the morning to look at the pictures? It's much nicer than trying to see them on my camera. And," I added, "why don't you bring over breakfast?"

Feeding people is one of Flori's favorite things.

I hung up the phone and pressed the blinking red light. The first two were from Flori. In the first message, she sounded a bit tentative (as if she hadn't left a message in five days and had forgotten how to bawl me out); in the second, almost hysterical (more normal).

The third one made shivers run down my spine. Perhaps, 'what happens in Las Vegas, stays in Las Vegas' is only a myth.

Chapter Two

"I think you're getting yourself in a flap over nothing."

Reg Smee, our local retired sheriff, sat across the table from me with a half-filled cup of coffee in one hand and a half-eaten banana muffin in the other. Several crumbs clung to his shirt and there was a neat pile of them on my tablecloth. Not that my muffins are dry and crumbly but when you eat three without hardly taking a breath, there will be crumbs.

I called Reg because I wasn't totally comfortable with Sheriff Jim yet. I'm not saying that he wasn't a good sheriff. I think it's mostly because I knew him and his deputy, Scully, when they were children. It's still difficult for me to look at them and see two mature adults. I am working on that.

"I think you're just trying to placate me because it's late and you want to go home, Reg. Now, put your ear closer and listen carefully. This person is threatening my life."

"Mabel, Mabel, Mabel." He shook his head. "No one is threatening your life. Besides, the recording is garbled and there's too much static and background noise to make out what the person is saying."

"Please, Reg, humor me. Listen again."

He gave an exaggerated sigh and said, "Okay. Hit the darn button again."

"... ... Wickles, listen .... get away ... . Las Vegas ... ... everyone in Parson's Cove ... . wicked. ... ... jail ... ... dying. ... ... your life. Watch out ... ... leave."

"See, Reg, that is definitely a threatening call. Don't you get it? Whoever this is, is telling me that I got away with something in Las Vegas; something very wicked. Now, they're out to get me, and everyone in Parson's Cove. And, I'm not sure, but I think they're telling me that I'm going to spend the rest of my life in the pen, until I die." A shiver passed through my body. "They're warning me to watch out and telling me to leave."

"Say you're right, Mabel." The Sheriff looked up at me over his reading glasses. (I have no idea why he had to put on his glasses to listen to the tape recording.) "Now, 'fess up, who did you exasperate when you were in Las Vegas?"

"Exasperate? That's a harsh word. I know you think I must have done something but I really didn't. This is what makes it so frustrating. What did I do? I did nothing. I was on my best behavior. I was a normal tourist. Well, not *normal* normal, if you know what I mean. I didn't gamble and everyone who goes to Vegas gambles, right?" My heart started pounding. "Do you think there are people in Las Vegas who come after you if you don't gamble?"

"No, Mabel. No one threatens your life if you don't gamble. It would be more likely someone would come after you if you did."

"I wonder if someone *thought* I gambled and now they're here to take my money?"

Reg drained his cup and stood up.

"I doubt it. Most thieves don't leave a message; they just arrive in the middle of the night." He slapped on his old hunting cap and headed for the door. "Thanks for the coffee. If I were you, I'd go to bed and stop fretting about this. It's almost ten and you'll probably have lots of customers in tomorrow again. Get a good night's sleep. Maybe whoever phoned will call back or pop into the store tomorrow and the mystery will be solved."

I shook my head. "I wish I could make out if it's a man or a woman on that thing."

"If you can't tell that, how can you tell that it's threatening?"

"I don't know, Reg. Maybe it's just the person's tone of voice."

He reached over and patted my arm.

"I'm sure it's nothing. Someone from here might be playing a crank call. Let's face it, there could be a bit of jealousy. After all, not many from here have ever been to Las Vegas."

"Do you think so? I never even thought of that." My heart pounded faster again but this time it was more excitement than fear. "I bet it's Esther Flynn come back to Parson's Cove to haunt me. Who else would do such a thing?"

"Now, Mabel, don't go making accusations like that. You can't blame Esther for everything in life that happens to you, you know. Besides, she doesn't even live in Parson's Cove anymore and I hear she's happily married."

"I know that, but I think you're right - it has to be a crank call. I'll bet you anything Esther did this to upset me because she's jealous."

"Mabel, you're not listening; I didn't say it was Esther who made the crank call. I didn't even insinuate it was Esther. And don't you tell anyone I did."

He might have said more but I shut the door.

That had to be it. I played the tape again. And, again. If I could only make out the voice. Reg was right, of course, I couldn't come right out and blame Esther Flynn or whatever her married name was now. She'd been gone from Parson's Cove for a few years but that wouldn't stop her from phoning. It certainly didn't stop her from coming into my shop every time she did come to town. I knew how to handle her though. At least, I should be able to after all the years of experience I've had.

Esther was a thorn in my side since the day we met. That was over sixty years ago. Flori, Esther, and I started school together. She was the most evil child I ever knew. Satan's spawn if there ever was one. I've forgotten most of the tricks that she played on me. I'm not the sort to keep track but getting me kicked out of school because she claimed I was cheating was unforgivable. Flori tells me that was in the past and I have to let go; however, some things cling to you for life. Flori, as you have probably surmised by now, has a much sweeter disposition than I have. Every once in awhile she still brings up the subject of 'intervention' even though Esther doesn't even live here.

"I think we should do this before old Mr. Braithwate dies," she says. (He was our principal, has dementia, and is almost a hundred years old.) "You should have closure on this, Mabel."

"Flori," I always tell her. "I do have closure. Don't forget, I took almost all my last year at home and I got higher marks than Esther did. That's enough closure for me."

"But that was so many years ago and you still haven't forgiven her."

"No, and I never will."

"That's not closure, Mabel."

"It's good enough for me."

After I say that, Flori sheds a tear or two and says she'll continue to pray for me.

Reg could possibly be right; someone was playing a trick on me. Parson's Cove is a lovely place to live. Although, to be honest, I've never lived anywhere else so I can't really speak from experience. No matter how lovely it is, however, a few living here have somewhat criminal minds. Not to mention names but even Sheriff Jim and Deputy Scully had a few run-ins with the law before they became the Law. That's in the past, of course. However, if someone finds himself or herself locked out of the house, Scully is quite handy at unlocking a door with a piece of wire or a credit card and Jim can hotwire a car in ten seconds flat.

I must say, I went to bed with total piece of mind. Well, perhaps, sort of a *fake* total. I did make a brief stop at the sewing room. This is the room where I was born so many years ago. My mother never let me forget the pain she had to endure giving birth to me so after she died I turned it into a sewing room. Even though it's much bigger than my bedroom, I'm sure I could never sleep in it. All night I'd be hearing my mother's screams. I never sew but I do hide my bottle of gin behind the old sewing machine. Flori has no idea. If she did, she'd pour every bottle down the drain. Flori thoroughly enjoys a glass or two of wine but gin is a sin.

So, I drained my glass of sin and fell asleep almost instantly. I dreamt about slot machines cha-chinging, the old singer with the young man's voice singing *Auf Wiedersehen,* but over it all I kept hearing someone screaming, "*Wicked ... everyone in Parson's Cove. Jail won't be enough. Watch your....*" And when the old guy transformed into the Canadian singer, belting out *Love Can Move Mountains*, her face suddenly changed right before my eyes and I was staring at Esther Flynn's ugly mug. I sat up in bed drenched in sweat, my heart pounding.

Chapter Three

The next morning, I was still a little shaky from my nightmare and headachy from the gin but managed to feed my cats and make it to the shop in time to put the coffee on before Flori came with breakfast. At eight forty-five, she rushed through the door. Her hands were empty. Not only that, she wasn't even dressed. She was wearing her pink cotton housecoat over her matching floor length nightgown. Her orange-red hair stood out in every direction and there were black smudges of mascara under her eyes. She stood staring at me with her mouth open and a hand placed over her pounding heart. I knew it was pounding because I could see her hand going up and down.

"Flori," I said. "For goodness sakes, what's wrong? Why are you panting like that? Why aren't you dressed? Where's our breakfast?"

"Mabel," she screamed between pants. "There's been a murder."

"What do you mean, there's been a murder?"

She finally caught her breath. "Just that. Jake went over to have breakfast at the Main Street Café because he didn't want to wait for me to cook up our breakfasts and I told him I wasn't cooking breakfast twice so he left (a pause to inhale) and when he came back, that's what he told me."

"So, who? Who was murdered?"

"I don't know. Jake said it was a stranger."

"Flori, we don't have any strangers in town, do we? Did some move in while I was gone? Or, is it one of the renters? Maybe someone renting a cabin on the lake?"

Flori walked over and plunked down in my wicker chair. She wiped the perspiration off her forehead and tried running her fingers through her unruly hair. She sighed.

"I have no idea. I told you all that I know."

"Where's the body?"

Flori gave me a look of dismay. "Who cares where the body is, Mabel? Someone visiting Parson's Cove has been murdered and that's all you can think about?"

"I want to know who it was. Don't you?"

"Mabel, if it's a stranger, it doesn't matter if I know her name or not. I would just like to know if the killer is still in Parson's Cove so I know if I need to lock my doors. Or, should Jake get out his hunting rifle for protection?"

"What did you just say?"

"I said I want to know if I have to keep my doors locked or should Jake get out his hunting rifle for protection." She made another feeble attempt at patting her hair down. "Is that the part that shocks you, Mabel? The gun part? You know I don't believe in violence of any kind but this is something entirely different."

"No, I thought you said, 'it doesn't matter if I know *her* name or not.'"

She nodded. "That's what I said."

"You mean a woman was murdered?"

"Yes, didn't I just say that?"

"No, you said it was a stranger."

"Okay, so it was a woman stranger. What difference

does it make?"

"I don't know but somehow it does."

Flori's eyes bulged; she gasped, clutched her chest again, and jumped up. "Oh, Mabel, I'm so sorry. Here you've been waiting for breakfast and I came empty-handed. You must be starving. I'll run home and make it right away." She hurried to the door, her housecoat floating behind.

"Don't rush," I called out. "You have time to get showered and dressed and put your make-up on. I'll give you a whole hour." I smiled at her. "I was getting used to having late lazy breakfasts by the pool anyway. I'll just pretend I'm back in Las Vegas, that's all."

"You had lazy breakfasts by the pool?"

"No, but I could have if I'd wanted them."

She came back, hugged me, and left. As soon as I knew she would be out of sight, I went out the same door, locked it, and walked in the opposite direction. I knew where the body would be.

I edged along the wall of our small brick county courthouse and peeked around the corner. The parking lot for the Parson's Cove hospital was directly across the street. If I wanted to get into the county morgue, I'd have to somehow get across that wide parking lot and enter the back door of the hospital. I certainly didn't want the sheriff or Reg to see me. They'd not only send me home, they'd make sure I never found out anything about the murder. That is, Jim and Reg wouldn't. I could usually squeeze info from Scully but sometimes it wasn't too reliable.

The patrol car with its cherry red light turning, sat at the front entrance. That meant Scully had either forgotten to shut it off or he wanted to let everyone know that he was working a case. The ambulance was already in its normal parking spot.

I had to not only get past Jim and Scully, or Reg if he was there, I also had to avoid Nurse Grappley. She ran the hospital with an iron fist. Even Doc Fritz makes a wide swath around her when he sees her coming down the aisle. Fritzy took over as head doctor when Lorna's husband died. Lorna Grappley, however, feels the hospital is still in the family and she's now the owner. Nothing goes on in that building without her knowledge or permission. Would she give Mabel Wickles permission to go and check out a dead body in the morgue? Not in her lifetime.

I looked up and down the street. There was definitely no hustle and bustle here. In fact, it was so quiet the only sound I could hear was a large bumblebee zinging around my head. The only person who might notice me was Charlie Thompson. He was sitting on a town bench in front of the library. It was quite a distance away but you never knew with Charlie. He's the type of person who is blind one time and has x-ray vision the next. I guess it's what you call selective sight. I didn't worry about him anyway. Charlie has very few friends in town but I happen to be one of them.

I sprinted across the street and hid behind a lilac bush. Now all I had to do was get across the parking lot without anyone seeing me. This wasn't going to be easy. There were four cars altogether and they were spaced as far apart as you could get. At least, none of them had to worry about getting their doors pinged. It just meant I'd have to make a mad dash for it and hope no one was watching. I took off running.

I would have made it clear into the morgue too except the moment I reached the door, it flew open. I let out a shriek. Bob Crackers stood there, staring at me. Bob is the town's electrician, plumber, and gravedigger.

"Hey, Mabel. Boy, you gave me a start for a second."
He shook his head and laughed. "By the way, good to see
you got home from your trip okay. Myrtle says you had a
real good time." He switched his toothpick to the other side
of his mouth. "Guess you heard the excitin' news here in
old Parson's Cove? Been a murder in town. Probably
nothin' to you, seein' you just come from the big city.
Don't think Jim's found out who the woman is yet. Even
brought in Reg this mornin'. Probably bringin' in some of
those city cops too. That's what I figure." He shook his
head again. "What's that now? First murder here in about
three or four years? Gettin' almost as bad as Vegas, ain't
it?" He stepped to the side. "Sorry. Here I am chattin'
away and takin' up your time. Were you wantin' to come in
the back door?"

"Actually, I was. Faster than walking all the way around
to the front."

"Well, old Grappely always insists I come in the
backdoor when I'm workin' on the plumbing. Toilets
plugged up agin." He sighed a frustrating sigh and moved
out of my way. "Here you go then." He paused. "You
visitin' somebody this mornin'?"

"You might say that."

He held the door open and I went in. There was no need
to tell me he'd been working on the plumbing - one whiff
and I knew.

The thing that hits me smack in the face when I walk into
a hospital, unless I run into Bob first, is the smell. I
immediately start to breathe through my mouth and if I'm
not careful, hyperventilate. The hallway leading to the
morgue smelled even worse. Or, maybe it was just my
imagination.

I looked to the right and the left but could see no one.

Was Jim or Reg in with the body? Knowing Reg, he wouldn't be there any longer than he had to be.

I wasn't surprised when Bob said Jim had called in Reg. Settling traffic disputes or neighbors fighting over garbage lids is one thing but murder is something else and this would be a new experience for Sheriff Jim.

The hallway was narrow, bleak, and appeared never-ending. To my right, at the end of that passage was a gray steel door. On the other side of that door was the morgue. Everything in the hallway was gray: the walls, the floor, and even the light fixtures. The most depressing color in the world.

I tried walking on my tiptoes but still my rubber-soled runners squeaked and echoed with each step. When I came to the steel door, I stopped to listen. Silence. I held my breath and pressed the door open. The room was empty; as least, of people who could still talk and breathe. I stuck my head back out; all was clear. Maybe Reg was going back to the police station with Jim and Scully now.

I stood just inside the door and looked around. It was not a large room. The one florescent light in the middle of the ceiling, along with the white cupboards and the steel table, made the room look colorless and lifeless - like the body, covered by a white sheet, stretched out on a gurney a few feet in front of me. Cold sweat formed on my forehead and my heart pounded in my ears. One thing, I couldn't do - I couldn't faint and have Nurse Grappley find me. Just imagining her wrath brought oxygen shooting to my brain. I tiptoed over to the motionless white mound, instinctively watching for any slight movement.

My hand trembled as I lifted the cloth from the woman's face. I didn't realize I'd gasped until I heard my own echo.

It sounded deafening, alien. I lowered the sheet.

This was a stranger to Parson's Cove but not to me.

Grace Hobbs looked exactly the same as I'd seen her only a few days before. The only difference was the small reddish-purple bullet hole between her eyes.

Chapter Four

Sheriff Jim, Scully, and Reg Smee stood staring at me as I burst into the police station.

Reg held up his hand. "Mabel, we don't have time for you this morning. Sheriff Jim has asked me to help him with something and Captain Maxymowich will be here any minute. If you're still concerned about that silly phone message, you'll have to wait. We have a much more serious crime to solve." Tiny beads of sweat covered his forehead and it looked as though he'd applied Flori's rouge to his whole face. "Why aren't you in your shop anyway?" he snipped at me.

I'd barely gotten my body inside the door and there Reg stood, glaring at me, judging me, and looking like he was stopping traffic in the middle of a busy intersection in New York city.

"Reg," I said, looking him right in the eyes and putting my hands on my hips. "I think you might want to hear what I have to say."

He shook his head. "No, Mabel, you have absolutely nothing that we want to hear. Scully," he said, as he turned towards the other side of the room, "show Miss Wickles the way out." With that, he turned, motioned to the sheriff, and they both walked into Jim's office.

"I know where the door is, Reg," I yelled. "I just walked

35

through it." I waited a moment and then yelled louder, "I also know who the dead woman in the morgue is."

Slowly, ever so slowly, the office door squeaked open. He and Jim peered around the corner.

"What did you say?" the two men uttered in unison. (Now I know what writers mean when they say a person's face is as black as thunder.)

"I said I know who the dead woman is. You know, there was a woman murdered right here in Parson's Cove?"

"Of course I know a woman was murdered right here in Parson's Cove." Reg stepped up to me and placed his finger on my chest. Well, perhaps, I should say just below my neck. "What I would like to know is how do you know *who* was murdered, right here in Parson's Cove?"

Sheriff Jim moved up beside Reg and out of the corner of my eye I saw Scully move closer too. I could swear there was a smirk on Scully's lips. Reg, on the other hand, was not smiling and still looking thunderous. His lips were set in a straight line and his breathing was not what I would consider normal. No wonder the man has high blood pressure.

"What's going on here, Mabel?" he growled. "If you think this is some kind of joke, you know I won't hesitate for one moment to lock you up for mischief. You know that, don't you? I've done it in the past and I'll do it again." And then realizing he really wasn't sheriff anymore, he removed his finger from my chest and placed his hands on his hips.

Sometimes Reg forgets he can't threaten anyone with jail time anymore.

He can be quite intimidating when he wants to be. After all, I'm barely over five feet tall and he's over six. He's also hefty. For a man who's almost three score year and ten, I imagine he could still throw a mean punch. With that thought in mind, I backed up against the door.

He continued, "I know your heart is in the right place; however, this woman is not from Parson's Cove. Trust me, Mabel, you do *not* know her. You have never seen her before in your life. Jim has asked me to help with this case and we don't have time for anything else right now. Understand?"

"But that's what I've been trying to tell you. Yes, I have seen her before. You just won't let me get a word in. I do know that woman. I went to the morgue and had a look."

I thought his eyes would pop out of his head. Sheriff Jim and Deputy Scully, on the other hand, replaced their smirks with unadulterated adoration.

"You *what*?" he bellowed. His face turned a brighter shade of red and a vein in his neck started to pulsate.

"I went to the morgue and had a look."

"I know what you said." He closed his eyes and ran his hand over his balding head. "All right," he said with a sigh. "Who is this woman? And, I suppose while I'm at it, I should ask if you already know who killed her?" The last sentence he said wearing a mordant smirk on his lips.

"Of course, I don't know who killed her. How would I know that? I can tell you her name though - it's Grace Hobbs. She won a trip to Las Vegas too. The same one I was on."

The three stood and gaped at me.

"Now, Reg," I said. "Do you believe that my life might be in danger too? That the message on my machine is threatening? That perhaps, there's a madman out there, killing everyone who won that trip?" My legs felt wobbly. "Do you think I'll be the next one to have a bullet through the brain?"

Chapter Five

When I opened my eyes, I was lying on the cot in the cell. Reg stood over me, looking very concerned and waving a magazine in front of my face.

"Would you stop that, Reg?" I said. "You almost hit me with that thing."

Jim pushed in front of Reg with a glass of water. "Here, Mabel, take a drink." He lifted the back of my head with one hand and put the glass to my lips.

I grabbed the glass and struggled to sit up. "I can drink by myself, Jim. What do you want to do? Drown me?"

Water was exactly what I needed. I took my time and emptied the glass. The three stood watching, not saying a word.

"What happened?" I asked.

All three started talking at once.

"Shut up, you two," Reg snapped. He turned to me. "You passed out, Mabel, but don't worry; we called Dr. Fritz and he'll be here any minute."

I stood up, feeling a bit shaky but not shaky enough to let Fritzy prod me.

"I'm not waiting for him," I said. "Flori will be at the shop with breakfast. She'll be worried sick about me. I'm fine."

Reg clasped his hand around my wrist. "I'm sorry, Mabel, but you aren't going anywhere. Sit right down there. Scully, you get hold of Flori and tell her where Mabel is."

"Sure thing, Reg. I'll head over to the shop right now."

"You don't drive over there - you phone."

"But I haven't had breakfast yet either."

"Never mind breakfast. We've got a murder to solve. I'll tell you when you can eat."

By the time Doctor Fritz arrived five minutes later, I was feeling much better. All he did was feel my forehead, look into my eyes, check my pulse and blood pressure, and then pronounce, "You'll live, Mabel. All you need is some food in your stomach." He then turned to Reg and said, "Next time, don't call unless it's an emergency. You know, blood and guts." With that, he whipped out of the room and disappeared. No doubt in search of blood and guts.

"Okay, Mabel," Reg said. "Let's talk about this woman now. Who is Grace Hobbs and what do you know about her?"

"Like I said, she was one of the women who won a trip to Las Vegas. I don't know much about her but she always carried a big brown leather bag. She never let it out of her sight. All her ID should be in that."

"There was no bag or purse. We searched the whole area. I guess the killer figured she wouldn't need it anymore."

"Where was the body found anyway?"

"You know I don't have to tell you things like that but I'm sure everyone in Parson's Cove knows by now so I guess it's no secret. I don't know where she was murdered but her body was dumped in the bush behind the nursing home."

"Parson's Cove's nursing home? I wonder what she

would be doing behind it?"

"We don't know where she was murdered. I said we found the body there. It looks like someone killed her and then tried to hide the victim's body. Guess they thought it would take awhile before she'd be discovered. The autopsy report will tell us the time of death." He reached into his pocket, pulled out his worn black book, and flipped it open. There wasn't much written in it but it was old.

"I thought you threw that old book out when you retired, Reg."

He gave me a hard look. I was beginning to get used to this soft kind retired Reg Smee and now I was back to battling with the old Sheriff Reg Smee.

"Shouldn't Sheriff Jim be writing this down?"

Jim, who was standing behind Reg, shook his head as if trying to tell me to be quiet.

"It's okay, Mabel, we're working together and Reg knows more about murder cases than I do. Scully and I can use his expertise."

"If you're finished now, Miss Wickles, may I continue?" Reg wet the end of the pencil with his tongue. "Now, what more can you tell me about this? What was her name? Grace Hobbs you said?"

"Like I said, she was on the trip with me. She was one of the prizewinners. I didn't talk to her much. She was friends with Andrea."

"Who's Andrea?"

"Andrea Williams. Or, Andy. She told us that some people called her Andy. No one on the trip called her that though, not even Grace. They didn't know each other before the trip but they were both from the same city. Some place in Texas. Not a big city. Yellow Rose. That was it.

They were both from Yellow Rose, Texas."

"You're sure of this, Mabel? You're sure this is the same woman that you were with in Las Vegas?"

"Reg, I just looked at a woman with a bullet hole through her forehead. I'm not sure of much but this I'm sure of: A few days ago, Grace Hobbs was alive. You know, talking and laughing." I paused. "Well, maybe not laughing so much the last time I saw her."

Reg's eyes popped. "She wasn't laughing? Why wasn't she laughing?"

"She and Andrea lost money, gambling. At least, that's what we all thought. You don't really ask something like that, do you?"

"Lots of money, do you think?"

I shrugged. "I have no idea, Reg. They didn't say. All I know is, they looked pretty gloomy all the way to the airport. Of course, Betty and Ralph were miserable too. Actually, I was the only happy one and that was because I was on my way home. Now, I'm not so sure; maybe now, I wish I were still there. Do you think someone is out to get me too, Reg?"

"Of course, not, Mabel."

"You don't sound all that confident."

There was a worried look in Reg's eyes. He sighed. "So far, there really isn't a connection, is there?"

"What do you mean, 'no connection?' I'm from Parson's Cove; her body was dumped in Parson's Cove. We have the Las Vegas connection. Besides that, are you forgetting the message I got on my answering machine?"

He was silent for a moment. "Maybe you'd better bring that in for me. I'll play that for Maxymowich and the city cops."

I nodded. "I'll have to bring my whole phone in. It's all

one piece. Flori bought it for me, you know."

"That's okay." He smiled.

"When is the Captain getting here?"

"He should be here soon." He touched my arm. "Sorry if I'm a bit short with you, Mabel. It's been awhile since we've had a murder in Parson's Cove."

I nodded. "I understand, Reg, and I'm sure Jim is happy to have you back with him. Is it okay if I leave? Flori will be worried. Besides, I don't want to be here when all those cops from the city take over."

He nodded; his mind on something else already. I escaped out the front door and headed for the shop. It was almost eleven and my stomach was aching for food. An hour ago, I couldn't have even thought about it without gagging.

As I walked, I was wondering whatever possessed me to go over to the morgue and check out that body. I mean, in hindsight, it was a good thing that I did but it still doesn't explain *why* I do such things. Flori says it's because I have an overactive imagination; Reg says I can't mind my own business, and Jake thinks I have some sort of mental disorder. I suppose it's a bit of all three combined. Sometimes, that's good; sometimes, that's not so good.

"Mabel," Flori screamed, when I walked in the door. She rushed over and hugged me. "I was sick with worry. I don't know if I felt any better after Scully phoned. Are you okay? I saved some breakfast for you. Are you hungry? Is it true that you had to go over to the morgue? I can't believe you could do that. I told Jake and he said he believed it. He said you were capable of anything." She proceeded to touch my hair and feel my arms.

"I'm fine, Flori. You don't need to touch me all over.

All I did was faint."

Her eyes widened. "You fainted? Nobody told me that you fainted!"

"Well, what did Scully tell you anyway?"

"He said that you identified the body and that you were at the police station."

"That's it? I identified the body? Flori, I went over to the morgue while I was waiting for you. It's a good thing I did too because if I hadn't, Reg and the boys still wouldn't know who the victim was. I ran over as soon as you left to get breakfast. I'm sorry, I thought I'd be back before you. Anyway, when I saw that it was Grace, I couldn't believe it. I had to rush over and tell Reg." My legs started feeling weak again so I decided I'd better sit down before I fell down. "Flori," I said, "she was one of the women on the trip with me."

As I spoke, Flori's face had changed from pinkish to chalk-ish; then, back to pink again. Her auburn eyebrows stood out like two neon arches.

"What are you saying?" Her hand clutched her chest. "Are you telling me that you went into Grappley's morgue by yourself?" Tears sprang up into her eyes. "Are you crazy?" She reached over and grabbed the front of my sweater. "Why did you do that?" Before I could even think of something that made any sense, she said, "You *wanted* to go and look at a dead body? Why? Why would you want to see a dead body?"

I pried her fingers from my sweater.

"Flori, it's okay. I'm all right. Please, don't ask me why I had to go and look; it's just a good thing that I did. Maybe it was Divine Providence that sent me over there."

"Oh, for Pete's sake, it was no such thing. You don't think, that's all. You don't think of the consequences of anything." She reached over, grabbed a couple of tissues, and proceeded to weep. I sat and waited, feeling dreadfully guilt-ridden.

"Are you finished now?" I asked when she finally stopped sniffling.

She nodded.

"All right, you might as well tell me now," she said.

"Tell you what?"

"What the dead woman looked like. Was there blood all over the place? How did she die? They say people who are murdered have terror etched right into their face. Did she, Mabel? Did she have terror etched into her face?"

I stared at her tear-stained face. "You're worse than me, Flori. Of course, there was no terror etched in her face. At least, not much. She looked exactly like she looked the last time I saw her. Well, she didn't have quite as much color in her face. And, of course, there wasn't the bullet hole..."

"There was a bullet hole?" Her hand went to her chest again. "Oh Mabel, I don't want to hear any more." She shuddered. "Was it a big one? Where was it?"

"No, it was really small. So small, in fact, I almost couldn't see it." I pointed to the spot between my eyes. "It was right here."

"Do you think she suffered?"

"I don't think she even knew what hit her."

"Well, I suppose that's a blessing. Did you print some of the pictures of her from the trip? I think I'd like to see what she looked like when she was alive."

"Actually, I have several pictures of her. I'll have to show them to Reg. Then, he'll know for sure I'm telling the truth."

Flori collapsed in the other chair.

"What's happening, Mabel? Why would a woman from your trip end up being murdered in our little town?"

"I don't know but I think it might have something to do with the threatening phone call I got."

"Threatening phone call? You got a threatening phone call? What are you talking about, Mabel Wickles?"

Well, I tried to explain in ten words or less, but it wasn't that easy; Flori tends to gasp and interrupt often.

"Which reminds me," I said, during a gasp break, "I have to take my phone over to Reg. He wants Captain Maxymowich to listen to it." I stood up. "Would you mind staying here and keeping shop a bit longer, Flori?"

Flori's eyes glistened with tears. "Of course, I don't mind. Please, be careful. Maybe I should see if Jake would walk home with you. I could phone him right away."

"No, Flori, Jake doesn't have to walk home with me. No one's going to shoot me in broad daylight. I'll be fine. Just try to keep my breakfast warm somehow. I'll be back in about ten minutes."

Poor Flori. That ten minutes turned into something much longer.

"You know Captain Maxymowich has been waiting for you, Mabel," Reg said, with a frown, as soon as I walked in the door as if I were telepathic or something. I knew he'd arrived because two strange patrol cars sat in the parking lot. Reg had been a good small-town cop but whenever there was something serious, like a murder, he was relieved of his duties. Not that they ever told him he was, that's just what always happened. They swarmed into his station and suddenly, there was no room for Reg and his two boys. It was no different now that Jim was sheriff. In fact, I think Reg was trying to shield the new Parson's Cove sheriff as best he could.

"Hello, Mabel." The Captain stood in the doorway to Jim's office. His voice wasn't loud and booming but somehow, it filled the room. It certainly got my attention. Captain Maxymowich hadn't changed much since the last time I'd seen him and that had been several years ago. In fact, I could swear he was wearing the same wrinkled navy suit. I might never have met him except it seemed so many people used the house behind mine for nefarious purposes that I could hardly not get involved.

At first, he terrified me. He was standoffish; he was insensitive; he slouched. His white hair was combed straight back. White hair on a young man. At least, to me, he was young. I doubt he was over forty-five. And those eyes - pale blue and piercing. All through that horrendous interrogation, he tapped his pen on the table and never once looked up at me. To say it was unnerving, would be putting it mildly. I didn't see him smile until the case was closed and then I got a glimpse of the 'other' Marlow Maxymowich.

"Hello, Captain," I said. My heart pounded at the same rate it had when I hit a patch of black ice last winter. He wasn't smiling and he was still intimidating.

"Why don't you come into the office and we can talk there?" He stood aside to let me in and then closed the door before anyone else could follow. I sat in the wooden chair facing him, still clutching my phone to my chest. Maxymowich sat in Jim's new leather chair with the armrests. I'm sure Jim would be cringing at the thought. He bought that chair to replace the one Reg had taken home after he retired and Jim was almost as possessive about that chair as Reg had been about his. Personally, I never understood it so I assumed it was a 'man thing.'

"So, how have you been, Mabel?" He didn't smile but there was a hint of one in his eyes. One thing I have to say about the Captain is that when he asks a question like that, he really *does* want to know the answer. Not, you know, how some people say, 'how are ya?' and then move on before you answer.

"Well, I have the usual aches and pains that everybody my age has, I guess. About a month ago, I had this terrible cold but I ate garlic and drank lots of orange juice. Flori made some chicken soup for me. She makes it for everyone who has the sniffles. Other than that, I've been keeping pretty well."

"I understand you won a trip to Las Vegas?" He raised his eyebrows.

I nodded.

"Tell me about it."

"Well, I saw this ad in the paper. Not our town paper - the city paper. I had no idea I'd win. I'd never even heard of the cereal they were promoting but I sent the coupon in anyway. Then, about a week later, this man phoned to tell me I'd won. All I had to do was answer a skill-testing question which was really easy and that was it. There were five winners: Sally Goodrich, Andrea Williams, Grace Hobbs, and Ralph Murphy. Flori said she would come with me but pay her own way, of course. Then, as usual, she had to cancel because of someone in her family. This time it was Jakie's wife giving birth. You remember Flori? She's my oldest and dearest friend." (No reaction from Mr. Maxymowich) I continued, "Of course, there was Mr. Hatcher. He was with the cereal company. We didn't see too much of him but he was helpful and polite. Well, I guess everyone seemed very nice. Our hotel was fancy, although, it was a bit too noisy for my taste. The others seemed to like it, especially the two women who spent all their time down in the casino. I don't know how they could do it; you know, with all the noise. I stood in the doorway for three minutes and my head started to pound. Then there were the other two: Ralph and Sally. They paired off on the second day. It's a good thing I enjoy doing things on my own. To tell you the truth, I was glad to get home."

"I understand the woman who was murdered was on this trip?"

"Yes. Grace Hobbs."

"What can you tell me about her, Mabel? What sort of woman was she? Did she appear worried or apprehensive at all?" There was the touch of a smile on his lips. "I know you're a very observant person. Tell me anything that might be helpful."

"All I know is that she and Andrea were upset that they'd lost quite a bit of money, gambling. Well, I guess I shouldn't say they did for sure. That's what the rest of us figured. I mean, if you'd lost a little money, you wouldn't be that upset, would you? Other than that, I really didn't notice anything. I'm sure she and Andrea would've gone on the tours if they hadn't been so occupied at the blackjack table. Well, there was the food. She told me to make sure to try the chicken fried steak at the buffet." A thought suddenly popped into my head. "I wonder if she was afraid to go home after losing so much money so she tried to borrow from a loan shark and couldn't pay it back so she got killed? Or, maybe her husband murdered her because she lost all their savings. Of course, that wouldn't answer why someone killed her and dumped her body in Parson's Cove, would it? Or, does it have something to do with me? Do you think her murder and the threatening message I got are connected?"

If he heard any of my questions, he didn't acknowledge it.

"Oh yes, the phone message. Could you leave it with me, Mabel?"

I handed him the phone.

He smiled - this time, a real one. There's one thing about someone who always looks so stern - when they smile, it's like the whole world lights up. It was only for a moment but it made me feel better. I knew that if anyone could find Grace's killer, it would be Captain Maxymowich. Well, either he would or I would.

"Now, what about the other people on this tour? What can you tell me about the man? Ralph?"

"Oh, well, he was okay. In his fifties, I think. He's divorced and has a boy in college. He and Sally were real chummy for the first couple of days but that seemed to cool off. One of those Las Vegas romances, you know." (Sounding as if I knew what I was talking about.)

He nodded as if he did know.

"And, the other women? This Sally? What can you tell me about her?"

I couldn't help but grin. "Well, she was something else. I think she's had every face lift and laser treatment there is. Half the time, I couldn't even make out what she was saying, her lips were pulled back so tight. And, trust me, she made it known to everyone that she was divorced and looking for a man." I shrugged. "That's about all I can tell you about Sally."

"But you say this Ralph had a thing for her?"

"Big time."

"Now, the other one? What's her name?"

"Andrea. Andrea Williams."

"What did you think of her?"

It was hard to make such an assessment because all of a sudden, instead of remembering positive traits, I was wondering if she was a murderer.

"What did I think of her? I don't know. I guess I didn't think anything. She was just kind of *there*. Know what I mean? Andrea didn't really stand out in my mind. She was nice enough. Maybe a little quiet compared to the others. That's about all I can think of."

He nodded. "That's good, Mabel. If you think of anything, write it down and let me know. Write down whatever comes to mind, even if it doesn't seem relevant."

He picked up a file and started to read. I think it meant that he'd dismissed me.

I stood up and walked to the door.

"Oh, there's one other thing, Mabel. Could you spare a couple of minutes right now and come down to the morgue with me? I'd like you to identify the body." He looked up. "We want to make sure it's who you say it is."

My stomach tightened and there went any thoughts of eating breakfast.

Chapter Six

It ended up that I not only had to part with my phone, Reg said Maxymowich wanted my pictures also. Not the ones of the desert or the dam or my hotel room unless, of course, some of my travelling companions were in it.

"Don't worry," Reg said. "If any of them get ripped or lost, we'll pay to have another one printed."

"Well, that's a nice offer," I said. "But, I erased them all from my memory card so this is all that I have."

He shook his head. "Now, why would you do that? Didn't Merlin tell you, you could save them on a CD if you wanted to?"

"Of course, he did. And, it might be a wonderful idea except why would I want CDs piled up all over the place and still not have pictures that I can't pick up and hold? Besides, it cost enough as it was."

He grunted. "Okay, we'll take good care of them." He slipped them into his inside jacket pocket and walked out the door. Before he got to the curb, he turned around and stuck his head back in. "Next time, get the CD anyway. Don't be so cheap." With that, he slammed the door and left.

Flori gave me a worried look. She tends to do this if she knows I haven't eaten in the past couple of hours. Or, if someone like a retired sheriff, is upset with me.

"Oh, Mabel, your breakfast is ruined. The eggs are gray

and dried out; the ham is as hard as rock." She looked up at the clock. "Besides, it's lunch time now." She gathered up all the dishes. "I'm going to run home and bring you some lunch." She looked at me beseechingly, "Please, try to stay here until I get back."

"Are you kidding? I will. No one is going to get me to leave, no matter what. This has been a dreadful morning. I hope I never see another dead body for as long as I live."

"Trust me; I hope you never see another one either. Or, go looking for one. This is as stressful on me as it is on you." Her eyes filled and her bottom lip quivered. "I wish you'd never told me about that phone call, Mabel. I told Jake that you should come and stay with us for a while. At least, until this murdering maniac is caught."

I walked over and put my arms around her and the dishes she was carrying in her arms. Mostly, I was hugging dishes.

"I'll be fine, Flori. I know Jake doesn't want me underfoot. Besides, I'm sure he didn't really agree, did he?"

"Of course, he did. I told him it was either you staying with us or me staying with you."

"Flori, go home and make lunch."

She grinned. "Okey dokey."

A half hour later, she was back and we were sitting, slurping up homemade cabbage soup with a dollop of sour cream on top and homemade bread slathered with butter. My eyes watered from the garlic fumes. When we were finished with that, I poured the coffee and Flori brought out two gargantuan cinnamon buns, which she proceeded to slather with more butter. At least, Flori comes by her weight honestly.

Gossip travels around Parson's Cove faster and gathers more momentum than a tidal wave does. All afternoon, people came in and out. Fortunately, I guess their consciences were starting to bother some of them; at least, I did make several sales. By the time, it came to close the store, I'd heard everything from Grace being stabbed in my backyard to Reg being shot in a high speed chase.

"Can you imagine?" I said to Flori, who had kindly come back to walk me home. "How do people come up with this stuff? You won't believe what Pattie asked me."

"What?" Flori's eyes were big. She loves good juicy gossip; especially, if it's something Pattie might print in the local newspaper.

"If it were true that I lost all my money, gambling. I said, 'Like I'm sure I'd tell you, Pattie. You'd have that splattered all over the front page of the paper tomorrow.' Actually, I am kind of worried about what she might print. I hope Reg didn't tell anyone about my threatening phone call. Do you think he would?"

Flori's face reddened. "I'm sure he wouldn't."

"What about you, Flori? Did you happen to mention it to anyone?"

She cleared her throat. "Well, I may have mentioned it in passing."

"In passing whom?"

"Obviously, I told Jake because I was worried about you."

"Anyone else?"

"It might have slipped out a few times while you were at the police station." Her chin started to tremble and after one giant snivel, she blurted out, "I'm so sorry. I didn't think what I was saying, Mabel. I was just so upset and worried." Her face screwed up and tears poured down. "Do you think it will make it worse? Will someone come after you for sure now?"

I handed her a tissue. The floodgates gave way.

"Oh Mabel," she said, through her sobs, "I've signed your death warrant, haven't I?"

"No, you haven't, Flori. You don't have to be quite so dramatic. Now that I think about it, maybe it's good that it's out in the open. Now, whoever called me knows that everyone will be on the lookout for me." I patted her back. "Maybe you did me a favor."

She wiped away the tears and patted her eyes. The tissue was smudged black and blue with eye shadow and mascara. We'd reached the front gate to my house.

"Look at this, Flori," I said. "Someone was here and left the gate open."

"Well, since you won't come and stay with us, I had Jake go through your house earlier, just to make sure no one was hiding in there. He should've known better than to leave the gate open." She stopped in her tracks and stared at me. "Unless, someone else was here, Mabel." Her eyes got bigger. "What if it were someone else? I'm sure Jake would've closed the gate. I'm sure he would've."

"Flori," I said. "Jake never closes my gate. He leaves it open to irritate me. And, besides, I figured you might get him to do a walk-through. By the way, you know I don't have a phone now so you'll have to trust that I'll be all right. No sending Jake over in the middle of the night to check, okay?"

"Oh, Mabel, you know I wouldn't do that."

"Promise, Flori?"

"Oh, all right if you insist, but I will call the store at nine sharp and if you're not there, I'll send Jake over to the house."

"I guess I can live with that. By the way, everyone is

talking so much about Grace's murder but no one told me who found her body. Do you know?"

We were standing at my back door now. The sun was sinking in the west behind the trees and there were streaks of shade across my lawn.

"I wish you hadn't asked me that."

"Why?"

"Because I know you're going to make a big deal of it, that's why."

"Why would I? I'm curious. Obviously, whoever found the body is not the murderer so why would I get upset? It wasn't Charlie, was it?"

I would be upset if it were Charlie. Not that he would be implicated in a murder but simply because he doesn't need such trauma. Charlie is different from other folks. Some are afraid of him but he's as harmless as a newborn. He spends most of his days, winter and summer, sitting on a bench in front of the library. He wears the same clothes, day in and day out, and he only talks to the people he wants to talk to.

"No, it wasn't Charlie."

"So, who then? Esther Flynn?" I laughed, imagining the look on Esther's face if she ever saw a corpse again. She was the one who found old Beulah Henry and that was traumatic enough. "That would be a good one - Esther returning and wandering around the bush behind the nursing home. How could she ever explain that?"

Flori scowled but didn't say a word. I stared at her.

"It *was* Esther, wasn't it? I can't believe it. It was really Esther? What on earth would she be doing back in Parson's Cove and walking through the woods behind the nursing home?"

She nodded. "I told you, you'd be upset."

"I'm not upset. In fact, for some reason, I find this almost exhilarating."

"You should wipe the grin off your face."

"I can't." I hugged Flori. "Good night. I'll see you tomorrow."

I started to shut the door but Flori's foot got in the way.

"I don't like it when you grin like that. What are you planning, Mabel?"

"Me? I'm planning on finding out why Esther was out in the bush when she happened upon that dead body. I'm also planning on finding out if she's the one who threatened me. And, in case you're wondering, Flori, I'm planning on finding out who killed Grace Hobbs."

And, with that, I gently pushed the door until Flori removed her foot.

Chapter Seven

I lay in bed that night, trying to figure out my first move. Light shone in from the street lamp and I watched the shadows from my elm tree bouncing back and forth on the ceiling. Where would a bona fide detective start? And, by that, I definitely wasn't including Reg. I'd read enough Agatha Christie books to know that I would have to start at the end and work backwards. Not only that, there had to be suspects and a motive.

The end, of course, was 'the body.' Grace Hobbs. What did I know about the woman? She seemed so ordinary. Why hadn't I paid more attention? On the other hand, I can't look at everyone and think that they might be a murder victim, can I? She was younger than me; perhaps, in her forties. Tall? Well, everyone is taller than me. Slightly over-weight. No cause for murder there. Did she have family? I closed my eyes and tried to remember. On the first evening in Las Vegas, we'd all gone out for dinner. It was our 'getting acquainted' meal. I closed my eyes and tried to picture the setting.

The dining room was downstairs in our hotel. It was crowded and noisy. A waitress with eyelashes at least two inches long and a waist about the circumference of a silver dollar, sat us at a round table. The smoking section and bar was on the other side of a five-foot divide. Great protection for all us non-smokers. The dusty artificial plants sitting on top looked very real. They had to be artificial because real ones could have never survived the smoky blue haze that drifted over into our section. I tried to concentrate on the people at our table but there were so many interesting characters in the room, it was hard. Half the men looked like Elvis, wearing sparkling pantsuits so tight it would've made Flori blush and most of the women looked like Marilyn Monroe with white-blond hair and enough cleavage to sink a ship. The laughter was earsplitting and rowdy so obviously drinking, smoking, and gambling must bring joy to many.

Mr. Hatcher stood up and tapped his water glass several times with a spoon. No one paid attention.

"People! People!" he shouted. Everyone at our table and the three tables beside us stopped talking and stared at him.

"Like I said, we'll take turns talking about ourselves. Mabel, you go first." With that, he sat down. I guess if you have to listen to life stories week after week, it gets boring, and a person might tend to be on the grumpy side.

What had I said? He'd caught me by surprise so I didn't have time to get too nervous but my knees were a little shaky.

"My name is Mabel Wickles. (I realized afterwards that if any of them had forgotten my name all they had to do was look at my nametag.) I've lived my whole life in a small town called Parson's Cove. I live alone except for my cats." Someone at the next table whispered, "Aww, poor thing" very loudly. I turned to look the woman in the eye and said, "That doesn't mean for one second that I'm lonely. I have some wonderful friends. In fact, my best friend, Flori Flanders, was planning on coming with me. It just happened, however, that her oldest son's wife was giving birth so Flori stayed home."

Someone asked a question. Who was it? Grace. That's who it was. Now, what was it she asked? My brain almost hurt from concentrating so hard.

"What's Parson's Cove like? It sounds so quaint."

That was it. That's what she'd asked. I said, "It's beautiful. About a hundred years ago, homesteaders built the town right beside a lake. We have quite a few tourists in the summer who rent cottages and houses in the area. In fact, the house right behind mine is a rental. Actually, it's become known as the house of crime." I got everyone's attention when I said that. It was Grace who said, "Why? There was a murder?" Of course, then I had to explain about the different people who rented it and how a few were ones you wouldn't want as your next door neighbors. I tried not to sound too self-important so I told them in my most humble way how without me, some of the cases might never have been solved. Out of all of them, Grace seemed the most interested in my story.

Now, could I remember what each person said? It isn't that easy when your brain cells are degenerating at the same speed as your eyesight.

Sally stood up next. When she stood up, her perfume wafted across the table. Perhaps, 'propelled' was a better verb. I was sitting across from her and it was all I could do to keep from gasping for air. I remember what she wore that day because she reminded me of Flori. She was wearing this dazzling blue-green outfit. Those happen to be Flori's favorite colors (along with bright orange). The only difference was that Flori's clothes flowed outward from the neck down and Sally's didn't flow at all. They clung. The neckline was on the low side and her ample breasts seemed ready to pop right over the top. That, of course, is not Flori. Flori is very prim and proper when it comes to things like that.

I missed most of Sally's speech, simply because she mumbled through her swollen Botox lips. I do remember she said that she'd tried out for the movies and would've been a big star except for some reason - which I couldn't make out. She spoke of being a ballerina and I overheard Andrea whisper to Grace that she was probably an exotic dancer. I was more inclined to think of pole dancing. Anyway, she really didn't have much to say. She'd lived in quite a few states but didn't say exactly where she was from. One thing she did make sure we knew was that she was happily divorced *again* and was on the quest for someone new. After saying that, she threw Ralph a 'look' and then, Mr. Hatcher. Ralph grinned and turned pink but Mr. Hatcher didn't even glance her way. He probably had women hitting on him all the time.

I could understand her making eyes at Hatcher. He was attractive in his own dark way. Sally was probably old enough to be his mother but that doesn't seem to make any difference nowadays. Especially, in Las Vegas.

Andrea was next. What's with Texans? I mean, Texas might be big but it's still part of the United States of America. Having one's own language doesn't qualify you to be a Separatist. After being around her and Grace for a few hours, I was starting to say 'y'all' at the beginning and ending of all my sentences. Not only that, I was leaving the 'g' off all my 'ing' words. A southern drawl is as contagious as the Hong Kong flu. It was probably a good thing those two spent all their time at the slot machines; if not, when I returned home no one would have understood me.

What did she say about herself? That is, besides the fact
that she hailed from Texas. Was she married? Yes, but I
detected a bit of anger when she said this trip had nothing to
do with her husband. She didn't tell us her husband's name.
In fact, I'm sure she wouldn't have even mentioned a mate if
Sally hadn't asked. I was all prepared to hear her call him
Bubba or Jimmy Bob but we never did find out. She didn't
tell us if she had a family either or if she carried a gun in her
purse. Since nearly all Texas women possess their own
firearms, there was a good chance that she did.

Grace Hobbs. She was from Texas also. Not only that;
she and Andrea were from the same place. Andrea, I would
think, would be a prime suspect. Why? Well, that I don't
know. It seems strange there's that connection and it
doesn't mean something. On the other hand, if Andrea for
some unknown reason wanted to kill a neighbor she claims
she never knew before, why do it after a trip to Las Vegas?
She could've just as easily drowned her in the Gulf of
Mexico. Maybe then, they wouldn't have found the body.
Why would someone from the same city, murder, and then
dump the body behind a nursing home in a little one-horse
unknown town hundreds and hundreds of miles away?

Perhaps Andrea wasn't the murderer but surely, the fact
that both of them were from Yellow Rose must mean
something. It seemed more than a coincidence.

I tried to remember what Grace had told us about herself.
Every time I thought about her standing there at the table
looking down at all of us, all I could envision was a bullet
hole in her forehead. My mind went blank. If she said
something of significance, I couldn't remember it.

Ralph stood up. He was a tall man with gray thinning
hair and the beginnings of a paunch. And, of course, the

dandruff. That told me he was single before he told us. No wife would allow him to wear dark shirts. He said he was also divorced. I didn't have to look across at Sally; I could hear her sigh. He was in sales, although I wasn't familiar with the company. It had something to do with installing lifts for beds in hospitals. His territory covered several states, so he had to travel. No wonder he was divorced. He did mention he had a son in college.

I asked Mr. Hatcher if he was going to tell us something about himself and he said, quite gruffly, "You have to be kidding."

Well, I wasn't but I left it at that.

For the time being, this was all I could recollect. I figured that as time went by, more memories would return. Solving a crime is like putting a jigsaw puzzle together and right now, my pieces were spread all over the place.

Chapter Eight

I made it to work with seconds to spare. Flori, true to her word, phoned at nine. I'm usually there much earlier but one of the cats decided to disappear and I had no choice but to make some sort of effort at finding her. I firmly believe that cats really do have nine lives and that no matter what, they return home … whenever it suits their fancy. My neighbor, ninety-two year old Hilda Whinegate, tends to differ. She spotted Dottie racing across her backyard chasing a rabbit and was sure the cat had either become lost or had returned to the ways of her primordial ancestors and would never return. I never argue with Hilda because who knows how much longer she'll be my neighbor; so, whenever she thinks one of my cats is lost, I make a good pretense at searching. The cat always comes back on its own steam.

This morning, I was thankful for her eccentric opinion. My chase took me right to the woods behind the nursing home. Well, perhaps, not right behind but I figure two blocks in one direction or the other is reasonable.

Parson's Cove's nursing home is situated on a street that runs parallel with the curvature of the lake. The lake is too far away for any of the residents to see but the forest separating the building from the water is very green in summer and white with snow and frost in winter. Lawn chairs and small tables clutter the back yard, year around. Once in awhile one of the residents wanders off into the woods but so far, we haven't lost anyone. I think every other day or so, the staff warns its residents of the dangers. I imagine in the same tone that a teacher talks to her first grade class.

Nothing in our town is exactly north and south or east and west. Personally, I think every street started out as either a covered wagon trail or simply a cow trail. The nursing home, built about forty years ago, is one building that is well maintained. After all, that's where the majority of us will be spending our last years. The front lobby and dining area faces east, letting the sun shine in on all the happy faces every morning.

"Here, Dottie. Here Dottie," I called out. If the cat were anywhere near, she probably wouldn't have any idea what was going on anyway. I usually call all of them Kitty, except for Phil. Who can keep track of every cat's name? Flori doesn't even remember the names of all her grandchildren.

The closer I got to the yellow police tape, the louder I called. No one was around and nothing was moving at the nursing home. I imagine everyone was eating breakfast. Captain Maxymowich and his men had undoubtedly combed the whole area looking for clues. It wouldn't hurt to have a fresh pair of eyes take a look, however. Even if those eyes don't work so good close up, as Flori would say.

I slipped under the tape. There really wasn't much to see. The tall wild grass and low brush were flattened somewhat. I had no idea who flattened it though - the murderer or the cops. About ten feet in front of me, beside an old oak tree, I could see stakes stuck in the ground so that must have been where Esther discovered the body.

Why would Esther Flynn return to Parson's Cove and be wandering around in this bush? I always thought she was a bit weird but to be out here at night? That's just plain creepy. More importantly, did she do anything to mess up the investigation? Knowing Mrs. Know-It-All, she probably touched the body, left her fingerprints over everything, and trampled all around it before having the sense to call 911. I wouldn't even put it past her to hysterically start performing CPR.

I stepped warily over the bent grass until I came to the stakes. I wasn't sure what I was looking for. There was no blood that I could see, only a larger area of flattened vegetation. I didn't even have to close my eyes and I could envision Grace lying there, all curled up in a fetal position. Whether she was or not, I don't know, but that's how I envisioned her. I shivered. The inside of my mouth suddenly felt dry and tasted terrible.

Beyond this point, the trees and brush became denser and on the other side of the bluff, perhaps about a quarter of a mile away, there was a lake. Everyone called it Parson's Cove Lake but I don't think it had an official name. There were various paths going through the woods. Everybody who wanted to take a shortcut to the lake created their own. About three or four feet to the right of the police tape, I could see the faint outline of a path. That area wasn't roped off. Obviously, the police took it for granted that whoever dumped the body entered the woods from behind the nursing home. I mean, who would carry a dead weight all the way up from the lake and then leave it so someone could find it so easily?

I heard voices in the distance and looked up. There were three cops standing on the street by their patrol car having a chat. I slipped under the tape, dashed down the path towards the lake, and kept running until I felt no one could see me or hear my puffing. It was probably best that I didn't return the way I came so I kept walking towards the lake. I'd simply take another route back and make sure I didn't come out where the cops were.

Now that I wasn't running, I had a chance to check the footpath. It wasn't one of the well-worn paths but someone had used it not all that long ago. Not that I'm a tracker, but it was quite obvious the grass hadn't been packed down a long time ago. Every few yards, there was the faint outline of footprints. As I neared the edge of the tree line, the ground became softer, probably still moist from our last rain. Now, the prints were clear. I bent down to examine them. As far as I could tell, there was only one set and they were going only in one direction - towards the nursing home. It wasn't a small print either. Offhand, I would say about a size ten. Most of the grass stood tall so no one had dragged a body through this area. I was sure if the murderer had carried the body, the footprints would've been much deeper.

There is a narrow beach on this side of the lake. It's made up of small pebbles so few people come to swim here. It seems this is where all the algae end up too and no one likes swimming in that. If you want to sit on the shore and listen to the water lapping or read a book in solitude, this is the spot to choose.

I spent some time on my haunches examining the shoreline. The footprints from the path disappeared. There were no discernible prints in the gravel, only little dips here and there.

It was disappointing. A theory isn't worth anything without proof. I stood up to leave when my eye caught something shiny almost buried under the coarse sand. An earring. I held it in my hand. A simple gold earring. Was Grace missing one? If that were true, I'd solved some of the mystery. At least, in which direction the murderer came. Had she been murdered on a boat? If so, why carry the body so far? Why not leave it somewhere well hidden in the middle of the bush? Unless, of course, the murderer hadn't planned on leaving it in the woods at all and suddenly someone, like Esther, showed up so he had to dump it and run.

I looked at my watch. I had five minutes to race through the woods and be at the store before Flori phoned. If I wasn't there, she would send Jake to my house and when he didn't find me home, Flori would be at the police station screaming at Jim that I'd been kidnapped or shot.

I caught the phone on the fourth ring.

"Why are you huffing like that, Mabel?" she asked.

Now I know how wise my father was to keep the back door unlocked at all times.

"Huffing?"

"You sound like you're having a heart attack. Are you all right?"

"Of course, I am. I thought this morning I'd jog to work, that's all."

"Are you telling me a story? You would never jog to work. Did you run because you were afraid someone might be after you? Be honest with me."

"To be honest, one of my cats ran away and I had to go looking for her."

"You never go looking for your cats."

"I know but now I can assure Hilda that I did my best."

"Where exactly did you look, Mabel?"

"Why?"

"Because I know you. If Hilda sent you out looking, you'd run across town, then sneak back to the shop, and have your coffee. That's what you always do."

I took the earring out of my pocket. Heck, I couldn't fool Flori anyway.

"I went searching in the woods, Flori, and guess what I found?"

"What woods? Not the woods where Esther found the body? Tell me you didn't do that. Oh, don't even bother. I know you went there." She sighed. "What did you find, Mabel? Please, don't tell me you found the murder weapon."

The murder weapon. It could be in the woods somewhere. The murderer could have tossed it somewhere into the bush. The cops might not have searched far enough.

"Next time, I'm going to take you with me, Flori. We could've searched together. I never thought of looking for the murder weapon."

"There won't be a next time. I forbid you to go into that wood again. Do you want to get into trouble? So, if you didn't find that, what did you find? Her shoe?"

"Her shoe? Was she missing a shoe?"

"Oh, for Pete's sake, I don't know. What did you find?"

"An earring. A gold earring. It was on the shore by the lake."

"I thought the body was found behind the nursing home. Why were you out by the lake?"

"Oh, never mind, Flori. Do you want to come and have a

look at it before I give it to the police?"

"I'm really not interested in some old earring, Mabel, but I will come over for coffee. I haven't had any yet this morning."

The coffee hadn't finished perking and Flori was in the door, looking quite summery in a pink and purple Hawaiian flowered sundress. It definitely made her reddish-orange hair and matching eyebrows look even brighter than usual.

I held the earring up for her to see.

"I'm going to check with Jim to see if Grace was missing an earring. If she was, Flori, it means she was probably murdered on a boat and then carried through the woods."

Flori took the earring out of my hand and looked at it.

She handed it back. "Don't bother," she said. "I'd recognize that earring anywhere. It belongs to Esther Flynn."

Chapter Nine

All morning, I waited, hoping and almost praying that
Esther Flynn would return to Parson's Cove and come into
the store. Not that I had much hope of that really happening.
She married some poor sucker in another small town and she
and her horrid daughter, Millicent, moved away. I actually
thought it would make me happy but in some ways I miss
having someone to take my anger out on. And, trust me, it
was easy for me to get angry with her.

Of course, if she did happen to come in, I wouldn't
accuse her of murder. Oh no, I knew she wasn't capable of
that. She got her kicks out of watching people suffer and
squirm. I should know. So would her estranged husband,
Chester, and perhaps her latest husband too. Chester left her
and their daughter, Millicent, years ago. It's true, he ended
up being a scoundrel himself but if he'd stayed with Esther,
who knows what would've become of him? He could easily
have decided, simply out of desperation, to plunge into the
lake with a couple of cement blocks tied to his ankles.

It was almost three when I caught a glimpse of Reg with
Captain Maxymowich driving down the street. I opened the
door and waved but they were at the end of the block by
then. Reg would have pretended not to see me anyway.

At ten minutes to five, when I was pouring out the
leftover coffee and getting rid of the grounds, Esther walked

in.

Let me describe Esther to you in the most glowing description I can muster. She's tall, skinny, has short dark hair that is usually tightly permed in an old lady's style and wears glasses that keep sliding down her long narrow nose. When she speaks, which is quite often, she has a high-pitched nasal voice. Flori says that's not her fault because she should have had her adenoids removed years ago. Personally, I think she does it to get attention and to irritate everyone. I realize this could describe a very nice person but with Esther, that's where the nicest part ends. Personality-wise, she's humorless, snotty, bigoted, abrasive, pig-headed and a nitpicker. One day I was reading a book and came across the word misanthropist. I looked it up in the dictionary and she is that, also.

"I've made the trip from another town and I believe I have fifteen more minutes in which to shop," she announced as soon as she opened the door. She stood, daring me, with her nose in the air.

"No," I said. "You only travelled ten minutes to get here and you have ten minutes in which to shop."

She upped her nose another inch as her glasses started to slide.

"You would think, Mabel Wickles, since your business doesn't seem to be all that lucrative, you would be pleased if your clientele came in even if it were last minute. Or, do you think you're above us since you won that ridiculous trip?" She wore the tiniest smirk. "Oh yes, I heard all about your trip to Las Vegas."

"First of all, Esther Flynn, you are not what I call clientele. When was the last time you even bought anything? All you do is come in to see what I have marked down and then try to get it cheaper. What do you want now anyway?"

"Humph. If that's your attitude…" She turned to open the door.

"No, no, it's not. You're right," I said. She gave me a surprised look. "No, I mean it, Esther. You take your time and look around." I tried very hard to smile. "The trip and then finding out that one of my friends was murdered has made me a bit irritable. I'm sure it would make you that way too."

"One of your friends? You knew the woman who was murdered?" Her eyes widened as her chin fell and her glasses slid. "I didn't know her. How did you know her?"

"We don't have to know each other's friends. I'm sure you have lots of friends that I don't know. And don't forget you left Parson's Cove a few years ago now."

"Yes, I suppose that's true. Besides, my husband and I have many friends. I've learned that Parson's Cove is really not a very friendly place in comparison to other towns." She turned and wandered down an aisle with a confused look on her face. I knew it was bugging her that I knew the murder victim. I also knew she didn't have any friends. She could move to Timbuktu and still wouldn't have a friend.

I waited by the register. She stopped every few feet to pick something up and then put it back.

"Find anything yet, Esther?" I called out. I knew what she really wanted was to find out how I knew the murder victim but she would be too proud to ask.

"Don't rush me. You know they say that the customer is always right."

"Depends on the customer," I said under my breath.

"I heard that."

After ten minutes, she walked to the door. "Sorry,

Mabel, I guess I made the trip for nothing; you don't have anything I'm interested in. Almost everything you have was made in some foreign country with cheap labor. I thought perhaps you'd finally acquired some new merchandise - something perhaps from Paris or Rome? But, no, there's nothing extraordinary at all. Just the same old, same old."

"Oh, but I do have something extraordinary. Well, it's not new. Used, but in very good condition and it's gold."

"Gold? You have something in gold?" Esther's eyes always light up when someone says the word gold.

I reached in my pocket and pulled out the earring.

She gasped. "Where did you get that? That's my earring."

Her hand shot out like a serpent's tongue but my hand was faster.

"I know it's yours, Esther, and you know what? When you tell me what you were doing out by the lake and in the woods, you'll get it back."

"What? Are you crazy? That's none of your business. I will *never* tell you what I was doing out there."

"That's okay. I will *never* give you back your earring."

She crossed her arms against her chest and put her nose in the air. "Humph. I will go to Sheriff Jim and we'll see about this, Mabel. He'll make you give that earring back."

"Oh, I don't think so, Esther. This is a murder case. It's one thing to simply drop an earring on the ground but I found this out by the lake. Right beside the path leading to the body. What would you be doing out there at night? Does your husband know you were out there? Or is he implicated in this murder too? And then, of course, there's the threatening phone call. How does that fit in with the murder, Esther?" I placed my arms across my chest and lifted my chin in the air, too.

I watched as Esther's face changed from white to scarlet.

"Phone call? What phone call?"

"You know very well. You can try and disguise your voice all you like but I know it was you."

"Well, I'll have you know, it was not me. If you were the last person on earth, I wouldn't phone you, Mabel Wickles."

She had a point there.

"You would if you were involved in a murder; so, what were you doing in the woods? You'd better tell me if you want your gold earring back."

"Never. And don't you implicate my husband. You say anything about him or to him, and I'll get you, Mabel Wickles."

"Aw, so you are threatening me now? Okay. I'll see what Reg thinks about all of this then."

Esther flew out the door, leaving me alone with a gold earring in my hand.

Chapter Ten

"She could be telling the truth, Mabel."

Flori sat in Father's chair, sipping her wine. There were three cats in the living room, all vying for Flori's attention. The others were outside, probably searching for a platonic relationship with any cat other than a family member. My cats are extremely naive so as a result, have returned home many times, beaten up by a bewildered tomcat. I guess in the animal world it's hard to accept the fact that a few are neither 'he's' nor 'she's' but only 'its.'

"No, I'm pretty sure she was lying. I could tell by the way she blushed." I picked up the bottle and topped off our glasses. "I would give anything to know why she was in the woods at night. What do you think?"

Flori rolled her eyes. "Like I know what Esther does with her time. Maybe she was out berry picking."

"At night? And leaving her husband? I'd say more like baying at the moon. No, she was up to something. I wish I knew; it's driving me crazy."

"Did you ask her?"

"Of course, I asked her."

"And?"

"She said that she would never tell me so I threatened to take the earring over to Reg."

"Are you going to?"

"I doubt it. It really doesn't have anything to do with the murder. I like to have some leverage with her, that's all."

"You just like to torture her, you mean."

"That, too."

We drank our wine in silence for a few minutes, which is very rare with Flori, but it was pleasant.

"So, you really think she's the one who made the phone call, Mabel?"

"I wish I knew for sure. It did rather catch her off guard. But the blush, Flori. Usually that's the giveaway with Esther."

Flori looked at her watch. "I'd better skedaddle home. Jake will be back soon."

She tipped her glass up and drained it. A few drops dribbled down her chin which she carefully caught with her finger and drove back into her mouth.

"I swear, Flori, you'd make a better beer guzzler than a wine connoisseur. It wouldn't surprise me if you didn't let out a loud belch about now."

She stood up and leaned over to place the glass on the coffee table. "Oh, for goodness sake, you know I'd never do that." She straightened up. "If you want me to bring over fresh cinnamon buns to the shop tomorrow, you'd better treat me really good."

"Enough said. You can down your wine any old way you please, my dear."

We hugged and Flori left for home. It was still early and I definitely wasn't going to spend a beautiful warm spring evening sitting at home watching television.

Phil (whose real name is Phyllis and is the mother to the rest of the brood) jumped up on my lap and started purring. I scratched behind her ears and under her chin until my hand was wet with drool.

"You're as bad as Flori," I said, and gently pushed her away. "But, you are one smart cat, Phil. So, who do you think might know what Esther was doing in the woods?" She gazed up at me with such devotion that I had to start scratching her again. After all, what's a little drool between friends anyway?

Sometimes I'm amazed how my brain works. Out of nowhere, a thought formed. There was one person in Parson's Cove who knows what everyone is doing. There is someone who walks the streets at night, always somewhere in the darkness but never seen. Charlie Thompson. To top it all off, he was my friend.

I grabbed my purse and headed for the door. Charlie would be sitting on the bench in front of the library now. That's where he is sitting when any crime in Parson's Cove takes place.

"Hi Charlie," I called out as I neared the bench.

Charlie didn't answer or move. Sometimes, it isn't easy talking with Charlie because if you don't get him in the exact right mood, he doesn't say a thing. Also, if you happen to say the wrong thing or say too much, Charlie clams up. He'll get up and walk away when you're in the middle of a sentence. It takes a very patient person to converse with this man.

Some of the older folk (I mean in their eighties) know Charlie's story. His parents were already up in years when they moved to Parson's Cove with a small boy. They claimed that Charlie was their son but the rumor was that he was, in fact, their grandson. A child born out of wedlock to one of their daughters. Who knows? It was juicy gossip for many years anyway. It soon became apparent that Charlie was a bit different from other children. All the teachers felt sorry for him so instead of keeping him in the first grade for years, they simply kept moving him ahead. I was already in high school but would walk to school with him whenever I could. At least, on those days, no one teased him. Maybe that's why he's my friend today. When his parents died, Parson's Cove's Town Council moved him from one home to another. No one wanted poor Charlie. Finally, when he was old enough to be on his own, they settled him into a little house at the end of Main Street. There he lives to this day, minding his own business and not bothering anyone. There are folks who think his place looks dumpy but personally, I think it looks like a small summer cottage. Besides, he keeps it as neat as a pin.

I sat down beside him. He was staring into the western sky.

"Beautiful, isn't it, Charlie?"

If he heard me, he didn't let on.

"The sunset, I mean."

Still no response.

When was the last time I'd sat like this and watched the sun go down? I couldn't even remember. No one does it anymore, it seems.

"You know, Charlie, I should get Jake to build a deck or something in my backyard. I could sit outside and watch the sunsets or the stars. That would be a good idea, wouldn't it?"

"What do you want me to tell you, Mabel?"

"Well, you could tell me it's a good idea, I suppose. Would you want to come over and sit with me? I could make coffee and we could eat fresh muffins. How does that sound?"

His mouth moved slightly. That meant he was thinking

about smiling. That's usually as far as it goes. It was encouraging though.

"That would be nice but I know you didn't come to tell me that. You want me to tell you something else."

Charlie is sometimes more perceptive than other folks.

"You know me, Charlie. I'll come straight out and ask you. Do you know what Esther was doing out in the woods when she found that body?"

He nodded.

My heart beat faster. "You know what she was doing out there?"

He nodded again.

"Can you tell me? I'd really like to know. Did you know that I knew the woman who was murdered? She was in Las Vegas with me. Maybe you could help me solve this crime. What do you think?"

Charlie sat for a long time and said nothing. I don't know if he blinked. This is where endurance comes in. I'm sure that at least ten minutes passed. I was actually thinking of getting up and walking back home when he spoke up.

"Esther didn't have anything to do with the murder, Mabel."

"Oh, Charlie, I know that. I just have to know what she was doing out there. I'll tell you a secret. She left a very nasty message on my answering machine and I'd like to find out why. That's why I thought you could help."

He turned his head and looked at me for the first time. "She left a nasty message?"

"Yes, she did, Charlie. She doesn't like me very much."

"Well, I like you, Mabel, so I'll tell you what she was doing out there. Esther was meeting someone."

"She was meeting someone? You mean she's being unfaithful to her new husband already? Who?"

Charlie turned back to the sunset and started to hum. This was the end of our conversation. Perhaps, he would tell me more tomorrow. Even this much probably wore him right out.

I patted him on the arm and thanked him. I found myself humming all the way home too.

Chapter Eleven

I couldn't stop worrying about the murder case. Every time Reg, Jim, or Scully saw me, they almost crossed over to the other side of the street to avoid me. The least they could do was fill me in on some of the evidence they had collected.

I clicked my bedside lamp on and checked the clock. It wasn't quite ten yet. My room was dark because I'd pulled the blind down. The days were starting to get long but there was no way I could sleep in a light room. I needed a drink of water, however, so I got up and went downstairs. While I was there, I thought I might as well kill two birds with one stone, as the saying goes.

Reg picked up on the third ring.

"What do you want, Mabel?" he said, without as much as a 'hello.' (I always forget that he has 'call display.' As does Flori.)

"Well, and how are you, too, Mr. Smee?"

"Never mind the niceties; I know you're after something."

"Maybe I want to talk to Beth."

"Do you?"

He had me there. "No, you know I want to talk to you, Reg. I have to know how the murder case is doing. You know Grace was my friend. I think you owe it to me to keep me informed."

He paused for the briefest moment and then he sighed.

"I guess I owe you something, Mabel. Actually, there's not much to tell. You know very well that when Maxymowich comes, I'm not exactly kept up to speed. All I know for sure is that they're having a hard time trying to find any of her family. It's like she doesn't even exist. Other than that, you know as much as I do. Does that help you any?"

"Has anybody gone down to Yellow Rose, Texas, to check things out? That's where she's from, you know."

"We know that, Mabel. All of Maxymowich's cops are here but he's probably in touch with law enforcement down there. At least, I would imagine. Maxymowich isn't stupid. He'll cover all the bases."

Reg wasn't much help but he did put a thought in my head. Why couldn't I go down and do some snooping? No one would be concerned about an older woman hanging around and asking questions, would they? The biggest problem to that would be how could I do it without raising suspicions? Not there but here in Parson's Cove.

Who knew the answer would drop right into my lap?

Flori entered the shop the next morning looking about as haggard and drained as I'd ever seen her. She usually bursts in like this tall, larger than life, sparkling sunbeam. Most days she radiates warmth, love, and joy. One look at her orange-red hair, her artificially arched auburn eyebrows, glossy pink lips and flamboyant orange and pink sundress and you can't help but smile. There are not enough adjectives to describe her.

"My goodness, Flori, what's wrong? Why do you look so forlorn? Where are the cinnamon buns? Please, don't tell me that Jake ate all of them. If he did, I'll never forgive him."

Just the hint that in some other world, I would even consider for one moment forgiving Jake anything usually makes Flori burst into laughter. Not today.

Instead, she burst into tears.

"What's the matter?" We met half way and I put my arms around her. Flori is the most wonderful person to hug because there's so much of her and all of it is soft.

"It's Jake," she managed to sputter before letting out a loud wail.

I steered her to the chair. She sat looking up at me, a torrent of tears streaming down her face, mixed in with mascara that eventually joined her very runny nose. I grabbed a handful of tissues.

"Here," I said. "Wipe your face and keep your mouth closed until you're finished."

She nodded and complied.

When she finished using up about ten tissues, I asked, "Now, what's this about Jake? And don't start crying again. That's my last box of tissues."

"Oh Mabel, I can't believe he would do this to me." With that, she did exactly as I'd told her not to do - she started wailing and blubbering again. I went into my back room and brought out an old hand towel; something I should've done in the first place.

"Here," I said. "Let it all out. When you're finished, we'll throw this in the trash." I did not intend to keep that towel. Or, ever use it again even if I washed it in straight bleach.

I grabbed her hand. "Are you trying to tell me that Jake is having an affair, Flori?"

That was the only thing I could think of that would make

a woman carry on so. Suddenly, Charlie's words came back to me. Esther Flynn was meeting someone in the woods at night. Surely, it couldn't be Jake!

"Is Jake having an affair with Esther?" I gasped.

Flori stared at me as if I were out of my mind.

"What?" she whispered. "What are you talking about, Mabel?"

"Oh, never mind. What are *you* talking about? Why, on earth, are you crying like this? What has Jake done?"

"He's going on a fishing trip with Mike Brown and Henry Brewster." She sniffed. "For a whole week. They've made the plans already and he never even told me. He didn't consult me. I always consult him no matter what I do." She covered her face with the towel and blew her nose. I shut my eyes and cringed. "I can't believe it," she said when her face finally surfaced. "He's never done this before. What's happening to our marriage? Do you really think he's going to meet another woman?" She looked at me, her eyes blank and confused. "Why did you say Esther? Do you know something I don't, Mabel?" The blank confused look turned to panic.

"Flori, he's not going to meet another woman. Forget I even mentioned Esther's name. I'll tell you about that later when you can handle it." I got up and poured a cup of coffee. "Here, drink this. You'll feel better afterwards. By the way, when are they leaving for this fishing trip?"

She blew on her coffee and cautiously took a sip.

"They're leaving next Monday."

"That's plenty of notice, Flori. He's obviously giving you time to give your 'okay' and to adjust your schedule. You don't want to smother Jake. He's retired now so you can't keep him home all the time, tied to your apron strings, you know."

"Oh, Mabel, do you think I do that?" Her eyes once again filled with tears. I have no idea where this woman gets all her moisture. If I cried as much as she does, I'd be on intravenous.

I patted her hand. "You have a tendency to smother, my dear."

She smiled through her tears. "Thanks. You are such a friend." She hiccoughed. "Thank you for being so honest."

I grinned. "So, do you know what we're going to do while he's on his vacation?"

"Do?"

"We're going to go on our own vacation. You didn't get to go to Vegas with me as you planned so we'll go somewhere else. I'll make sure you don't think or worry about Jake Flanders for one second."

The tears of sadness had been hardly mopped up when out poured the tears of gladness.

"Where will we go? To the city to shop? I would love to do that. We could stay at a fancy hotel for a few days. That would be wonderful, wouldn't it? Is that what you had planned?"

I shook my head. "Do you still have your money from the trip you never took?"

"Of course, I do. What are you saying? You want to go back to Las Vegas?"

"No, I'd like to go somewhere different this time. I have some money saved and I'll get Delores to watch the shop and the cats. I know she'd like a break from the restaurant anyway."

"Mabel, don't keep me in suspense. Where will we go?"
"Let's go to Yellow Rose, Texas."
Flori screamed as the hot coffee splashed onto her lap.

The coffee mug hit the floor, bursting into a few dozen pieces.

I'd say that was a good sign. She was obviously overcome with excitement.

Chapter Twelve

Flori sat on a bench at the William P. Hobby airport in Houston, Texas, surrounded by two suitcases, a purse, and a plastic bag containing three pairs of shoes. Personally, I had taken one small carry-on case. As usual, she was weeping. It didn't bother her that people stopped and either just stared or walked over and asked if she was all right. It didn't bother her that I was the one who was mortified. It was the last straw when a tall man with a cowboy hat and droopy mustache went over to her and said, "Is there anythang I can do for y'all, darlin'?" and she looked up at him with those big watery eyes and said, "No, there's nothing anyone can do. I left my husband to go to Yellow Rose with Mabel. I don't know what I was thinking. He should've stopped me but he didn't." She sniffed. "Now, we're stuck here at this horrible airport and I don't think we'll ever get home again."

I ignored the hateful look he threw at me. "Flori, we are not stuck here," I said. "I told you that there's a taxi waiting outside to drive us to Yellow Rose. Now, pick up your suitcases and let's go."

"Now, just one minute here," the cowboy said. He turned to Flori. "You can make up your own mind; do you really want to go with this woman to Yellow Rose, or go back to your husband?"

Flori sniffed and wiped away a tear. "There's a taxi

waiting for us?"

"Yes. I told you I was going to get one."

The cowboy put his hand on her arm and said in the gentlest voice, "Y'all sure you want to do this, honey? Remember, you have a faithful husband waitin' back home."

"Oh yes," Flori said, with a most enchanting smile. "I have never been anywhere besides Parson's Cove and Mabel says Yellow Rose sounds wonderful. Besides, she's the one who is going to try to find Grace's murderer." She stood up. "I'm going to relax in the sun. Right, Mabel?"

The last I saw of the Texan was his back as he walked outside, shaking his head. I didn't have the energy to explain anything.

After two hours of speeding along a country highway, barely slowing down as we whipped through dull forlorn looking little towns, we were in our hotel room, unpacking. Well, Flori was. All I had was clean underwear, a shirt, and another pair of jeans. It took all of three minutes to take care of that. Flori would put something away and then rush to the window for another look at the Gulf of Mexico, which slapped up against the abandoned beach, several feet away. There was no traffic on the street that ran in front of the hotel and stretched out along the coastline. Our hotel matched all the other stores and restaurants - old, weather-beaten, but somehow managing to look quaint and welcoming. This was a quiet place, too out of the way for most tourists.

"Isn't this wonderful, Mabel? I'm so glad Jake thought this was a good idea. I can't believe he really encouraged me to go, can you? And, with such short notice. Did you know, I didn't even have time to tell the kids. Jake said he would. He's so good to me sometimes." She grabbed a tissue and wiped her eyes.

I didn't want her to ever find out that I'd had a private talk with Jake and had succeeded in giving him a mighty huge guilty conscience. I mean, if he could traipse off with the boys for a week of drinking and carrying on at some secluded lodge, so could she. Not the drinking and carrying-on part, but definitely the traipsing off part. I really had no idea what men do at those places but Jake seemed to think I did so he agreed to let Flori go. On one condition, I told him, no one in Parson's Cove must know where we were going, especially Reg or Sheriff Jim. I wouldn't worry about Scully. He'd think it was a hoot.

"What'll I say to someone who asks? And, what about the kids?" he said. "They're going to think something's weird if I don't even know where their mother is."

"Tell them I still had some free time left from my Las Vegas trip and we were using it up in Florida."

I knew Jake had no problem lying.

Flori pulled out some brochures she'd picked up in the lobby and studied them.

"I've circled all the places we should tour, Mabel." She looked over at me. I was on the other bed, studying a map of the city and surrounding area. "You are going to come with me, aren't you?"

"Of course, I am. I have to look like a normal tourist. I'll just have to keep my eyes and ears open. You can too. I showed you all the pictures of the people on that trip so if you see any of them, let me know."

"I'm sure I wouldn't recognize any of them in person. Surely, the police are checking out where this Grace lived. Wouldn't they have to contact her family to send the body back?" Flori shivered as she always does when she says the word 'body.'

"I have no idea. Reg knows about as much as I do. Obviously, I'm not about to ask Captain Maxymowich."

"So, where are you going to start?"

"I have started; I'm looking up Hobbs in the phone book." I flipped through the phone book, which wasn't much bigger than the *Parson's Cove and Surrounding Communities White and Yellow Pages.*

"There's only three. One must be Grace's husband. Of course, they could all be related. We'll sort of wander past each house tomorrow while we're sightseeing."

"What if there's nothing to see on that street?"

"Flori, everything in Yellow Rose is something to see. Everything is old and historic. We could go to almost any house and ask to look inside."

Her eyes widened. "They let you do that?"

"Of course, it's an honor. Especially if it survived a hurricane."

She looked doubtful.

"When was there a hurricane?"

I shrugged. "There are always hurricanes on this coast. Don't worry about it. It's not hurricane season. Let's go to eat and then we'll start out tomorrow. We can walk along the beach to a restaurant and back."

That cheered her up. We walked to a small Mexican restaurant that advertised cheap margaritas. By the time we'd downed two drinks each, emptied two bowls of homemade salsa with their own made-on-the-premises chips, it was hard to look at the large platter of food that was plunked down in front of us. Especially the generous plop of runny beans. The helpful server suggested that we have another drink so that's what we did. After that, we cleaned our plates.

I'm not sure who was up the most that night but I do know we went through a half bottle of anti-acid pills. We both vowed never to eat beans and drink margaritas again. Actually, Flori would never have even smelled a margarita except I told her it was an authentic Mexican drink and the folks in the restaurant would've been very hurt if we hadn't had some of their national drink.

In between trips to the bathroom, I slept but somehow in the background of every dream I could hear Esther's voice on the answering machine, threatening my life.

The next morning, the sea mist was so thick we could hardly see the water from our window. Even with the morning traffic, however, we could still hear the constant soft rumble of the ocean. We made coffee in our little coffee maker, added the powdered creamer, and sat on our balcony. I drank half a cup and threw the rest down the sink.

By the time we had showered and dressed it was almost nine. Flori looked exceptionally colorful in her flowered sea blue and lime green tent dress. Of course, she wore her wide brimmed straw hat with the matching blue and green band. No one would even notice me in my jeans and white cotton shirt. I did put on some light pink lipstick so I wouldn't be too outshone.

All the way to the restaurant, Flori 'ooed' and 'aawed' over every wave that hit the shore. I was thankful that I was the one who had the camera. I'd learned from all the pictures of the Hoover Dam that every water picture would look almost identical.

This time we tried the Yellow Rose Family Restaurant. Over eggs, bacon, and grits, we discussed our plans. Well, they were Flori's plans and they were my strategies.

"What street did you say you wanted to visit, Mabel?"

"Avenue P½."

"Avenue P½ ?"

I nodded. My mouth was full of egg.

"What kind of street is that?"

"It isn't. It's an avenue."

"I mean, why would they have the ½ ?"

"No idea. Maybe it's to confuse everybody." I shoveled in another mouthful.

"What's on that street that you want to see anyway?"

"Hobbs."

Her eyebrows went up and disappeared under her bangs. "That's where your friend Grace lives?"

"Lived, Flori. *Lived*. Past tense."

"Well, I know that, for Pete's sake. It just came out, that's all."

"I know. It hasn't really hit me yet either. Hard to believe I was with her, laughing and having a good time, a week ago."

"You were laughing and having a good time with her?"

I buttered and salted my grits. "In a manner of speaking."

"Oh." Flori concentrated on her food. "This bacon is not cooked enough," she muttered to herself.

After breakfast, we took a leisurely walk along the beach. The morning mist had lifted and the sun shone. The sandy beach was quickly filling up with some of the locals. Already, girls with very little on were sunbathing and boys in skintight rubbery suits were heading into the water with their surfboards. We went back up to the street and caught a bus to the downtown area. The driver was talkative and as he pointed to different houses, he told us some of Yellow Rose's history and some of the latest gossip.

"Did you hear about the murder of Grace Hobbs?" I asked. Flori poked me and gave me a dirty look.

"Can't say I did," he said. "Was that before or after the big hurricane in 1900?"

"No," I said. "That was during the warm spell about a week ago."

"Oh," he said. "Nope, didn't hear about it. Strange, too. There's not too many murders here in Yellow Rose. By the way, if you want a good cup of coffee, I'll drop you off right in front of the coffee shop," he said. "Tell him Tom sent you and you'll get it cheaper."

I'll do anything for a good cup of coffee so that's what we did. There wasn't much point in explaining the murder to him. If he knew Grace, he would've expressed some surprise. He did seem to be a storehouse of knowledge though so he might prove useful to me at some point.

The coffee shop was at the corner of 23rd street and some letter of the alphabet, but I forget which one. It was long and narrow with hardly any customers and the few who were there, were nursing a cup of coffee and reading. How long did this fellow expect to stay in business? Paintings from local artists covered the walls and Flori gushed over all of them.

Flori and I wandered around through the shops on J Avenue. Although I wasn't interested in buying anything, it did give me some ideas as to what I might like to stock on my shelves. Flori had a long list of things to buy for her husband, kids, and grandkids.

"You better wait, Flori," I said, as she started grabbing everything in sight in one of the souvenir shops. "Don't forget we have to do some walking. Besides, you still have a few days to buy things. Why don't you look for now and then you can compare prices?"

"Oh, you're so right," she said, and started putting the t-shirts back. The young sales girl curled her lips at me.

We caught the bus back to the hotel. It was getting hot and humid and the cool room was refreshing. Flori flung her hat on the chair, flopped on the bed, and was soon asleep. I left a note for her and slipped out the door.

How far away could Avenue P½ be anyway?

Chapter Thirteen

P ½ was farther away than I'd expected. Well, I don't know what I expected. I found it difficult trying to remember the alphabet backwards. The street was in an older section with houses probably built in the 20's or earlier. I'm not sure why I picked this address to investigate first. Perhaps, it sounded more ominous. P ½. Murder on P½. Hmm…of course, the murder couldn't have taken place here. Unless the body was transported in a refrigerated truck or something back to Parson's Cove. Did that mean that Grace never returned home after her vacation in Las Vegas or did return and then, for some reason, went to Parson's Cove? Was she coming to see me? No, why would she do that?

I kept walking until I stood right across from the house. It looked like a small square box painted light green. The paint was peeling, the steps going up to the porch were falling apart, and almost every other shingle on the roof was missing or flapping in the breeze. In comparison, the house next door looked like it had just been painted, not a shingle was out of place, and the yard with its shrubs and flowers was immaculate. I realized as I looked down the street that seemed to be the trend. One lovely house could have something resembling a chicken coop on either side.

I stood and waited for a few minutes. There was no sign

of life. The whole street was silent. A couple of dogs barked back and forth from somewhere. There were two or three cars parked further down. I waited a bit longer.

I checked the street once again before I crossed. The wrought iron gate was sagging and permanently held open by the weeds that wound their way around and through the railing. The yard was cluttered with plastic weather-beaten Christmas decorations (a faded plastic Santa Claus, a cardboard snowman lying on its back staring up at the sky, and a reindeer with one leg missing), two garden gnomes on each side of the steps, and several rusty gardening tools tossed under a window. A ceramic pot filled with plastic flowers sat on the floor beside the door. There wasn't one home in Parson's Cove to compare with this.

My heart was pounding as I banged on the door. Silence. Before knocking again, I walked to the side of the house and looked towards the backyard. I was actually quite surprised at how far back the building went. Did I dare walk back and knock on the back door? Before I could decide, I heard someone yell, "Can I help y'all with somethin'?'"

I looked around but couldn't see anyone. "Where are you?" I yelled back.

"Never mind. I'll be right down, darlin'."

Now I realized the voice came from next-door, behind an upstairs window covered with hurricane shutters. No wonder I couldn't see anyone.

In about two minutes, a large black woman was standing at the fence facing me. The first thing I noticed, besides her size, were her clothes. She was a black version of Flori.

"You lookin' for somebody?" she said.

I didn't want to say Grace Hobbs so I just nodded.

She shook her head. "Haven't seen anyone round here

for a few days now. You some relative or something?"

"No," I said. "I knew Grace from a trip we took together. I wondered if this was where she lived. Did you know she was in Vegas?"

"Lord, no. I hardly see anything of that woman. If she were away for a month, I probably wouldn't notice." She sighed. "Now, if the yard were cleaned up, you can bet I'd notice that!" She laughed and showed off the whitest teeth I'd ever seen in my life. "What'd you say you wanted with her, honey?"

"Well," I said. "I really didn't want her for anything. In fact, the truth be told, no one will be wanting her for anything ever again, I'm sorry to say."

"What on earth are you sayin'? Grace might not be the most Christian person in this world but there's no need to be talkin' bout her like that. We being neighbors and all, you know."

There's really no nice way to put some things. Now, I understand how those cops feel when they have to tell the family a loved one has been murdered.

"What did you say your name was?" I asked.

"I didn't." She glared at me.

"Oh, I'm sorry. Of course, you didn't." I held out my hand and smiled. "My name is Mabel Wickles. I'm from a little town called Parson's Cove, a long ways away from here. It's much smaller than Yellow Rose, if you can imagine. I came down with my friend, Flori Flanders. Actually, Flori is sleeping right now at the hotel. I left a note saying I was going for a walk on the beach to collect shells and not to expect me back for at least an hour or more." I looked at my watch. "My time is almost up and I seem to be babbling a bit, so I guess I'd better tell you."

She frowned so hard, there was a wrinkle from the

middle of her forehead right down to her chin.

"Tell me what? You *are* babblin' and you ain't makin' much sense."

"Grace was murdered. Maybe a week ago. I don't know for sure when, because her body was dumped in the woods behind our nursing home." My legs started feeling rubbery so I inhaled deeply and exhaled before continuing. "We only have one nursing home because as I said, Parson's Cove is small." My tongue seemed to keep moving without any help from me. "Anyway, someone found her body there. I won't go into detail as to who found the body. Well, I'm the one who identified her. It was really a fluke because when I snuck into the morgue I had no idea I'd be looking at someone that I knew. You can imagine the shock when I lifted the cloth and saw it was Grace. As I mentioned, we were on a vacation in Las Vegas together. We both won it. I'd never met Grace or her friend, Andrea, before. In fact, that's the first time I ever won anything and now I'm hoping I never win anything again."

The wrinkle disappeared, as her eyes got bigger.

"Grace was murdered?" Her voice softened and her eyes watered. She swallowed. "How? How was she kilt?" She didn't wait for an answer. "Did her good for nothing husband murder her?" Now her watery eyes blazed with anger. Again, she didn't wait for an answer. "I knew it. I knew someday, he'd get into some kinda trouble. There was always somethin' not right goin' on in that house. Sinister lookin' men and women, comin' and goin'. More than once, I had to call the cops. Lotta good that did." She grunted. "Can't say Miss Grace was mixed up in things but you know sometimes they looks good when they's doing bad. Not that I want to speak ill of the dead, you understand. "

She sniffed a couple of times and shook her head before turning her attention back to me. "My goodness, darlin', this has got to be awful for you. Imagine lookin' at a dead body like that. Here," she grabbed my arm and started pulling me along the fence beside her. When we reached the end, she said, "Can you come around to me all by yourself now, sweetheart?"

I almost said, "I think so, Flori." Instead, I just nodded. I walked out the gate and she met me on the sidewalk.

She put her arm around me and half-carried me to her house. We walked up wooden steps with a wooden railing to the second floor. I realized then that there was a garage on the bottom floor. It was a house on stilts.

Her kitchen was dark and cool. She walked over to the sink and poured a glass of water.

"Here," she said. "This will make you feel better." It did help.

"Now," she said, "what's all this about Grace? Was it Cecile who killed her?"

"Is Cecile her husband?"

She nodded. "He's one of those cagey guys, you know. Always looks out the corner of his eyes at you. Wouldn't trust him for a minute. Not that fellow. All he does is fix cars on the side. When I say, 'on the side,' you know what I'm sayin'?" She cocked her head to one side.

I shook my head. "No, what are you saying?"

"I'm sayin' that's just a front. He's been dealin' drugs or maybe somethin' worse for years. I don't know if Grace ever got involved but then again, like I say, I never saw much of her lately. By the way, honey, I never did tell you my name, did I? Guess I just got so caught up in this murder thing." She held out her hand. "My name's Stella.

Stella Townley."

This handshake was much firmer than the first one.

I looked up at the clock. I'd been gone almost two hours.

"Stella, would you mind if I called my friend at the hotel? She might be starting to worry about me."

'Might' was putting it mildly. It took almost ten minutes to calm Flori down and convince her that I was okay. Finally, I just handed the phone over to Stella. I slipped out the door and hurried back to the hotel.

Chapter Fourteen

I walked, gasping and puffing, into the room. Flori was still on the phone with Stella. I showered, dressed, and blow-dried what little hair I have, and Flori was still on the phone.

It wasn't until I stood in front of her doing charades and wanting her to guess, 'let us eat supper,' that she finally said, "Oh Stella, I think Mabel is here now so I'd better go. We'll see you bright and early in the morning then."

"You *think* I'm here now?" I said when she finally put the phone down.

"Yes, I think you are, Mabel."

"We'll see her bright and early in the morning?"

Flori looked flushed with excitement.

"Yes, isn't it wonderful? Stella is going to help us solve the mystery."

"Stella is going to help us solve the mystery?"

"That's what I said. Aren't you happy about that? We'll have someone right here from Yellow Rose to help us. She'll know all the hideouts and everything."

"Hideouts?"

Flori stood up and scowled. "Mabel, why are you repeating everything that I say?"

"Well, pardon me, Miss Detective Who Doesn't Want to Get Involved, it's just that you keep saying *we*. If I remember correctly, you distinctly said, 'I will not get involved in this murder case. I will only come with you so you don't get yourself killed.' And, if I further remember, you repeated that to me at least ten times before we even got on the plane."

Flori blushed and her eyes filled with tears. "I know but it just seems different now. Now, there's someone else to watch over you, too. It will be so much easier if I have someone to help me."

I knew she was ready to burst into a flood so I handed her the box of tissues and said, "You're right. It will be easier for both of us." She blew her nose and I gave her a hug. "Now," I said, "where do you want to eat? I'm starving."

"How about seafood? I think I'd like to avoid Mexican for another day or so."

We strolled down the seawall to a little establishment that said it had the freshest seafood on the Gulf coast. It was another warm evening and the breeze off the water was just enough to make a person wish they'd brought their sweater. Flori, of course, remembered hers. The food was delicious. Flori splurged on a bottle of wine, which she insisted we finish before we leave because even though it was the restaurant's cheapest, it was expensive. At least, to anyone from Parson's Cove.

"And not as good as Sadie MacIntosh's chokecherry wine," she said. "Not by a long shot." Her tongue slid out to catch a drop that almost escaped from the side of her mouth.

"Don't worry," I said. "The taste will improve the more you drink."

Flori giggled until everyone at the surrounding tables began staring and I gave her a gentle kick under the table.

"Flori," I said, "everyone is staring. Here, have another drink," and I filled her glass up to the top again. At that point, she totally lost control and the people beside us burst out laughing too.

Well, by the time, we were finished the wine and ready to go, Flori had everyone's address and knew pretty much everything there was to know about anyone. Except Big Bill's little prostate problem. That was something, he said, he didn't like to talk about; at least, in public. Perhaps, he and Flori could go out for lunch. If I hadn't given her a kick and the evil eye, I'm sure she would've hauled off and hit him with her handbag. It was bad enough that she gave him a three-minute lecture on fidelity. I didn't need that much attention. We were getting too much as it was.

"I think you've missed out on a lot of things in life, Flori, because you've been stuck in Parson's Cove." We were almost at the hotel now and the sun was settling down in the west. The sky in the east was pink and powder blue. "If you were let out on the loose, I think you'd pretty much know someone in every state or maybe every country."

Flori was still smiling when we reached our room. In fact, I think she slept with it plastered to her face because when I woke up in the morning, there she was, smiling down at me.

"I let you sleep in a bit, Mabel, but now you'd better get up and shower. Stella is going to be here any minute. She's taking us out for breakfast. She knows this little restaurant down on 25th, I think she said it was. Anyway, she has a car so she's going to be driving us." She flung the covers off me. "I've already started the shower running. Now, scoot."

I stared up at her. "You are my best friend, Flori, but now I remember why I never wanted to go on a vacation with you. My own mother never started the shower running for me or told me to scoot."

"That's because you were an only child and your mother didn't know how to handle you."

There was no use in arguing with her so I trudged to the bathroom. Little streams of steam were seeping through the opening along the floor.

"By the way," I said, before entering the steam room, "did I tell you that Stella is black?"

Flori looked a bit confused. "Black? Black what?"

"Black skin. What do you think I meant?"

Just before I shut the door, I heard her say, "She didn't sound black."

Chapter Fifteen

"I think we should set up surveillance on Cecile's house." That was my first idea – with the emphasis on *my*.

Flori whispered, "Since you live next door, Stella, and have all those windows facing his house, I think that should be your job. What do you think?"

Stella replied, in a hoarse whisper, "I s'pose I could. Only thing is, I might not know what to watch for. Don' forget, I ain't done no sneaky things before. I'm innocent like a little lamb." She roared. Flori did too but I'm not sure she knew why. "My bedroom faces Grace's house," she continued to whisper. "I s'pose I could sit in the dark and keep watch. That little weasel comes home, I'll let you know."

"What about your husband?" I asked.

"Oh, she doesn't have one," Flori said. "Her husband, Rocky, died seven years ago. He was a firefighter. She lives with her oldest son, Spencer. He's a fireman too, but he works in Houston. Right now, he's on a two-day shift so he won't be there."

Why did I feel like I was the one out of the loop?

Stella opened her huge handbag and pulled out a sheet of paper. "Here," she said, as she handed it over to Flori. "I made a list of some of the places drug dealers visit." Realizing her voice was back to normal, she looked around and whispered, "Not that we'd go in or anything but we could sit outside and watch. Surveillance, you know."

There was actually no need to whisper, the place was so noisy, you couldn't hear yourself think. All I could do was wonder how this woman knew where all the drug deals were going down.

Not to be outdone, I opened my handbag. It was about one-third the size of Stella's bag. I laid my envelope of pictures on the table.

"I thought you gave all your pictures to Reg," Flori said.

"He doesn't need all of them." I spread them out. "Here's every picture I kept that has a human being in it."

Stella gasped. "That's him," she said, pointing to the picture of the man in front of the mechanical cowboy. "Why do you have a picture of him?"

"Who's *him*? Why do I have a picture of whom?"

"Grace's husband, that's who." Stella looked at me as if I might be joking. "You're telling me you don't know who that is?"

"I'm telling you, I had no idea who that was. Flori and I just thought he was some creepy guy who accidently got into one of my pictures." I looked at the man. "That's Grace's husband? Are you sure?" I handed the picture to her so she could get a better look.

She took it and nodded. "I recognized him upside down." She gave it back. "See how evil he looks?" She shook her head. "That's Cecile Tucker, sure as I'm sittin' here."

"Cecile Tucker? But Grace said her name was Grace Hobbs."

Stella raised her eyebrows almost as high as Flori raises hers.

She nodded. "Sad, ain't it? Now, why would she say that? Maybe she's ashamed to use his name cause it connects her to a drug dealer. Come to think of it, I guess I never really knew if she used his name or not. Some women don't, you know. I gotta say I was always proud to use my husband's name."

"Me, too," Flori stated. Then, she bowed her head and whispered, "Maybe they weren't even married. I bet they were living in sin. Those kinds of people do."

Stella nodded and murmured in agreement.

"Flori," I said, "one of your kids lives in sin."

"All right, Mabel, I'm just making a point. You didn't have to bring that up. You know it breaks my heart."

"It's all right, darlin'," Stella said. "One of mine does too. Nothin' I say does any good. Young people nowadays got no moral sense a'tall."

"Okay, you two, let's get back to what's at hand here. Now we know why the name in the phone book was Hobbs. Grace is the one who took care of the phone bill."

Stella leaned forward, glancing around before she spoke. "Or, it could've been in her sister's name. She used to live there but then she died. Maybe Grace and Cecile never changed it."

"She died?"

Stella leaned over farther and nodded. "That's what I hear. Strange circumstances, too. Mind you, this is mostly hearsay but I'm sure there's truth to it. Nothing anyone could prove but it was a suspicious death. Know what I mean?" Her eyes looked like two black marbles floating in a sea of white milk.

Without realizing it, I had started leaning over the table too. "How suspicious are we talking about?"

Stella did another quick look around. No one was

watching; certainly, no one could hear over the din.

"Ginger lived there first. Everybody called her that 'cause of her hair. She was a real nice friendly girl. Not sure where she worked. She seemed to be comin' and goin' a lot too. Onct I happened to notice a gun layin' on her kitchen table when I walked past the window. 'Course, lots o' girls have those for protection, you know. Kept her yard all nice and neat. Then, along comes Cecile and Grace. Grace, I don't mind. All of a sudden, I notice Ginger isn't lookin' so healthy. Kind of limpin' around. I axe her, 'what's wrong wich you, honey?' She say, 'I'm okay. Just got injured from some fall.' But, you know what I'm thinkin'? I'm thinkin' gunshot wound. That's what I'm thinkin.' Next thing you know, Ginger is nowhere to be seen and Grace and Cecile take over the house. Do that sound suspicious to you?"

Flori and I nodded in agreement.

"Do you think Grace left Cecile?" Flori piped up. "Maybe that's why he was in Vegas. He was checking up on her. If that's the case we might've come all the way down here for nothing. Who knows where he might be."

"Not for nothing," I said. "I'm sure he would've come back to his house. Where else would he go? It would all belong to him now. Not that's it's anything to brag about." It sounded to me like it was a cursed house no matter which way you looked at it. "Somehow," I said, "I have a feeling that he's probably the killer."

Stella and Flori widened their eyes, raised their eyebrows simultaneously, and nodded in agreement.

"So what can we do?" Flori asked. "I don't want to make a citizen's arrest, you know."

"Oh sugar, you wouldn't want to make a citizen's arrest

on this guy if you were armed with a bazooka. Trust me; he's nobody to fool with. It's a good thing he's never in his yard because when he's out there, I go inside."

"We won't make any arrests. When we spot him, we'll simply call the police and tell them what we know."

"What about Grace's friend?" Stella asked. "Didn't you say she had a friend who lived here too?"

"Well, they weren't friends before. They met on the trip. I think they sort of paired off because they both spent all their time in the gambling rooms."

The server cleared away our plates and filled our cups up for the third time. There were people still standing by the door, waiting for a table. I tried not to make eye contact. I was glad Flori was facing me because she would insist we get up and give our table to someone. She would for sure if she knew there was a woman with crutches waiting there. There were people sitting, nursing a cup of coffee, who'd been here much longer than us, so let them move on.

"We should really let her know about Grace, don' you think?" Stella asked. "That would be the Christian thing to do, wouldn't it?"

"Yes, it would," Flori gushed. "It would be and besides," she looked at me, "she might be able to tell us something about Grace."

"What'd you say her name was?" Stella asked.

"Andrea Williams."

"Hmm. Williams is a common name. Lots of folks by that name here in Yellow Rose." Stella seemed to be trying to conjure up a face. "Don' think I know any Andrea though. What'd she look like?"

I shrugged. "Sort of everyday looking. Her hair was dirty blonde. She was a bit on the heavy side."

"Honey, that's about how every woman in Texas looks."

She and Flori burst out laughing.

"'Cept for us black folk, that is." And she burst out laughing again.

Flori blushed. She'd already forgotten that their skin tones were different.

I sorted through the pictures that I'd brought.

"Here. This is Andrea." I handed her the picture I had of Andrea and Grace standing together in the hotel lobby. I hadn't thought about it before but now I remembered how Andrea hated getting her picture taken. I thought it was because she didn't like the way she looked. That's why, when we were in the lobby, I snapped it quickly before she noticed. She wasn't facing the camera but there was enough of her face showing to be able to identify her easily. Grace was looking the other way so I only got her back.

Stella picked it up and examined it carefully. "Can't say I've ever seen her around here and I pretty much know everyone. Yellow Rose ain't exactly that big, you know. Her face looks familiar but that's all I can say. Unless, she's from the west end where all the rich folk live and I happened to bump into her on the beach."

"No, I'm pretty sure she isn't from any rich area."

"I don' think so either. She look more like po' folk. Isn't dressed too sharp, is she?"

I looked at the picture. Now that Stella mentioned it, Andrea did look more like po' folk than rich folk.

She grabbed hold of the waitress' apron as she walked by.

"Honey, you gotta phone book I can look at?"

"Si. Up by the register."

Stella slid out of the seat and went to the counter by the entrance. Before grabbing the phone book, she walked over to the woman with the crutches and said, "How y'all doin,' sweetie? We'll be out of here soon as anything, sugar. Can you jus' hang on a bit longer?" The woman gave a little hop as she tried straightening her crutches, nodded, and smiled. Stella gave her a hug that sent one crutch flying. I kept talking to Flori so she wouldn't see.

The server filled our cups again.

"Aren't these the friendliest folks you ever met, Mabel?" Flori said.

I had to admit they were right up there in the top ten. It was quite all right, however, to let a handicapped person keep standing, as long as you called her 'honey' and gave her a hug. It's the same in Parson's Cove, except we don't call just anyone 'honey' and Flori is about the only person who hugs.

Stella came back and opened the phone book.

"Lots of 'Williams' here," she said. "Can't find an Andrea though." She slid her finger down the row.

"Oh, shucks, I never thought of it, Stella, but that's probably because she's married and unlike Grace, the phone is listed in her husband's name. I got the impression she was glad to be rid of him for a few days. Just the way she talked, you know."

"Wouldn't it be a coincidence if the two husbands knew each other?" Flori said.

Stella grunted. "If this Williams guy is a jerk, for sure Cecile will know him."

She took a piece of paper out of her purse and wrote down the addresses of all the Williams in the phone book.

"Do you think we should leave?" I said. Our cups were empty and the waiter was heading our way with the coffee pot again. "There's quite a line-up at the door waiting for a table."

"Good idea." Stella stood up, waved to the woman with the crutches, and shouted, "Y'all can have our seat now, baby."

The young woman hobbled over and gave Stella a kiss on the cheek before sitting down.

We got back into her car. Stella drove a 1975 pink Cadillac. I love my 1969 Buick but riding in this was like floating on a massive cloud - an earsplitting cloud that emanated gas fumes. I sat in the backseat with several empty paper coffee cups, French fry containers, and at least two dozen ketchup packets, some empty and some unopened. There was a child's car seat in the other corner, filled with several stained and worn stuffed animals.

I moved the refuse off my seat and let it fall to the floor. Flori looked around at me. Not that I'm a neat freak but I'm sure she thought I might say something offensive so before I could, she said, "Stella has almost as many grandkids as I do, Mabel. She babysits every week so that's why she has a car seat back there." Then, to make sure I got the point, she added, "They always have to eat on the run because Stella has a very hectic schedule."

"Thank you for that information, Flori," I said. "How many places do we have to check out, Stella?" I asked.

"'Bout five or six. Seven, I think."

It was almost ten by this time. We started on the houses closest to the beach, driving along the avenues from east to west and sometimes, detouring around schools or churches. Most weren't home and the ones who were had never heard of Andrea. Or, maybe she was someone's second cousin who moved to California back in 1973. When it was almost noon, we decided to try one last house before going for lunch. I was still burping up eggs and salsa from breakfast.

Stella and Flori announced that they were starving.

The house was close to Avenue K. It was old and had seen much better days. If it had survived any of the hurricanes, no one would've known the difference. I went to the door alone. The small yard was overflowing with weeds. The sidewalk was heaving and cracking. I banged on the wooden door. I heard some movement inside. I banged on the windowpane this time. Someone from inside yelled something. No one came. I took my fist to the window again. Maybe if they thought the window might break, they'd come to the door.

"Who is it and what do you want?" The voice was raspy and sounded like someone who'd smoked a pack-a-day for at least forty years. It was hard to tell if it was male or female.

I yelled, "It's Mabel Wickles and I'd like to talk to you."

The voice was louder and closer. "Mabel who?"

"Mabel Wickles."

"Do I know you?"

"I'm looking for Andrea."

"She ain't here."

"Do you know where I can find her?"

"She don' live here no more."

"Can you tell me what her husband's name is?"

"Ha! Far as I know, she ain't got no husband."

"Who are you?" I asked.

"Who are you?" she demanded.

"I met Andrea on a trip to Las Vegas. A friend of hers, Grace, died and I wanted to let her know."

I could hear several latches clicking and the door slowly opened.

"Andrea won a trip to Vegas? I'm Veronica, Andrea's momma."

Veronica was about my age and my size. And, she was black.

Chapter Sixteen

"There are obviously two Andrea Williams," Flori said when I got back into the car and explained our conundrum.

I nodded. There had to be. "I showed her the picture but she'd never seen our Andrea. I guess that means we stop to eat and then start up again. It's a bit disappointing though."

"Wait one minute," Stella said. "Seems to me, if I remember right, I used to know a Veronica Williams a few years ago. I'll be back in a minute." She climbed out of the car with as much agility as a three hundred pound woman can and waddled almost gracefully to the door that I had just exited. She knocked, the door opened instantly, and she was inside. We waited for ten minutes.

"Do you think I ought to go in and see if she's all right?" Flori wondered.

"Somehow, I think Stella can look after herself. Veronica is about my size. I wonder what she's finding out." I reached over and patted Flori's arm. "This was a good idea having Stella with us; she can get into places we never could."

Flori beamed and pointed toward the house. "Here she comes."

Stella heaved herself back behind the wheel, a smug look on her face.

It took several seconds for her to catch her breath and

then she said, "Thought I recognized the name. Her and me used to work at the same store years ago. We used to have this shoppin' center called the White Mall. An' trust me, that's mostly who was in it too. The white folks. We was doin' the work and they was spendin' the money." She laughed. "Never had two nickels to rub together. I guess it ain't changed all that much."

"Oh surely, it has," Flori said. "Your home sounds lovely and look at all the people in the restaurant this morning. Everyone was laughing and talking."

"Oh, sugar, you don' understand unless you come from the south. But, let's not talk about that. I got some news to tell you and I'm startin' to think there's more goin' on in this little town than I ever knew. You wanna hear it?"

"We aren't sitting here hanging on to your every word for nothing, Stella."

"Oh Mabel, be quiet and listen. What did you learn?" Flori leaned over until her face was about five inches from Stella's face.

"That Veronica's daughter don' live with her no more because she disappeared several weeks ago. The police did a decent search for the first week or so but now it's kind of on the back burner. She didn't get along all that good with her momma so they think she mighta just took off." She twisted around to face me. "What do you think, Mabel? Isn't this a strange coincidence?"

"I'm with you. I think there's somethin' comin' down here."

"So, what's our next move?"

Flori said, "Let's eat."

I knew enough not to come between Flori and her food and Stella and her food, so I went along with it.

Stella pulled up in front of a small Cajun Greek restaurant. It wasn't quite noon yet but it looked packed inside. One thing I had to say was the people of Yellow Rose sure did know how to eat. They swarmed to restaurants at breakfast and noon like seagulls diving for a breadcrumb.

After stuffing ourselves with blackened chicken 'po' boys,' we decided to check out the last two addresses we had on our list. As it turned out, one house was vacant with a No Trespassing sign stapled across the falling-down door, and a miserable old man with his humongous dog sat on the steps of the other one. I got as far as the gate, saw the man guzzling beer, saw the pit bull watching me, and I was back in the car before the dog hit the fence, running full speed.

"Okay," I said. "Forget about finding Andrea. She can read about Grace's murder in the newspaper like everyone else. So, Stella, I was thinking, what if you and I check out the drug dealers' places tonight? And, Flori, you could do surveillance from the house. How does that sound? That way, if Cecile comes to the house, you can phone Stella on her cell phone. What do you think?"

The two women looked at each other and sort of shrugged.

"I s'pose so," Stella said, without too much enthusiasm. "You just make sure you keep the lights out, Flori, and he don't see you." She turned to me. "What did you want to do now, Mabel?"

"After all that food, I want to go back to the hotel and have a nap."

They both looked as if that was the best suggestion they'd heard all day.

Chapter Seventeen

I stretched out on my bed, trying to shut my brain off, and trying to piece everything together at the same time. The air conditioner in the window blasted out cold air, moving the drapes and blowing in my ear. No matter how much we tinkered with it, there seemed only the one setting so I was huddled under the covers with a comforter on top of that. Flori was lying on her bed on top of the covers, snoring softly.

Were we on some wild goose chase? I mean, the only thing we knew for sure was that Grace was dead. We knew that she was from Yellow Rose. Now, we knew *who* her husband was but we didn't know *where* he was. Had he followed her to Las Vegas to murder her? Why had he dumped her body behind the nursing home? Was there any connection to the murder and the nursing home? Had she lied to me when she said she wasn't related to old Mr. Hobbs who used to live there? And, what about Andrea Williams? Where the heck was she?

I fell asleep and dreamt that Captain Maxymowich came down to Yellow Rose to take me home… in handcuffs.

When I next opened my eyes, Flori was already up and sitting in front of the window, watching the water. I don't think I'd ever seen such a tranquil look on her face. Even after giving birth.

"This is what you needed, Flori. You needed a break from Jake and all your kids."

Flori's face turned pink and her eyes got watery. "Oh, Mabel, and I was sitting here, thinking how wonderful it will be to get back home and have everything back to normal." She dabbed her eyes with a tissue. "I'm really not into the detective thing, you know."

"After knowing you for all these years, Flori, I should've known you couldn't stay away for more than a few hours. Do you think you can last out another day or two?"

Flori smiled. "I can do that."

"Why don't you phone one of the kids before we go to Stella's? That will give you a new lease on life."

She managed to catch one of her sons but he was on his way out. He didn't seem to know where she was or whom she was with or what she was doing but it made Flori feel much better. She had made contact.

Stella was picking us up at six and she told us not to eat anything before we came. I didn't intend to, not after all that lunch. She informed us that there was no point in searching for drug lords before nine. In all actuality, she said, it would be better to start after midnight but Flori and I vetoed that. We didn't want to appear like country hicks but our usual bedtime was ten in the summer and nine, in the winter. She picked us up exactly at six. When we walked into her place, the dining room table was overflowing with food and there was country music playing.

"Oh, Stella," Flori said, her eyes lighting up. "This looks wonderful."

"Do you think," I said, "it's wise to play the music so loud? You know, with all the surveillance we're going to be doing? Could it draw too much attention?"

"I thought about that," Stella said, "but decided it would

seem more natural. 'Cause you know, if we were doing surveillance, it would all be quiet. This way, they'll figure nobody's surveillin' with all the racket. What do you think, Flori?"

I knew Flori would agree to flying to the moon if Stella suggested it, so I spoke up and said, "Maybe you're right. They'll think there's just some party going on here."

While Stella was in the kitchen getting the appetizers, Flori said, "Wasn't that a good idea she had? She's going to be such a help, Mabel."

"You don't have to whisper. If you yelled, she wouldn't hear you." I leaned over and spoke into her ear, "It actually seems a little weird to me."

"Oh, Mabel, don't be so critical." She smiled as she gazed at the table. "Look at all this food. Isn't it grand?"

For the next forty-five minutes, we ate, drank, and giggled hysterically. If you're a skinny person like me and have sat at a table with two jolly over-sized people who laugh until they cry every few minutes, you'll understand the situation. Even when the music was so loud we couldn't hear, we still laughed. Of course, the wine may have had something to do with that.

Our laughter came to an abrupt halt when Stella heard a car door slam. She raised her hand.

"Listen," she said. "I'm sure that's comin' from next door."

Personally, I hadn't heard a thing and even Flori looked doubtful.

We tiptoed over to the window and peered through the wooden slats. There was a car parked on the street and a man was walking to the door. He glanced up at the house, obviously attracted by the music. Which was exactly what I didn't want.

"Who's that?" Flori whispered. "That doesn't look like that man in the picture."

"It isn't," Stella whispered, in return. "That's not Cecile Tucker. I don't know who that guy is."

"I do," I said, in a somewhat louder voice. "This is crazy. That's Mr. Hatcher. He's the representative from the cereal company. What would he be doing here?"

"Do you think maybe it has to do with the trip?" Flori asked. We were no longer whispering. "Maybe Grace left something behind. You know, like her passport."

"We didn't need passports. We weren't traveling to Canada or Mexico."

"What about her credit card? Or, a suitcase?"

"No, Flori. I don't think so. Besides, if that happened, the company would get UPS or FedEx to deliver it."

Mr. Hatcher didn't return to his car.

"Where did that man go?" Flori asked. None of us had taken our eyes off the house for a moment.

We waited for about five minutes.

"He's gone inside. That's where he is." I looked at the two women. "I don't think we'll have to visit any drug houses looking for Cecile, Stella. We might be busy enough keeping watch here all night."

Flori let out a sigh. "Oh, I'm so glad, Mabel. I was worried about you doing that."

We decided that two of us should stay at the window, in case one missed something. The other would rest, in case this surveillance went on all night.

About nine, when the sun was just going down, we started to get some action.

"Mabel," Flori whispered. "Come here. There's another car pulling up."

There was a light on in the house now.

The car door opened and a man got out. He was average height, dark skinned, with longish black hair and wore a black overcoat that went down past his knees. He reminded me of Cecile but Cecile looked a lot shorter in his picture.

"Do you know who that is, Mabel?" Stella whispered.

I tried to remember if I'd seen the man anywhere. Maybe in the casino in Las Vegas? No, I'd never set eyes on him before. I should have paid more attention on that trip. But then, how was I supposed to know there was going to be a murder?

Whoever it was, hurried to the door, hair and coat both flapping. He disappeared from sight and we assumed he must have entered.

"You know what I'm going to have to do," I said. "I'm going to have to go over there and see if I can hear something. It looks like that one window might be open a crack. If I sneak over, I can stand under it and listen."

"Are you crazy? I won't let you do that." Flori grabbed my arm and glared at me. "You are not going over there."

"Then who is, Flori? You or Stella? Not that I want to mention anything about your size but I think I'm the one who can do this and not get caught. What would you do if you had to run? You'd never escape. But I could. Besides, I'm the one who's most involved. You two are just helping me out. Isn't that what you said, Flori?"

Before Flori could get hysterical, I rushed over to the door.

"Make sure, Stella, that if you see anyone coming or if you think one of them has discovered me, give me a warning of some kind."

Stella nodded. "I know just the thing, darlin'. I got this

whistle my son gave me. It's loud nuff to wake the dead. That'll confuse them so's you can race back here."

"I don't know, Mabel. What will you do if they have guns? What if Grace was trying to find something out like you are now and that's why she got shot?" Flori was starting to cry.

"Don't worry. I'll be very careful. And, Flori, you might have discovered the reason she was killed. I'm proud of you. Now, all we have to do is find out for sure."

Flori wasn't sure if she should acknowledge that compliment or not. I could see the confused look on her face as I let myself out the door.

I would have preferred complete darkness but the men might be gone by then so I had to take the chance. Instead of trying to slip through the front yard, I went around to the back lane. There were two derelict cars sitting in Cecile's back yard. I snuck alongside the one and up to the side of the house.

In fact, the closer I got to the window, the better it got. The voices were loud. The two men were arguing. I crouched down and listened.

The man I didn't know was shouting, "What's wrong with you? I can't trust you anymore? And, where the hell's this Grace? I warned you about using someone you didn't know." He had a Mexican accent.

Hatcher answered but he spoke too softly. I think if Stella's music hadn't been so loud, I might've heard him. Whatever he said didn't sit too well with his companion.

"I don't want to listen to your excuses. You promised me this woman would be here. Where is she?"

Another mumbled answer but I was sure he said something about losing her in Denver.

"Why didn't you wait for her then?" the Mexican

screamed. "Where's the money? Are you telling me that this woman took off with the money? Is that what you are saying, Amigo?"

This time I heard Hatcher's answer. "Keep your voice down. You want all the neighbors to hear?"

I lifted my head to get closer to the window. What were the chances they would see me? After all, if you're in the middle of an argument, you don't usually start checking out all the windows, do you?

My head was up and as I strained to see through the dirty window, an earth shattering shrill filled the air. Stella's whistle! I turned, tripped over a water hose, caught my balance before I hit the ground, and raced to the back. There wasn't time to run into Stella's yard or I would've been seen so I went the other direction, down the back lane, heading west. I was moving as fast as a woman my age could run without having a heart attack. If there were gunshots, I could never have heard anything over the blood pounding in my ears anyway. When my heart was about to burst, I slipped into the opened door of a garage. There was a van inside. I tried the door. It was unlocked so I climbed inside and slid down in the driver's seat.

Why had Stella blown that darn whistle? Was there anyone searching for me? I had no idea. All I knew was that for the time being, I was safe. I stayed there, praying the owner wouldn't come out as I had no idea how I would explain my predicament.

It was dark when I crawled out. Perhaps, a half hour had passed. Instead of going back through the lane, I decided to circle the block and come up behind Stella's house. All was quiet as I approached and as they say, the coast was clear.

There was only one worry. Stella's car was no longer on

the street. I snuck under the steps and tried the garage door but Stella had locked it. Cautiously, I crept up the stairs to the living quarters.

"Flori, Stella," I called out, trying to be heard above the music but not down the block.

No one answered. The door opened into the living and dining room. Although the room was in darkness except for some light from the street lamp shining in through the slats, I could see that dirty dishes and three empty wine bottles still covered the table. Flori and Stella were gone. Either they were out looking for me or they were trailing the men who had been in the house. I was hoping it would be the latter.

I walked over to the window and looked down. The house next door was in darkness. There were no cars sitting in front. Mr. Hatcher and Associate were gone.

I'd had about all I could take of Country and Western music but instead of shutting it off completely, I turned the sound down. Stella's water heater or pipes knocked a few times but even that sounded better than the CD.

Chapter Eighteen

No one can imagine how hard it was for me to stay in that house and feel so utterly helpless. Where could the girls be? I had no idea. I dared not turn the lights on so I lit one of the candles on the table and proceeded to clear away the dirty dishes. At least, by keeping busy, I wasn't going to worry so much. Every time I walked across the room, the water pipes seemed to rattle and bang. If I remembered, I would mention to Stella that her son might want to check it out for her.

Every few minutes, I went over to the window to see if anything was happening at the house next door. It was still dark. I carried the candle into the kitchen and was about to fill the sink up with water when I realized that there was one thing I could do; I could go over and check out Grace's house. That is, if it wasn't locked.

This time, instead of sneaking round the back, I went straight up to the front door, turned the knob, and walked in. No one suspects you of anything when you do that. Did everyone in Yellow Rose leave front doors open? Kind of like Parson's Cove ... at least, Parson's Cove, before it became a murder town.

The small living room appeared filled with furniture. This I discovered when I tried to walk a few steps and banged my knee against the coffee table.

"Shitrophsky," I mumbled, and rubbed my knee. That is my swear word of choice. Flori says it's the same as swearing because she knows what I want to say but since she'd rather hear me say that than the real thing, she keeps quiet.

A mixture of stale tobacco smoke (or maybe something a little stronger?) mixed in with old food odors and the faint tinge of garbage that needed to be taken out filled the air. Not very inviting, to say the least.

As I was standing there, in the middle of the room, in the dark, it suddenly dawned on me - why was I there when I could hardly see my hands in front of my face?

The phone rang, piercing the silence with as many decibels as Stella's whistle had. Or, so it seemed in that small room. I stood there, unable to move, my heart hammering, waiting for the deafening sound to stop. All of a sudden, I got this sinking feeling that maybe I wasn't alone! What if someone were to emerge from the back part of the house and flip the lights on? If that happened, I would have a heart attack. I couldn't think of anything else to do. The ringing stopped after four times and the answering machine kicked in.

In the darkness, I heard a woman say, "We are unable to take your call. Please, leave a message." I wasn't certain but it sounded an awful lot like Grace's voice. Then again, it might've been the recording that came with the machine.

It is very creepy thinking you might be listening to a dead person's voice even when you know it's a recording. There was this moment of silence and then a loud beep.

"Grace? This is Andy. Give me a call. I'm getting worried."

By the time, my brain went into gear and I grabbed the phone, Andrea was gone. I had only the dial tone.

However, my little trip over to Grace's house was not in vain. I learned two very important things: Andrea was alive and she didn't know that Grace was dead.

Why was she worried?

I was definitely ready to go back to Stella's house. After all, Cecile still lived here and I wasn't too keen on meeting up with him in a dark room - especially one that belonged to him.

I'd been brave going into the house but before I left, I stood on the step for a moment to take a good look around. The street was quiet. Most of the houses were in darkness. I could hear the faint sound of traffic, probably coming from the seawall. Dogs barked and a car door slammed.

The pink Cadillac drove up just as I was about to open Stella's door.

I waited for them at the top of the stairs.

"Mabel," Flori called up from the bottom step. "Are you all right? Where have you been?"

She rushed up the steps at an amazing pace and crushed me to her bosom. Stella was right behind.

"You can let go now, Flori. I'm fine." She pulled me into the room. Stella shut the door, then walked over, and turned the music up again. At least, this time it wasn't quite as loud.

"Could we put the lights on now?" I asked. "I'm really tired of trying to maneuver in the dark." My knee was still hurting from its encounter with Cecile's coffee table.

Flori looked at Stella. "Do you think we should? He might be searching for us."

"Who's searching for you?" I turned to Stella. "Why'd you blow your whistle, Stella? I nearly had a heart attack."

Stella got a funny look on her face. Flori started crying.

I looked from one to the other.

"Isn't anybody going to tell me?"

"It was my fault," Flori said between sniffles. "I'm sure I saw that Mr. Hatcher walking towards the window. You know, Mabel, the one you were so foolishly going to look through. I saw you start to stand up so I grabbed the whistle out of Stella's hand and blew." She started to wail so I walked over to the table, fumbled around until I found a napkin and handed it to her. She blew.

"Then what happened?" I said.

"Things were happening so fast." She snorted. "Maybe Stella could tell it better."

"No, you tell me."

She cleared her throat. "Well, both men ran out of the house. While they were looking down the street at the front of the house, we saw you running down the back lane. We figured you'd be okay. When the men didn't see anything…"

"But," Stella interrupted, "they sure did look up here for a long time."

"That's true, they did. We were so frightened. It seemed like they could see right through those storm blinds, didn't it?"

"So, where did you go?"

Stella picked up the story. "Both men jumped into their cars so we thought we might follow at a distance."

"This was not my idea," Flori said.

"I'm sure it wasn't but it was better than staying alone in the house, right?"

"Right, Mabel." She blew her nose but the tears continued to drip.

"It was hard to know which man to follow," Stella said, "but it seemed to me that since you knew that Mr. Hatcher,

it was best we follow him. In hindsight, maybe we
should've gone the other way."

"Why?"

"Because Mr. Hatcher drove straight to the pen."

"The pen? You mean, Mr. Hatcher drove to the jail?"

They both nodded in unison.

"And we think he got a good look at us when we drove
by."

"Why would he go to the jail if he was involved in the
murder? Isn't that the last place he'd want to go? And,
what about the money? Where is it?"

"What money?" Stella asked.

"I think we should sit down." It felt like my legs were
going to give out on me. I reached for a match and lit one of
the candles. There looked to be a few swallows of wine in
one of the bottles so I tipped it up and drank it down in three
gulps.

Stella said, "Should I get another bottle of wine?"

Flori and I both nodded. "Yes," I said. "I think we'll
need it."

We settled in with our wine and I lit another candle.
Stella spoke first. "Now, what's this about money?"

"That's what the two men were arguing about. Mr.
Hatcher and the other fellow. He had an accent. I think he
was Mexican. Anyway, he'd come to collect money from
Grace but as we know, Grace wasn't there. He was very
upset but I couldn't hear what Hatcher was saying.
Whatever it was, I'm sure he didn't tell him that Grace was
dead."

"Does Hatcher know she's dead?" Flori asked.

"Good question," I said. "He might not."

"Or," Stella said, "do you think he's the killer?"

"Why would he go to the jail" Flori said, "if he were the killer?"

"Why would he go to the police anyway?" I asked. "He works for a cereal company."

We shook our heads.

"Oh," I said. "We do know something more. I went into the house just before you came."

Before I could continue, Flori gasped and said, "You what? What house?"

"I went into the empty house next door. While I was there, the phone rang. The answering machine picked up and guess who it was?"

"Grace?" Flori whispered, her eyes bulging and her eyebrows up under her bangs.

"No, Grace is really dead, Flori." I paused a moment. "It was Andrea."

They both looked at me for a moment as if they couldn't remember who Andrea was.

"So," Stella said, "which Andrea are we talkin' about here?"

Chapter Nineteen

Sleep didn't come too easily that night again. We drove almost all the way back to the hotel with the lights out. If we saw a car coming behind or meeting us, we pulled over and parked. None of the cars, however, looked like the two we'd seen at Cecile's house. Flori had a long hot bath to help her sleep. It worked too because within ten minutes, she was snoring. It took my brain quite some time to stop running in overdrive. Question after question kept piling up in my mind. I had no answers and I knew Flori wouldn't want to stay much longer. One more day would be about it.

Before I drifted off, I realized there was one place we'd have to check out - the jail. Why, on earth, would Mr. Hatcher go there? Would someone rotting on Death Row be the answer to our mystery?

The next day, we woke up to rain. The gray and depressing kind. Flori doesn't function well in dreary weather. I tend to enjoy having an excuse to feel and act miserable once in awhile.

I knew the day wasn't going to be all that great for her when she woke up without her usual smile. She groaned when she got out of bed. Her knees bother her when it's damp outside. I don't have the heart to tell her that if she lost a bit of weight, she wouldn't have so much pain. We never go there.

"I don't think we'll solve anything today, Mabel. Look at the sky." She stood up and walked to the window. "Look at the water; it's so rough this morning." Her eyes got big. "Do you think we could be in for a hurricane?"

"No, Flori. This isn't hurricane season. It's only a little rain. We can still solve a crime in the rain, you know."

"I don't know if I have any energy left to solve anything. We're way over our heads with this and you know it, Mabel. Besides, it's up to the police to solve murders, not you. There's nothing more we can do. I want to go home."

"You're saying that because you don't like the cloudy gloom. As soon as the rain lets up a bit and we have some breakfast, you'll feel much better." I rolled out of bed and stretched. "Besides, there's one place that we have to go, Flori. It will hold the answer to Grace's murder."

Flori moaned. "I hate it when you talk like that. Nothing holds the answer. We are not going to solve anything. Period."

I didn't say a word.

She watched the rain and rolling waves for a few minutes and then said, "What do you mean; you have one place to check out? Please, don't tell me you're going into Grace's house again. I won't allow that."

"No, I don't think we'll find anything there. Unless, Cecile came home. If he did, Stella would call us immediately, I'm sure. By the way, where is she? I thought she was coming to pick us up for breakfast."

"Not until nine," she said. "It's only seven-thirty now."

"Okay. Well, I'm heading for the shower then."

I'd started the water running before Flori stuck her nose up to the door and shouted, "What place did you say we had to check out?"

"The jail," I shouted back. "We have to check to see

who Mr. Hatcher visited."

Flori rarely, if ever, says an indecent word but if I were a betting person, I'd say a very foul word came out of those innocent lips of hers. Good thing I flushed the toilet at that exact moment.

I should tell her to start saying shitrophsky too.

Chapter Twenty

We were back in the small crowded Mexican restaurant for breakfast. It was after nine and the place was packed. Flori and I were in the minority - everyone else was either black or Hispanic.

"Hmm." Stella was trying to concentrate on her food and pick her own brain at the same time. "I must know somebody who's in jail."

"There has to be some way that we can get in and find out who Mr. Hatcher was visiting," I said. "Is there a way to check all the inmates' names?"

Stella's eyes brightened. "We have a little newspaper called *Police News*. I wonder if we could check out some of those at the library." She filled her mouth with the last piece of her burrito and chewed. "What're we lookin' for anyway, Mabel? Do you have a name?"

"Not yet. I will if I see it though."

"Sort of a shot in the dark, isn't it?"

"No," Flori said. "It's not even that; at least, in the dark you might hit something. Mabel has no clue who to look for at all. Right?" She turned to me with an accusing look in her eye.

I ignored Flori and turned to Stella. "When was the last time you saw Cecile? Did you see him within the past few days?"

Stella's eyes got bigger. "I don't think so but he could've been comin' and goin' and I missed him. He's always been a sneaky kind of person. You think maybe he's the one Mr. Hatcher was goin' to see, Mabel?"

"That would make sense, wouldn't it? Hatcher was in Cecile's house and they seem to be partners in crime, don't they? Of course, it would mean he would've been arrested sometime after leaving Las Vegas. Could he have come straight home and been picked up by the cops?"

They both nodded but looked doubtful. Flori was getting back into it again.

She turned to Stella and said, "Why don't you go to the jail and ask if they know Cecile Tucker? Tell them you're his neighbor and you thought you saw some people breaking into his house. You felt it was the only Christian thing to do … to report the crime. Even though you don't condone his way of life. Make sure you say that. You wouldn't want them interrogating you."

I stared at Flori. "Flori," I said. "That's brilliant. That's the answer. Will you do it, Stella? After all, you won't even have to lie. You did see two men breaking into his house. Well, maybe not *breaking* in but how were you to know, right? They went in and you were quite sure neither Cecile nor Grace were home."

"And, you, Mabel. You really *did* break in." Flori added.

"She didn't see me."

Stella grinned. "Oh lordy," she said. "What have I gotten myself into with you two ladies?" She and Flori burst into laughter and I had to walk over to the counter to bring back more napkins.

By the time we drove into the prison parking lot, the rain was over and there was blue sky showing in the west.

The Yellow Rose Correctional Facility looked about as bleak as the weather had at seven that morning. It was a six-story gray stone building, with black bars covering every window. Even with the bars, I could see that the windows were almost black with dirt. There were cameras on each corner of the roof, and two more pointed straight down at the front doors. I couldn't tell if they were moving or not so I preferred not to make eye contact.

Flori and I sat and waited for what seemed to be an eternity.

"Quit looking at your watch, Mabel. She'll get here when she gets here." Flori looked out over the parking lot. She sighed. "If I ever go on a vacation with you again, Mabel, remind me to bring my knitting."

I looked out over the lot too. There was a variety of cars - mostly, older models. The cars that had pulled up in front of Grace's house weren't there. Where was Mr. Hatcher?

"You know, Flori, I was wondering. Do you think Mr. Hatcher stayed in a hotel while he was here? If so, I'm sure Stella could find out where. She knows almost everyone. Of course, if we had to, we could even bribe someone, couldn't we? You know, like the desk clerk?"

"Pardon me, Miss Wickles? We could *not* bribe anyone. Get that thought out of your head. And, stop thinking of your next step until we get through with this one." Worry furrowed Flori's forehead. "I hope Stella will be okay. Now, I wish I'd never come up with this stupid idea."

"Well, it was really my idea, Flori. You just came up with a good reason for going in, that's all."

"That's what I mean; I wish I'd kept my mouth shut."

I glanced at my watch again. All of three minutes had passed since the last time I had looked. Stella had been behind those prison walls for almost half an hour.

"I hate sitting here," Flori said, "and watching all those cops going in and out. Do you notice how every one of them looks over here? I keep thinking that any minute one is going to come over here and arrest us."

"They can't do that. We haven't committed a crime."

"Right, Mabel. You don't think it's a crime to break into someone else's house? What if there's a warrant out for your arrest? What if someone saw you going into the house last night and the cops are out looking for you? Have you thought about that?" Her eyebrows went up and disappeared under her bangs.

"Nobody's out looking for me." I looked towards the jail again. "Here she comes, Flori. Do you think she looks like she's found anything out?"

"I have no idea how that looks."

Stella climbed in and let out a long breath of air.

"Are you okay?" I asked. "What did you find out? Did you tell them about Cecile?"

She reached over and started up the car. "Let's get out of here," she said. "I'll fill you in later."

"How much later?"

"Oh, Mabel, be quiet and let Stella collect herself. It's not easy going into a prison all alone. Not that I've ever been there but I'm sure it's awful. It isn't like going into the little police station in Parson's Cove, you know." Flori gave me a disparaging look before turning back to Stella. "Did they do that strip search thing with you, Stella?"

Stella laughed. "Are you kiddin'? Honey, nobody wants to strip search me. I could conceal weapons in my rolls of fat but nobody wants to go there."

She pulled in front of a doughnut shop.

"This has made me ravenous," she said. "Let's have

coffee and a chocolate croissant. I'll tell y'all about it while
we eat."

This had made her hungry? It had completely erased any
thought of food from my mind. How can people think of
eating every hour when there's a murder to solve?

We settled into our booth. I had coffee. They were out
of croissants so Flori and Stella both ordered something
called a Bismarck. I had no idea where the name originated
but it must have had something to do with enough deep-fried
dough and jam to blow a ship out of the water.

"How much longer do we have to wait?" I asked.
Watching them sit there, silently filling their mouths was
killing me.

Stella shook her head; her mouth was full. She
swallowed.

"Well, one thing I know is that Cecile Tucker isn't in
jail."

Deflated doesn't even begin to describe how I felt. I was
hoping he'd been picked up for murdering his wife and the
mystery would be solved.

She grinned. "I did find something else out though. As
an afterthought, I said to the very nice police officer, 'you
don't know if my other neighbor is here, do you? His last
name is Williams.'"

"And?"

"He said, 'You mean, Ben?' and I said, 'Is that Andrea's
husband?' And, guess what he said?"

"I'm not in the mood for a guessing game, Stella. What
did he say?"

"Mabel, don't be so rude. Stella will tell us in her own
due time." Flori shook her head and went, "Tsk. Tsk."

"Oh, that's okay. My husband, God rest his soul, was an
impatient person too. Used to always say, 'get to the point,

woman.' That's what he always said."

"I bet you'd give anything to hear him say that again, wouldn't you, sweetie?" Flori said, with watery eyes.

"Well," I said, "if it makes you feel better, Stella, I can say it: *get to the point, woman.* So, now, what did he say?"

"Oh for goodness sake, Mabel," Flori said, "be patient. What did he say, Stella?"

"He said, 'Yeah, Andrea's husband. He's off duty right now. Not sure when his shift starts.'"

I stared at her and then at Flori. Stella was grinning.

Andrea's husband was a cop! At last, we were getting somewhere. I figured the answer was in that jail. Of course, it didn't tell us whom Hatcher was going to see.

"You didn't happen to find out if Andrea was black or white, did you?"

Stella took a big slug of coffee and swallowed it.

"Honey, I was finished askin' questions. That's somethin' you're gonna have to find out yourself."

I nodded. After all, Stella had already been a big help and I didn't want to discourage her. Not when there was work still to do and only one day in which to do it.

"I was wondering, Stella," I said. "Do you think we could check out Ben Williams' house? I'd sure like to see what his wife looks like. It's hard to believe she could be *our* Andrea. Also, I was wondering if we could find out if Mr. Hatcher was staying in any of the hotels?"

"Why you want to find that out?"

"I'm wondering if there's a chance he's still in town."

Stella turned to Flori. "You want a refill and another Bismarck?"

Flori's eyes lit up.

They settled in with their calorie, cholesterol, and sugar-laden treat, while I had another cup of coffee. I had to admit it was almost as good as mine was.

"I wonder," I said, thinking aloud, "if that cereal company was legit?"

"Of course, it must have been," Flori said. "Don't forget you got a free plane trip and free lodging in a very expensive hotel. It had to be legitimate."

"But what about Hatcher and the rest? Do you think they were who they said they were? It could've been a front for something."

"What do you think?" Stella asked. "You're the one who met them."

"Right now, I'm thinking the whole bunch were crooks. What I can't figure out is why one of them would murder Grace."

"We don't know that any of them did. Maybe," Flori said between mouthfuls, "Grace wasn't who Grace said she was."

"That's for sure. But, murder? And, why dump the body in Parson's Cove?"

"You don't have a picture of Grace, do you?" Stella asked as she wiped some jam off her chin.

"I thought I showed one to you."

"No, you just showed me Andrea. Remember? I told you I wasn't sure if I'd seen her before."

I searched through my handbag for my envelope of pictures. I was glad I hadn't given all of them to Reg and Maxymowich.

"Here," I said and handed her the one and only picture that I'd kept of Grace. It was a good one. She was standing beside Mr. Hatcher at the door to the hotel. Neither of them knew I'd taken the picture.

Stella held it towards the light from the window.

She put it down on the table. "You know," she said, "this ain't no picture of Grace. You had a picture of Cecile but this isn't his wife, Grace. I don't know who this woman is. Never saw her before in my life."

Why wasn't I surprised?

Chapter Twenty One

"I'm not even shocked," I said, as we made our way back to the car. "This whole thing is just one big charade. It's like *Alice in Wonderland*. No one is as they seem." I turned to Flori. "I might lose my mind over this."

"No, you won't, Mabel. I won't let you. You know very well that it's time to let Reg or Sheriff Jim know what's going on. It's up to them to tell that nice Captain. They can solve it. You don't have to." She turned to give me one of her motherly looks. "He should really know that the Grace you thought was Grace, really isn't the Grace you thought she was."

I settled into the back with the baby-seat and the wrappers.

"There's only two things that I still want to do before I phone Reg. And, Flori, I *will* phone Reg afterwards. Let's go and see if we can find Andrea Williams. We know now that her husband's name is Ben so that should be easy. Since Ben is a cop, his wife can't be a crook, can she?"

Stella laughed. "I've heard of worse things. Who knows?" She backed out without looking and started down the street. "Here in Yellow Rose lots of cops ain't what they seem."

"Well, let's check her out first. Do we need to get a phone book?"

"No," Stella said. "Ben and Andrea live on Avenue P ½. Now, you know why he trusted me. He axed where I lived and when I said P ½, he said, 'Oh, you *are* neighbors.' Then, I said, 'Didn't they live close to 39th street before?' and he said, 'No, I think they've always lived at 3602.' Now what kind of a cop is that dumb, givin' out personal information like that?"

"Stella," I said, "you should've been a private investigator. You are awesome! I don't think I've ever known anyone who could think on their feet like you can."

In three minutes, we were parked in front of 3602 P ½. Stella's house was two blocks away.

"So, what do we do now, Mabel?" Flori asked. She was starting to fidget.

It was noon and the sun was right overhead.

3602 was the second house from the corner. It was an older home too, like most in the area. Compared to Cecile's house, this was a mansion. The yard was neat and there were no shingles dangling from the roof. This was a small brick house, looking sturdy enough to resist any hurricane.

"I suppose," I said, "I could go up and knock. If it's the Andrea that I know, I can tell her about Grace. Well, at least, the Grace who was on the trip. The Grace who she thought lived with Cecile. Or, even if she didn't know about Cecile, she knew where she lived and what her phone number was."

"Maybe Stella should go with you. You don't know what you're getting into. This Andrea person might already know who the real Grace is. She could even be the murderer, Mabel."

"No, she couldn't, Flori. She's the one who phoned Grace while I was in Cecile's house. Plus, her husband's a cop. Remember? Don't worry, I'll be all right." I stepped out of the car, not feeling exactly as though I would be all right but putting on a brave face anyway.

There was a little overhang above the door and it provided a bit of shade from the sun. The rain was finished and it was hot and humid now. First, I rang the bell and when no one answered, I knocked. Everything was still and silent. It did seem strange that these two women had lived so close to each other and had never met. Something like that would never have happened in Parson's Cove. In Parson's Cove, everyone is your neighbor, even if you wish a few of them weren't.

As I walked back to the car, Flori was frantically waving her hand as if to say, hurry up.

"What's the matter?" I asked as soon as I shut the door.

"Mabel," she said. "There was someone there. We could see the curtains moving. Let's get out of here. It could be the murderer for all we know."

I'd never given any thought to the murderer lurking about. After all, we were at a cop's home. I guess it wasn't on Stella's mind either because as soon as Flori mentioned it, she stepped on the gas and left a puff of exhaust on the street.

She turned left and we drove up to the beach road. Before I could mention which hotels I thought we should check out, she pulled in front of a fast food restaurant.

"What are we doing here?"

Flori looked at her watch. "It's lunchtime, Mabel. We thought we'd grab a quick bite."

"But, you just finished having your coffee break."

She nodded. "I know. That was our coffee break. This is our lunch."

"But I'm still burping up breakfast."

She turned in the seat to face me. "So, what do you want to do? Do you want to wait in the car?"

"Or," Stella said, "you can take the car and then come back and pick us up. Do you want to do that?"

"You don't mind me driving your car?"

"Not at all." She and Flori waddled into the restaurant and I scooted into the front seat.

It took several minutes to get the seat and mirrors adjusted. Stella said she'd never moved anything since she bought the car twelve years before so everything was a bit stiff.

I really enjoyed working with Flori and Stella but suddenly on my own, I felt like perhaps I could accomplish more. Now, I would only have to worry about myself. There would be no voice from behind saying, "Don't go there, Mabel."

The first thing on my to-do list was check the hotels to see if I could find the elusive Mr. Hatcher. What would happen if I met him face to face? What possible reason could I have for coming to a small, unknown city in Texas? Of course, I could show utter shock at seeing him. I mean, why was *he* here? I could say I'd come to tell Andrea about Grace's death and had he heard about it?

I was almost hoping I would meet up with him just to see the look on his face.

Most of the hotels were on the street facing the water. There were only three newer ones; the others looked sun-bleached and shabby. I decided to start at the farthest western end and work my way east.

The Gulf Motel was first. The office faced the street and there were twelve rooms hidden behind. There were no cars anywhere and the only movement was a housekeeper moving her laundry cart from room 8 to room 9. She stopped in between to take a long drag off her cigarette and knock the ashes off.

It was hard to imagine him staying in a place like this; especially after that grand hotel in Las Vegas. However, since Hatcher was obviously a crook and/or murderer, this might be the sort of place he'd hide out in.

Before I went into the office, I pulled out my pictures and selected the one of Grace (I had to keep calling her that so I wouldn't be completely confused. Or, more confused that I already was) and Mr. Hatcher.

The office was small and crowded with an over-sized couch, chair, and giant television. The air was thick with a mixture of garlic and curry. Mostly curry. It stung my eyes. The man behind the desk was short, dark, and greasy looking but extremely friendly.

He stood up the moment the door opened.

"Yes, miss. What can I do for you? You would like a room? We have very good prices. Very clean rooms. How long would you like to stay?"

"No, no, thank you. I don't want a room."

"Well, what you want then? I am busy. I do not want to buy anything, thank you very much."

"No, I'm not selling anything." I held up the picture. "I'd just like to know if you've ever seen these two people." I walked over and laid the picture on the counter. "Either one. Have you ever seen this man or this woman?"

Without looking down, he said, "No, these people have never stayed in my motel."

"But you didn't even look." I held the picture in front of his eyes. "Now, can you say that?"

"I have told you, these people have never stayed in my motel. I do not keep criminals here. This is a place for

148

families, not criminals."

"I didn't say these were criminals. I'm trying to locate them because someone has died and I need to notify them. Look at the pictures. Have you ever seen them?"

Finally, his eyes rested on the photo. He squinted as if trying to remember.

"Perhaps, I've seen the woman, but not the man. I have never seen this man before."

"Do you remember where you saw the woman? Does she live around here?"

He shrugged. "I said that maybe I've seen this woman. She looks a little familiar, that's all I'm saying. I don't know for sure."

On the way out, I stopped and showed the picture to the housekeeper. She studied it for a moment, took a drag off her cigarette, blew smoke out the side of her mouth, which blew back into my face, and said, "Kind of looks like someone I seen. What'd you say her name was again?"

"Grace Hobbs."

She shrugged. "No, I never heard of anyone by that name. She kinda looks like that Williams woman who lives on P ½."

"Well, kind of, but no, this is Grace Hobbs. You know Andrea Williams?"

She shook her head. "Nah. Not personal like. Somebody pointed her out to me one day, that's all. I gotta get back to work now." She took another drag, blew the smoke straight out in my direction, threw the cigarette on the ground and stomped on it. I turned and stomped out of there. This gal knew more than she was telling me.

I made less headway with the next three hotels. If any of them did recognize Grace or Mr. Hatcher, they definitely weren't going to tell me.

By the time, I hit the fifth place, I was ready to call it quits. Besides, it was almost time to pick up the women. I'm sure they would be anxious to leave. After all, no one wants to sit in a fast food restaurant longer than one has to. Well, maybe I shouldn't speak for Flori and Stella.

This was one of the newer hotels and the last one I was going to visit. There were several cars in the parking lot. There were a couple of black newer models. Could it be Hatcher and the other man?

I knew by the startled look on her face that the young blonde-haired woman behind the desk recognized at least one of them.

"Do you know these people?" I asked.

She nodded. "They were both in here awhile back."

"Really? When was that?"

"Oh, maybe a week or two ago. Can't say for sure." She smiled very sweetly, showing off a row of perfect white teeth. "I can't remember everyone but I do remember them." She rolled her eyes and snapped her gum.

"Oh? How come you remember them?"

"What are you, a cop or something?"

I laughed. "Are you kidding? Do I look like one?"

She grinned. "No, you look kind of old to be one but you never know."

I let that one slide. "Actually, I'm trying to find Mr. Hatcher. The woman beside him in this picture is dead. I thought he should know."

She grabbed the picture again. "She's dead? What happened?"

"Well, I might as well tell you - she was murdered."

Her eyes got big. She blew a large bubble with her gum, sucked it into the back of her throat, and snapped it.

"Wow," she said. "Did that Mr. Hatcher kill her?"

I shrugged. "I don't know. Maybe her husband did."

She scowled. "Her husband?"

"Well, I'm not sure on that one. Someone already told me that she isn't his wife. To be perfectly honest, I'm not sure who anyone is anymore."

"Who's her husband?"

"Maybe a man named, Cecile Tucker?"

She looked down at the picture again. "Well, I can tell you for sure, that's *not* Cecile's wife."

"You know Cecile's wife?"

"Sure and that's not her."

"What's her name?"

"Cecile's wife? Her name's Grace but that's not Grace Tucker." She shrugged. "Unless, Cecile's got two wives." She grinned. "Wouldn't that be a hoot!"

"That would be a hoot, wouldn't it? What does she look like?"

"Who?"

"Grace Tucker, I guess. Cecile Tucker's wife."

She shrugged. "Oh, I don't know. Kind of plain. Sort of dirty blond hair. A little overweight."

"I know; like almost every other woman in Texas."

"Pretty much. So, how was this woman killed?"

I pointed to my forehead. "Bullet, right there."

"Shut up!" She blew another bubble, sucked it in and snapped it.

"Can you tell me now why you remember these two in particular? What did they do?"

"I was going to say that they caused a ruckus but, it was more, you know, one of those silent deadly fights. Started in the restaurant, over there, and worked its way out to the parking lot. I had the feeling they were both trying hard not to attract too much attention."

"So, how did you notice them then? I mean, if they were arguing quietly, they could've been talking, couldn't they?"

She shook her head and laughed. "Not those two. You should've seen the looks. Anyway, we were waiting for one of them to pull out a gun."

"Shut up! What happened then?"

"Mr. Sloan, that's my boss, went out and said he was going to call the cops if they didn't leave. They each jumped in their car and drove away."

"Really? That's very interesting. So, Hatcher knew Grace before the Las Vegas trip." I tried not to show any excitement. If she thought I'd completely lost my mind, she didn't show it. I reached across the counter and touched her arm. "What's your name?" I asked.

She pointed to her nametag. "Cindy Sue."

"Cindy Sue, can you think of anything else you could tell me about these two?"

She squinted. "You're sure you're not a cop?"

"Would it make any difference if I were?"

"Maybe. I drive."

"That's illegal in Texas?"

"No license."

"Well, I suppose that could be a problem. However, not my worry at all. Now, can you think of anything else?"

After several bubbles and snaps, she said, "There is one thing."

"What?"

"I'll tell you but you have to promise not to tell my boss. If he finds out, I'll lose my job. You promise you won't say anything?"

"Cindy Sue, my lips are sealed; all I'm interested in is

finding out who killed Grace Hobbs or Andrea or whatever her name is. Or was."

She leaned forward. "Well, I actually saw them earlier. You know, before they had the argument in the restaurant. I was in the closet where the cleaning supplies are, sneaking a smoke, when they came out of their room."

"They had a room together?"

"Yep. Well, I mean, they came out of it together. I assumed they were a couple." She looked around. "I can bring up the date and room number if you'd like."

"I'd like that." I wasn't sure what good the info would be but you never know until you've heard it.

"You know I'd get fired for this, right?"

"I'm not going to tell a soul. I mean it."

She plunked down in front of the computer and in a couple of minutes, smiled.

"I'll write it down for you. And also what I heard them talking about," she added. "When I'm finished," she whispered, "maybe you'd better go, in case someone starts wondering what we're up to."

I nodded. "Good idea, Cindy Sue."

An elderly couple came in, each pulling a small suitcase on wheels, and stood behind me.

She scribbled on a page of hotel stationery for a few minutes, folded it, and handed it to me.

"Here, you are, Mrs. Smith," she said, in a loud voice. "This is the information you wanted about our hotel. We'd love to have you come and stay with us."

I took the paper. "And, I would love to come and stay here," I replied with a matching voice. "Thank you so much." In a whisper, I said, "I'm staying at the Firebird Motel. If you think of anything else, call me. Room 301."

I smiled at the couple. "I'm sure you'll enjoy your stay here."

As I walked out to the car, I felt good, knowing there were other kindred spirits out there. Cindy Sue was just a younger version of me, younger and more hip; I never could snap my gum like that.

When I reached the restaurant, Flori and Stella were waiting in front, leaning against the wall. Flori's nose was taking on a nice red hue. Beads of sweat were dripping off Stella's forehead and forming little streams down her cheeks.

"Mabel, where on earth have you been?" Flori exclaimed as soon as she got in the front seat and I settled into the back again. "We had three meals just sitting there and waiting for you. I don't think I'll ever eat anything again."

"Oh Flori, trust me, you will. Probably in about two hours."

"No, Mabel, this time I think I've sworn off food for good. Well, fast food anyway." She rubbed her stomach, belched, and groaned. "If I never see another cheeseburger, it will suit me just fine." She turned in her seat to look at me. "I hope you accomplished a lot, Missy, after putting us through such torture."

"First of all, you didn't have to sit and eat all the time. You can just sit and talk; no one would notice. For goodness' sake, Flori, it's a fast food joint, not some high-class restaurant and yes, I did accomplish a lot. You won't believe all the things I've found out," I said. I carefully removed the paper from my jean pocket.

"Well, what, Mabel? Don't keep us in suspense."

"Okay, here goes. First of all, Cecile's wife might not be named Grace; she might be called Andrea."

"Just a minute," Stella interrupted. "I know Cecile's wife

is named Grace. It just isn't the Grace who was killed, that's all. But, Mabel, her name has always been Grace. I should know; I live next door."

"Okay, but the Grace who was murdered, who *wasn't* Cecile's wife, was really named Andrea."

"Well, that makes more sense, doesn't it?" Stella said.

"It does?" Flori said. "That is logical to you?"

"Well, sure. She obviously wasn't who she said she was. She must've been pretendin' to be Cecile's wife and all the while she was somebody named Andrea."

"But why? Why would someone take on another person's name and pretend to be someone else's wife? Do you know why, Mabel?"

"You're asking me, Flori? This whole thing is just plain ludicrous. But, hey, that's why we came here, right, Flori? We have to find out who Andrea really was. Was she pretending to be Cecile's wife? I don't even know if she was. Also, why was Cecile Tucker in Las Vegas and where is Cecile's real wife? Is she dead too?"

Flori moaned and shook her head. "This is too much for me. This is too much for you too, Mabel. You have to call either Reg or Jim."

"That's not all though. Get this - would you believe that Mr. Hatcher and Grace, or Andrea, were sharing a hotel room right here in Yellow Rose? I was going to say, before someone killed her, but that's sort of a 'given,' isn't it? Obviously, that was before the trip to Vegas. And, not only that, they had a big fight. Cindy Sue thought they were mad enough to shoot each other."

"Cindy Sue? Who's Cindy Sue?" Flori asked.

"She works at the hotel where the two were staying. They booked in that morning, had the fight, and never returned. Weird, isn't it? I'll tell you, I would've sworn on a stack of Bibles that they were strangers when I saw them together. But, you will never believe what else I found out. Flori, you were right. This whole Las Vegas thing? It *was* a hoax."

Chapter Twenty Two

"Let me see that paper again."

We were back in our hotel room. Stella was with us. Flori took Cindy Sue's note out of my hand and read it aloud for the fourth time.

Room 322. Registered to Bob Hatcher. Heard the woman saying the Las Vegas trip was a great cover up. Nobody suspected. It sounded like she didn't want Cecile Tucker involved and he said she was crazy if she thought he'd trust her. Last thing I heard was him saying Cecile recommended you so you'd better live up to our agreement.

"Aren't those what you call, famous last words?" Stella said. "I wonder what they were coverin' up? If Cecile was involved, you're knowin' it was somethin' bad. Maybe drugs or guns."

"Do you think Grace was the one behind it? You know, the one who planned it all?" I wondered, aloud.

"Tucker would be my bet," Stella said. "I tell you, I wouldn't want to meet up with Cecile or that Hatcher character in an alley, I'll tell you."

"No," Flori said. "It's never the one you think. Mark my words, there's always some nameless person behind these things - someone who never gets caught. Someone who keeps doing more diabolic crimes and keeps getting away with it. You see it all the time on TV. I bet Maxymowich could torture Hatcher forever and he would never divulge any information."

"Flori," I said. "Your imagination is getting away on you. This isn't a television series or a mystery book. Those things don't happen in real life. You know that."

Stella snorted. "Yeah, but this isn't real life. This is Yellow Rose, Texas. Flori could be right." She shook her head. "There's people here who'd do most anythin' for money. Trust me, I know. Some of the most law-abidin' citizens have done things they never thought they'd do. Even me. It ain't easy bein' poor."

Flori looked at me with an 'I told you so' look.

"So, now, Mabel," she said, feeling a bit more confident. "You'd better give Reg a call. I think you have enough information to make him happy."

She was right. It's just that I would've liked to call and tell him who Grace really was, why someone killed her, and why that someone left her body behind the nursing home in Parson's Cove. Of course, handing over the killer would bring me the greatest joy, but I had to be realistic and surrender to the circumstances. After all, I should leave something for the authorities to solve, shouldn't I?

"You're right." I checked my watch. It was after five. "But, you know what, Flori? He's at home having dinner now so why don't I phone later? You two probably aren't hungry but don't forget - I didn't have any lunch."

They both looked at me as if I were nuts.

"That," Stella said, "was hours ago. I'm famished, aren't you, Flori?"

Flori giggled. "This detective work really gives a person an appetite. Where should we go for our dinner?"

So much for never eating again.

Flori got out the phone book and they checked the

restaurants. Stella had eaten at every one. We decided it was time for Chinese. I was excited too; not so much about the food but I felt, for the first time, that we were close to solving this mystery.

The restaurant was small and, as usual, packed. I don't know much about Chinese food so I let the other two order for me. When the plates arrived, they were over-flowing with steaming fried rice, sweet and sour chicken, and Chinese vegetables. We shared a pot of green tea. The cups were small but after four of them, I made a dash for the washroom.

"Do you know what I noticed?" I said, after getting back to the table. "The door to the kitchen was open and all the cooks back there are Mexican."

"That's why we came here," Stella said. "They make the best Chinese food in town."

We stopped on the beach road, down from our hotel, and watched the sunset. I took out my camera and snapped a few pictures of the sun reflecting on the water. In the west, the sky was orange and in the east, it was pink and powder blue.

"I'm going to try and remember this," Flori said. "It's so beautiful."

"And," I said, "if you forget, you can always look at my pictures."

"Or, y'all can come back for a visit." Stella had been quiet all evening. "I'm going to miss you two." She started to tear up. "I never realized what a boring life I lead. Ever since you came, things have gotten lots more excitin'."

I grabbed a box of tissues off the back window and passed it up front. Stella, I found, almost matched Flori in the crying department.

When the sobbing, hiccoughs, and snorts had desisted, I said, "Well, we don't have to call it quits. After all, we still have to find out who the real Grace was. Besides that, we don't know who Hatcher was going to see in prison. Do you think there's any way you could get back in there, Stella?"

They both turned in their seats and glared at me. Okay, so they didn't want to do any more detective work tonight. I took the hint.

Instead, they decided we would rather spend a lovely evening in the hotel room, watching a movie. Stella stopped at a little corner store and came out with a gigantic bag of snacks. Much to Flori's horror, in the other arm, she had a six-pack of beer. Beer isn't gin but it's better than soda pop. We'd barely stepped foot in the lobby when the young man from behind the desk came rushing over to pounce on us. Well, me in particular.

"Miss Wickles?" he said. "There's been an urgent message for you from someone in someplace called Carson's Cove." He handed a piece of paper to me. There was a phone number on it. "The gentleman who called sounded extremely upset. I hope everything will be all right." The faster he talked, the more his freckles and pimples reddened. He placed his hand on my arm. "If there's anything we can do to help, let us know. I told the manager and he said that if, and heaven forbid this might be true, but *if* someone has been in an accident or something like that..." His grip got tighter. "Perhaps, a death in the family, and heaven forbid this might be true, we can make arrangements for a shuttle bus to take you and your friend, to the Houston airport immediately."

Flori gasped and made a low moaning sound. "Are you sure it was for Mabel?" Her voice shook. Stella put her arm around her to steady her. "Did this man say Mabel or was it

Flori?"

"No, it was Mabel. Mabel Wickles."

I looked down at the phone number.

"Flori, there's nothing to get excited about. This is Reg's phone number." I looked at the young man and smiled. "By the way, it's *Parson's* Cove, not *Carson's* Cove. And, don't worry. I doubt there's an emergency. Did he happen to leave any sort of message? Knowing Reg, I'm sure he must have said something."

The boy blushed. "Well, I thought because he seemed so upset that there must be something terribly wrong. I'm sure he didn't mean what he said."

"I'm sure he didn't either. Can you remember the exact words?"

He cleared his throat. "I think he said something like: 'Where the hell's Mabel Wickles? (Pardon my language but you said 'exact words.') You tell her that if she's not home on the next flight, I'll send a posse out to search for her.' At this point, I said, 'Are you threatening one of our guests?' Because, you know, Miss Wickles, we would never allow that. However, this very upset gentleman then said, 'If I don't hear from her within the next four hours, I'll be there to collect her, myself.' At which point, I said, 'I'll get this message to her as quickly as possible.' He seemed to settle down a bit when I said that because then he said, 'She better be all in one piece when I see her.' I think that was very nice of him. I mean, to say that, wasn't it?"

"Yes, it was. And, you did a very good imitation of Reg." I removed his hand. "Don't worry. I'll call him right away. He tends to worry too much."

He smiled. "He must be a very good friend to be so concerned."

"No." I rolled my eyes. "He's just an old retired sheriff."

Chapter Twenty Three

Half way through the first ring, Reg picked up.

"Mabel," he bellowed. "Who gave you permission to go to Yellow Rose, Texas? And, who said you could take Flori all the way out there? Are you out of your mind? Flori's kids are worried sick about her. Well?" He paused. "What do you have to say for yourself?"

"First of all, Reg Smee, I don't need *anyone's* permission to go on a vacation to Yellow Rose, Texas. Or, to any other place, for that matter. Secondly, Flori's kids are not worried sick about her because she's been phoning them and most of them couldn't care less where she is. Well, I mean, they care but they're not worried at all. And, thirdly, I'm not out of my mind. Is there anything else you have to say to me?"

"Yes, there is something I have to say; this is the most bone-assed trick you have ever played."

"Don't you think you're getting a bit carried away, Reg? I have no idea what you mean by saying I'm playing tricks. And, for another thing - you can watch your language."

"If you weren't playing tricks, why'd you tell Jake to say you were in Florida? Why'd you try to hide it from the police? Tell me that, Miss Wickles."

"Okay, I will. I didn't want you or Jim or Scully or Maxymowich to know because I knew you would react exactly as you're reacting right now. And, besides that, I was going to phone you tonight. There was no need for you to scare that young desk boy half to death."

"You were going to call me, were you? Easy to say that after I called, isn't it?"

"Just one second, Reg." I handed the phone to Flori. "Here, tell the old coot that I was going to phone him this evening anyway."

"Hello, Reg? This is Flori. How are you? I'm sorry we didn't phone sooner. It's really true, we were going to talk to you tonight. We're having a wonderful time, Reg. I wish you could meet our new friend, Stella. The folks here have to be the friendliest in the world. And, the sunsets over the water? They are marvelous. Pink and orange and blue. Something you never see in Parson's Cove. And, you know, Reg, we have a room that looks right out onto the water. Oh, and another thing, the food is wonderful. Stella has taken us to so many different places. I never thought I would enjoy Mexican food so much. Well, the first time, we drank too many margaritas and we were up all night." She giggled. "Did you know that's a Mexican drink, Reg? Mabel says they get very offended if you don't have one or two with your supper."

Flori stopped to catch her breath and Reg must have asked to speak to me again.

"Here, Mabel. He wants to talk to you." She handed me the phone.

"Okay, Wickles, I'll hand it to you; it sounds like Flori is having a good time. At least, I'm glad you're looking after her. You? I know you're up to something. I haven't known you for all these years for nothing. There's no way you would've traveled all that way unless you were going down there to find Grace Hobbs' killer."

"Hey, Reg, I know I can never pull one over your eyes. I

have to admit I did do a bit of investigating while I was here."

"I knew it! All I can say is you better not be upsetting Maxymowich's investigation. You'll be in big trouble then. This isn't some little game you can play, you know. You get mixed up with these thugs and you might end up like Grace. Did you hear me, Mabel? You could very easily end up like Grace - dead in a morgue."

"Well, you don't mean like the *real* Grace because she's probably still alive."

"What real Grace? What on earth are you talking about?"

"That woman who was murdered and whose body was discovered behind the nursing home in Parson's Cove? That's not the real Grace Hobbs. Actually, as far as I can figure out, there might not even be a Grace Hobbs. Her name might be Grace Tucker. Unless, she didn't want to use her husband's name and I wouldn't blame her at all. Grace Hobbs was the name the dead woman gave when she was on the trip to Las Vegas, but that's not her real name. Her real name was Andrea."

"You're not making much sense, Mabel, as usual. Are you trying to tell me that the dead woman's name is Andrea, not Grace?"

"*Was.*"

"Okay, say you're right; then, who was the Andrea who went to Las Vegas? Isn't that what you said her name was? The one you said was Grace's friend?"

"That's something I'm still working on, Reg."

"Well, you can quit working on it. I thought I'd save the best until last. Maxymowich and his men are headed for Yellow Rose and I don't want them to see you. If you mess things up, I'm the one who'll get H, E, double L hockey sticks. I want you out of there tomorrow morning, latest. Got that?"

"Maxymowich? Here, in Yellow Rose? You're kidding. As for leaving in the morning, you're coming through loud and clear, Mr. Smee." I put the phone back in its cradle.

I looked at the two women.

"Well," I said, "Reg says we have to leave tomorrow which is no big deal because we were planning on leaving soon anyway. Except he said tomorrow morning and how does he even know we could get a flight? Just shows what a county bumpkin he is."

"Oh but, Mabel, we're going to listen to him. If we don't, he'll talk to Jake and then I'll be in trouble. Besides, didn't I hear you say that Maxymowich is here?"

"Can you believe it? Let's hope we don't run into him. Don't worry, Flori, we'll get a flight sometime tomorrow for sure. We're on standby for an evening flight anyway."

Flori and Stella sat looking at me, not saying a word.

"Which means," I said, "we can either waste the time we have left watching some movie or we can get back out there and try to find a killer." I smiled my best smile. "What do you think? All ready to find a killer?"

Both of them looked at the television set and then the bag of junk food. I could see already that this was going to be a hard sell.

"Okay. How about if we don't solve anything by midnight, we come back and eat all our snacks? Or, better yet, what if we take all the snacks with us?"

"I don't think so, Mabel," Flori said. "How about we go out until nine and if we don't find our killer, we come back and eat our snacks here and watch a movie?"

"Ten and it's a deal."

The women looked at each other and nodded.

I looked over at the alarm clock by the bed. It was already seven-thirty. Only two and a half hours to solve a murder?

Stella went out and brought back some ice for the beer and placed everything in the sink. Flori and I used the washroom and then we were ready to go.

"Okay," Stella said, "where to, Mabel?"

"Let's go back to the houses on P ½. We might see who the Andrea is at 3602 or we could check and see if Cecile Tucker is at home."

"It's so confusing," Flori said. "Why would Andrea change her name to Grace Hobbs? I don't understand that."

"Maybe," I said, "they're all undercover cops. Why didn't we think of that before? What if the whole thing was to expose Cecile and his drug deals?"

"Okay, but remember when you were in Tucker's house? You said someone named Andy phoned and left a message for Grace. You also said, the woman's voice on the recorder sounded like the Grace Hobbs and the woman who left the message sounded like Andrea Williams," Stella said. "So, why would this Grace be with Hatcher? They were obviously in something together."

"Just a minute," I said. I grabbed the hotel notepad and pen. "I'm going to write down all the things that we know for sure. There isn't much but it might help us to get it straight in our minds."

I looked up at them. "Okay, start. What do we know for sure?"

"Well," Flori said. "We know that Grace Hobbs is not Grace Hobbs but is Andrea somebody. And, we know she was white so the dead Andrea Williams isn't the Andrea

Williams who is black and missing."

"Hold it! We don't know that she's Andrea *William*s, do we? All we know is that her first name is Andrea. I mean, lots of people have the same first name, right?"

"You're right," Stella said. "Do you think because she's a crook, that when she found out the other woman on the trip had the same first name, she decided it would be best to use different name?"

"I have no idea, Stella, but it sounds logical, doesn't it?" I looked at them. "So, what else do we know?"

"We know that Hatcher is a shyster and that he and Andrea or Grace were involved in this thing together. Which is a good motive for murder; especially, since we know that they were arguing about it. Oh yes, and we know that the whole Las Vegas thing was just a front for some illegal goings-on. What it was, we don't know but it could've been drugs or guns."

"We don't know if there were any guns involved, Flori. It could've been illegal gambling of some kind, couldn't it? After all, that's what goes on in Vegas."

Flori shook her head. "We don't really know much at all, Mabel. I think we should've stayed home."

"Don't say that," Stella said. "We had lots of fun doin' this. Hey, maybe someday, I might even make a trip up to Parson's Cove, if y'all say it's okay."

"That would be wonderful," Flori said. "Mabel and I both have lots of spare bedrooms."

I don't but I didn't want to spoil Flori's moment. Besides, it would serve Jake right if he had another 'Flori' in the house.

"Okay, girls," I said. "Humor me. Let's go and check out those two houses on P1/2."

It was almost dark now and the streetlights were slowly

coming on. First, we checked out Cecile's house. Nothing had changed. There were no lights, no movement of any kind. It looked as deserted as Stella's house, next door. Disappointed, I asked if we could go by the Williams' house.

This time, the light in the little overhang above the front door was on but with all the blinds down, it looked as if no one was home. We drove slowly down the street and came back through the lane. There were two cars parked closely together by the back door.

"Look," I said. "Somebody might be there. Stella, can you move over into this yard so we can watch?"

She pulled up, almost touching bumpers with one of the cars, and then whipped into reverse. I don't know if she had her eyes open or not; I know I didn't. At least, we were off the back lane and sandwiched between a dilapidated shed and garage. If a car drove down the lane, no one would bother to look. The old Cadillac seemed to blend in with the shed and garage quite nicely.

We sat in silence and watched for about ten minutes.

"I wish we would've brought the snacks with us," Flori said.

"I wish we would've brought the beer," I said.

It was after nine before we saw the back door open. None of us said a word. A man walked out first, followed by a woman. They walked over to the car closest to the door and got in.

"Do you know who they are?" Stella whispered.

"Maybe," I whispered back. "The woman might be Andrea Williams. It's hard to tell. I'm sure I don't know who the man is."

"I wonder," Flori said. "I wonder if she knows that

Grace Hobbs is dead. I mean, she would think her name was Grace Hobbs, wouldn't she?"

"I would think so. Unless, everything was a lie and they knew each other before. Maybe they just exchanged names?"

"No," Stella said. "Grace Hobbs was really Andrea Williams and Andrea Williams was really Andrea Williams. Isn't that how it is?"

"So, now," I said. "One Andrea Williams is dead and one is alive."

"Then," Flori said, "where is Grace Hobbs?"

"You know what?" I said. "As soon as those two leave, let's go and watch a movie. This is too perplexing for me."

"Wait," Stella whispered. "There's someone else comin' out. A woman. You know who they are, Mabel?"

It was obvious that the woman wasn't a willing companion. The man behind her either had one of her arms shoved behind her back and he was propelling her towards the car or he had a gun in her back and that's what was propelling her. The woman inside the car reached back and opened the back door. It swung open and the couple on the outside tumbled inside. It all happened quickly and I'm sure they didn't notice our car.

I shook my head. "I couldn't make out who those two were. Somehow, the woman looks familiar. It's just too dark out."

"And, you need glasses," Flori interjected. "Why did you think the other one was Andrea?"

"Mostly by the shape. And her hair. Oh, I don't know. I didn't realize that all of them seemed to be shaped the same."

The car's backup lights came on and we ducked.

The car drove away. No one stopped to check us out.

After all, who would suspect anyone driving an old pink Cadillac, right?

Chapter Twenty Four

Flori and I were sound asleep when the banging started. Stella had left about an hour earlier. We'd tried our hardest to watch the movie but none of us could stay awake. No matter how many chips we put in our mouths or how many jellybeans we popped, our eyes kept drifting shut. The beer definitely didn't help. All it did was make Stella and me run to the bathroom every twenty minutes. Flori tried making coffee in our little coffeemaker but it tasted awful so we dropped that idea. Finally, when Stella woke herself up, snoring, we decided to call it quits. As soon as she shut the door, after promising to pick us up for breakfast, Flori and I crawled under the covers, clothes and all.

When the banging started, I thought it was part of some dream so I turned over, believing it would eventually stop.

"Mabel," Flori yelled. She was sitting up in bed. "Wake up. Somebody's banging on our door."

I pulled the bedspread over my head. "No, you wake up. I'm too tired."

She slid off her bed, took two steps over to mine, and started shaking me. The room was black. I don't know how she even found me.

I grabbed her arm. "Flori, what are you doing? Stop that."

Another sharp bang on the door soon brought me to my

senses.

I sat up. "Flori, who's at the door?"

She started to whisper. "I don't know. Should we call the front desk? Whoever it is, is waking up the whole building."

"Just wait. I'll go and look through the peephole."

Before I could get to the door, someone called out, "Mabel, Flori. Open up!"

"Is that you, Jake?" Flori shouted.

By that time, my eye was at the peephole.

"No, it isn't." My heart was in my mouth. Or, someplace because I don't think it was beating in its right spot.

I took off the chain latch and undid the deadbolt.

Before I could open it all the way, Captain Maxymowich had pushed it open. I flipped the switch and two bedside lamps came to life. Flori and I both started blinking.

"Well, well, what do we have here?" he said. He kept coming towards us and we kept backing up until Flori's bed got in the way. He was so close; I could smell his aftershave and see the hairs inside his nose. That was much too close to be to Captain Maxymowich. Flori grabbed my hand and we stood there; nowhere to hide. "A couple of private investigators? Is that what you are? What do you have to say for yourselves, Mabel?"

The poor, undoubtedly harangued, night clerk was hovering in the background, his acne and freckles brighter than before. A deputy in khaki pants and shirt, with all sorts of paraphernalia drooping from his waist, stood beside him. We took turns staring at each other for several seconds.

"What do you mean, Captain Maxymowich?" I asked. "And to be fair, it seems you're singling me out."

"It does, does it?"

He turned to the clerk and said, "You can leave now." The young man hurried away, probably heading for the nearest restroom to relieve himself. The Captain nodded towards the other law officer. He walked in and closed the door.

Maxymowich looked exhausted. Not that I was feeling tenderhearted all of a sudden, it was only an observation. His wrinkled suit and slouch didn't help. He looked at me and then at Flori.

"So?" He raised his eyebrows. "You didn't answer my question."

"Isn't a person allowed to take a vacation without the police getting involved?" I asked.

"You came here strictly for a vacation, did you?"

I could hear Flori starting to pant. She can't stand it when I start lying. Which I wouldn't do if I wasn't put on the defensive.

"Yes, among other things."

"Like sitting in a back lane spying on a house?"

"Which house?"

"The one on P½. You probably remember being there."

"Oh, *that* house."

"We're being very patient with you, Mabel. You tend to forget that if you interfere with the solving of a crime, I could arrest you. Or, worse yet, you could get hurt. Even killed. Are you aware of that or do you think you live in some kind of bubble and no harm could ever befall you?"

"How could I be arrested if I'm helping?" I turned and looked at the young deputy. "That shouldn't be a crime, should it?" He blushed and looked uncomfortable.

"We wouldn't want you to get hurt, ma'am," hc said.

The Captain straightened up. "You aren't aware of this,

girls, but not long after you left, someone was almost killed in that same back yard."

I looked at Flori and she looked at me; we both looked at Maxymowich.

"*Killed?*" we said, simultaneously.

He nodded. "You could've screwed up the whole investigation."

"But," I said, "how did you know we were there? Who told you?"

"Ben Williams got hold of us and asked us to come and have you removed. It seems the Yellow Rose police force thinks I should be looking out for you. Fortunately, by the time we got to the lane, you were leaving."

"How did he know it was us? It could've been any car sitting back there. And, we did duck down. He couldn't have seen us."

Maxymowich sighed. "Mabel, you were sitting in an old pink Cadillac. You got out of the exact same car when you went to the house, earlier in the day. How stupid do you think the police are anyway?"

I could feel my cheeks getting hot. Flori looked ready to burst into tears.

"Now what are you going to do with us?" I asked.

"I'm going to ask a big favor."

"We'll do anything," Flori said, her voice quivering.

"Within reason," I said.

The deputy glanced down at the floor but not before I caught a glimpse of his smile. I knew he wasn't a bad sort the moment I saw his face. I mean, there has to be at least one officer of the law who isn't narrow minded and stubborn. Perhaps, it was because he was young and hadn't faced all the terrible situations that dear Mr. Maxymowich had. Also, he wasn't retired out to pasture like Reg was. Old age can make one cynical too, I suppose. Besides, I liked his clean-cut look, his shaved head, and lopsided grin.

"This," the Captain said, "is within reason. I don't want you leaving this hotel until it's time for you to take the shuttle to Houston to catch your plane. Got that?"

"What about food?" Flori asked. "Can we go out for breakfast? Stella is coming to pick us up."

The Captain blinked several times, sighed, and rubbed his eyes. Flori, I knew, was waiting with great anticipation for that breakfast. If we had to cancel our last meal with Stella, my friend would be heartbroken.

"I can keep an eye on them, if you like," the deputy said. "I'm off duty at eight so I could accompany them for breakfast." He looked at me and grinned. "I have to go for breakfast anyway, might as well go with a couple of lovely young ladies."

Maxymowich shrugged. The man comes up against hardened criminals every day but five minutes with two old women and he can't seem to get it together. It was clearly frustrating for him. "Up to you, Bumstead. Just keep your guard up, that's all I can say. They aren't as innocent as they look."

"Okay, girls, I'll be back at eight-thirty. Think you can manage to stay here until then? And, out of trouble?" He winked.

"We'll try our darnedest," I said. "Thanks so much, Sheriff Bumstead."

"Well, I'm just a deputy. You can call me Kyle, ma'am." He made a slight bow when he said, 'ma'am.'

Maxymowich stopped with his hand on the doorknob and said, "I haven't slept in two days, girls, and I get cranky. You don't want to see me cranky." For some reason, he seemed to keep his eyes peeled on me. "Don't do anything to upset me, Mabel."

He held the door open for the deputy. Kyle gave us one last wink and they were gone. Flori and I stood for a minute or two, just looking at each other and not saying a word.

"Mabel," Flori said. "I don't even want to talk about this murder thing again. I want to get into my nightie, go to sleep, and pretend none of this ever happened." With that, she grabbed her nightgown, went into the bathroom, and the last thing I heard before I fell asleep was her electric toothbrush.

Chapter Twenty Five

Deputy Bumstead arrived right on time. Flori had phoned Stella to fill her in. Of course, she tended to exaggerate somewhat. From her perspective, it sounded like an old Western. *Gunfight on Avenue P ½*. Personally, I was wondering if it were even true. Maybe Maxymowich was just trying to scare us. Scare us into submission. I wouldn't put it past him.

"He wouldn't do that and you know it," Flori said. "The Captain is not a liar. Besides, he was right. We had no business being there." She stared at me until I made eye contact. She does this to me. I hate it. "Wouldn't you feel terrible if we spoiled their whole investigation? What if there had been a real killing and it was our fault? How would we be able to live with ourselves, Mabel?" Her eyes filled with tears.

"But, that's not what happened, Flori, so don't get all upset. Don't forget, we got out of there before there was any gunfight." I bent down and tied my running shoes. "I wonder who the target was? What do you think, Flori?"

"I don't want to talk about it," she said. That was that, for the time being.

Stella was a little flustered when she found out that a policeman was escorting us to breakfast in a cruiser but it

178

didn't take long for her to adjust.

"Say," she said to Kyle as soon as we were all settled in the back seat, "Didn't you go to school with my son, Spenser?"

"You mean, Spenser Townley?"

She beamed. "That's him. He's a fire fighter, jus' like his daddy."

"Sure, I remember Spense." He turned around and smiled. "Glad to hear he's doin' so good. We didn't go to school together but we did have some contact at one point. Something he probably didn't share with his mama." He grinned and winked. "So, where we headed? Any special place y'all were fixin' to eat at?"

"How about you choose, Deputy Bumstead?" I suggested.

"All right, but y'all better start calling me Kyle or you'll be in big trouble with the Law." He turned around and winked again.

"We don't have any problem with that, do we, girls?" I said.

"And, it doesn't mean we don't respect you as much," Flori had to add.

Kyle took off flying out of the parking lot while Stella, Flori, and I hung on for our lives. In three seconds or less, he pulled into a small dumpy diner.

"Oh, oh," Stella whispered. "Maybe we should've chosen. This is a dive."

"Why would a cop eat here then?" I whispered back.

She shrugged. "All of them come here. I don't know why."

The three of us spilled out of the car as soon as Kyle opened our door. We would've opened it ourselves except there weren't any handles in the backseat.

Stella was right; the place was a dive. You could cut the tobacco smoke with a machete. If there was a non-smoking area, it wouldn't have made any difference because it was so small. I'm not sure what color the walls were; there was an inch or so of soot on them. There were windows along two walls and Kyle headed for a booth that was empty and faced the Gulf. We trailed after him while everyone in the place stopped eating or drinking, including talking, and watched. After we sat down, I looked around. Most of the people appeared to be city workers. One or two looked like homeless men. There wasn't one man in a suit. The only other woman was a very pregnant one who sat a couple of booths down. She was puffing away on a cigarette. Flori was sitting across from me beside Stella so she couldn't see. I was glad because if she had, she might've gone over and knocked that cigarette right out of her mouth. Not that I would blame her. I've never been pregnant but even I know that's a big no-no. There should be a worldwide law that no one can smoke in any place where there are people - never mind these silly 'no smoking' areas.

I also didn't mention the cockroach creeping up the side of the wall and disappearing somewhere behind the window frame.

There was a breakfast special but before we could say anything, Kyle raised his hand and yelled to the waitress, "Four Specials here." Then, he turned to us and asked, "You want coffee?" We nodded and he yelled, "Four coffees too, Selma."

"Sure thing, Kyle," she yelled back and that was that. No menus, no asking what we would prefer, nothing. Flori looked a bit flustered but then again, she would never argue with a cop.

"So, Kyle," I said, trying to put us more at ease. "You should come and visit Parson's Cove sometime. Maybe Maxymowich told you, that's where Flori and I are from. We have a young sheriff not much older than you are. We had an old sheriff but thankfully he's now retired. We could always use another deputy, that's for sure."

Kyle laughed. "I'm sure it would be a blast. I'm sort of attached to Yellow Rose though. It's usually a quiet place. Haven't had any real bad crime, you know like murders, here in a long time."

"What about that li'l girl who was kidnapped awhile back?" Stella said. "An' that old man who was beat up and had all his money stole?" She glared at him and then looked at me. "I'd say that was some real bad crime, wouldn't you, Mabel?"

Before I could try to quell the argument, she continued, "You should live where I live on P ½. I tell you, there's a crime goin' on every night on that street."

Kyle cleared his throat. "Well, all you gotta do is phone the police, Stella. That's all you gotta do. We'll take care of it all."

The waitress, a skinny thing with her hair pulled back in a pony tail and with crooked front teeth, brought four cups of steaming coffee on a tray and plunked one in front of each of us. How she did it without spilling was a miracle. There was barely enough room in the cup to add a teaspoon of cream.

Stella didn't even take the time to thank the server. "You don' think I bin doin' that?" she said to Kyle. "I quit countin' how many times I dialed 911."

"Where you live on P ½ anyway?"

"On the corner of P ½ and thirty-eighth."

"You're right next door to Cecile Tucker? Heck, woman, you didn't need to worry at all. He'll be looking out for y'all." He grinned and winked.

Stella glared again. "Yeah? Well, I don' think I need his kind lookin' out for me."

"What happened last night anyway?" I asked, changing the subject. "Was there really gunshots fired or are you boys trying tell us in a nice way to stay out of your way?"

He shook his head. "Hey, we don't go making up stories. 'Specially when it comes to murder. And, especially that Captain. He's one serious dude." He paused for a sip of scalding hot coffee. "Williams called to tell us you were there but by the time we drove down, you were pulling out. That's when we saw the other car coming so we took off and waited down the street. Saw this guy back into the exact spot you were in, and then after sitting there for a few minutes, he went over to the house. We saw he had his gun drawn so we got out of the car and spread out. I guess he must've seen some movement or something because he fired at one of the officers as he was running back to his car. The officer returned fire but neither one got hit. The fellow took off and that's the last we saw of him."

"So, that means he came for someone in that house. Was it a man for sure? I mean, is there a chance it could've been a woman?"

He shook his head. "Naw. It was a man. You could tell by the way he moved."

"Could you see what he looked like?"

"Nope. Too dark. Couldn't get a license plate number either. All we know is that it was a dark late model car. That's it."

I looked at Stella. I figured she was thinking the same as I was. That matched the description of Hatcher's car and the stranger's car - the man at Cecile's house. Just down the road on P½ .

Our breakfast arrived: three fried eggs, three fried sausages, three pieces of slightly undercooked bacon, a pile of slightly burned hash browns, and toast saturated with butter. On a separate plate, there were three medium-sized pancakes served with three packets of butter on the side and a pitcher of hot maple syrup. I guess everyone in Yellow Rose must take their eggs over-easy, their bacon dripping with grease, and white bread, toasted, because every plate was identical. There wasn't an inch of space left on the table. If I would've thought about the cholesterol and sodium content, I would have had a heart attack right then and there.

We ate in silence for the next ten minutes. It wasn't that our eating was silent; it's just that there was no conversation.

After our first coffee refill, Kyle said, "So, I don't understand why you came down here, Mabel and Flori. I don't think that Captain of yours... What's his name again?... Maxymowich? ... was too happy about it all." He looked up at us over his cup. "In case you didn't know, he doesn't have any jurisdiction down here. Obviously, he could've gotten the info he needed by phone, so it seems he headed down here to make sure you two left town. Maybe he was worried that you'd screw up the case. Or more'n likely worried you might get shot."

"He doesn't have any jurisdiction down here?" I asked. "You mean, he can't come down here and arrest somebody?"

"Nope, that's up to the folks in Texas now to catch these crooks."

"That's interesting." I drained the last of my coffee. "So, really, then, Flori and I could do more good solving a murder down here than he could?"

Flori's eyes got big and she looked like she was sipping on a straw, except she didn't have a straw, but she didn't speak.

Kyle pulled a toothpick out of his shirt pocket, picked off the lint, and stuck it in his mouth. "Well, I wouldn't go that far. We don't like ordinary folk getting involved in crime fighting. It's a dangerous sport to get mixed up in, that's for sure. Besides, we got this one pretty much figured out anyway."

All three of us stared at him.

"You do?" I said. "You know who murdered Grace? Or, Andrea, or whoever she was?"

He shifted in his seat. "Well, that we don't know yet. But, this whole thing has to do with drugs and gambling. Cecile's been working undercover for years."

"Pardon me," I interrupted. "You said that *Cecile* was working undercover? You mean the person who lives next door to Stella? The creep who looks like a convict? He's a cop?"

He nodded. "That's why he's so good at it. Nobody suspects. He lives the part. Gets in there, real mean and dirty. Been doing this for years. His cover's been blown now so I imagine he and Grace will be moving on. Some other city, some other crime scene, some other name…"

"Just a minute, Kyle. You know that the Grace Hobbs who was murdered was not his wife? She was somebody named Andrea."

"Well, sure. That's right." He shook his head as if trying to erase something from his brain and then yelled, "Time for some coffee refills here, Selma."

"Well, sure? That's all you're going to say? What's going on here, Kyle? Flori and I came all this way to find out who killed Grace Hobbs, only to find out she's not Grace at all. I think the least you can do is fill us in on a few things. Like, are all of you just plain crazy or is there some sense to this?"

We all stopped talking while Selma filled our cups, pulled a handful of creamers from her pocket, placed them on the table, and cleared away our plates. She started with two plates in her hand and she lined all the rest up from there to her shoulder.

"So?" I asked, when I saw Selma disappear behind the swinging doors that led to the kitchen.

"So, I have to say this was a tough one." He reached for four sugar packets and proceeded to add them, one at a time, to his coffee.

"Thank the Lord, we don't lose good officers too often," he continued. He started stirring his coffee. "Still can't figure it out." He shook his head. "She was always right on her game. Things can happen when you're in the line of fire. Go wrong, you know. Gotta be prepared for the worst. All the time. You just never know." He kept stirring.

Flori was trying not to weep and at the same time, looking a bit confused because she really had no idea for what or whom she should be weeping.

"Could you explain that a little more?" I said. "What do you mean, 'line of fire'? What do you mean - lose good officers?"

"Well, here's all I can tell you: Andrea Williams infiltrated that gang because Cecile Tucker recommended her and Hatcher fell for it."

Flori gasped. "See, Mabel. Her last name was Williams.

I thought it would be. That's why she had to take on a whole new name."

Kyle laughed. "Yeah, that's quite a coincidence, isn't it? Imagine two women with the same name."

"So, that's why Andrea changed her name to Grace Hobbs? Because she would've had the same name as the other woman on the trip? How come when I went to look for her number in the phone book, I ended up at Cecile Tucker's house?"

"Well, for one thing Cecile'd never use his name. I think it was from the person who lived there before."

Stella leaned forward. "There was somethin' funny going on there when Cecile and Grace moved in. I think they might've done something to that nice young woman who used to live there."

"No," Kyle said. "That was Ginger Hobbs and she moved on. Got shot in the knee or something, if I remember correct."

"Wouldn't Hatcher have known Cecile's wife?" I asked.

"Hatcher knew Cecile real good but Cecile kept Grace out of the scene as best he could. Don't know if any of them did business when Grace was around."

"What about Grace, the wife? Where does she fit in?"

"We never had Cecile and Grace work together. They just do that in the movies. No, when it was time to start closing in, Cecile said he wanted another undercover agent to infiltrate. By this time, everybody trusted him so that's when we called in Andrea. She's been doing undercover for years."

"How long was Cecile working on this anyway, Kyle?" I asked.

He shook his head. "A long time. I remember thinking Cecile was a drug dealer when I got on the Force. Guess it must be almost three years now."

"Is it okay that you're telling us this?"

He laughed. "It'll be plastered all over the news within the next few days, I'm sure. You know, big crime bust. Probably say that Cecile Tucker has been put away for the next twenty years. That means Cecile and Grace will be pulling out. Hate to see them go. It was kinda fun, treating him like a crook. Y'know, bashing him up once in awhile." He grinned.

"You're being really quiet," I said to Stella. "What do you think of all this?"

She shook her head. "I don' know. Some things still don' add up for me."

"Well, I'm glad it's coming to its end. But, just think, Stella, you don't have to worry about Cecile anymore. Too bad about Andrea though."

"Yeah," Kyle said. "Seemed like this one should be an easy bust after taken' so long but instead it ended up in tragedy." He started stirring his coffee again. "Still can't figure out what went wrong. Course, nobody tells me too much. Probably that Captain, Maxymowich, knows more than I do. One thing I do know, the drugs went through okay and Andrea collected the gambling money. Cecile made sure of that. He followed them all the way to Las Vegas. Said he always had her back. Then, he lost Andrea in Denver. Suddenly, she just disappeared. Doesn't know where she went or who she went with. Next thing you know, her body's found in some little town somewhere." He cleared his throat, pulled out a tissue and blew his nose. "Yes, sir. Sure is tough when you lose one of yer own."

I gave him a second or two to get the handle on his emotions and re-establish his macho image. That's about all the time it took too. Flori, however, was having a harder time but I ignored her. Stella sat, looking like she was still in a state of shock.

"Okay, Kyle," I said. "For the last time, let's see if I have this straight. You're saying Andrea Williams was an undercover cop, and that she took on the name, Grace Hobbs. Cecile, who is married to a different Grace, is also an undercover cop."

"That's about it. As far as Hatcher and his associates knew, Cecile Tucker and Grace Hobbs, were both into the drug and gambling scene."

"Does that mean that Grace Tucker was an undercover cop too?"

"She used to be a cop up north some place. Seems to me that's where the two met. She knew Cecile was undercover but she lived the life. It's a rough life, you know. Never knowing what's going to happen next. Never knowing if your husband will come home alive. Having to stay away at times so as not to interfere when deals are going down. Not something I could put my wife through. Was she still a cop? Well, she obviously couldn't walk the beat anymore but she did work sometimes. Nothing ever to do with Cecile and his assignment though."

"Okay, so who's the other Andrea Williams then? The *real* one who went to Las Vegas? Or, was she real?"

He moved the toothpick to the other side of his mouth. "Ha! The real one? Oh yeah, she's the real McCoy all right. She's a tough one, that one. We've been waiting a long time to catch old Hatcher and Williams. Them and Cecile were the ones involved in the drug trafficking and gambling. They started trusting Cecile and he brought in Andrea. Or, Grace, as they knew her."

Stella spoke up. "Must be a real poplar name, that one.

There's another girl named Andrea Williams livin' here in Yellow Rose."

Kyle laughed. "You mean, old Veronica's girl? Yeah, that's another Andrea Williams, except I think she's married now. Maybe not. She run off with some old guy a while back. I don't know how many times we got called over to that house. Mama and daughter almost killing each other." He laughed again. "Talk about cat fights."

"I don't think that's very funny, Kyle," Stella said. "It's a downright shame when family's don' get along. How 'bout you? You get along with your momma, Kyle?"

Kyle seemed to have hit a sore spot with Stella so I thought I'd make an effort at redirecting the conversation.

"You have any idea why the body ended up in Parson's Cove?"

He shook his head. "That's a mystery."

"Well, that and who killed Andrea Williams and why they killed her? Yes, I guess it is quite a mystery, Kyle."

He slid out of the booth and stood up. Maybe the Captain gave him money to pay for our breakfast; whatever, he said our money was no good so we didn't argue. We followed him outside.

"There's really no point in you driving half a block to our hotel," I said. "We can walk that far. I'm sure the Captain won't mind."

Kyle grinned. "I don't know, Mabel. He said to watch you like a hawk."

"What about Flori and Stella? What did he say about them?" "Nothing. Absolutely nothing."

Chapter Twenty Six

"What time does that shuttle come to pick us up, Flori?"

"Not for another two hours, Mabel, but you know what the Captain said. We aren't to leave the hotel. And, this time, we're going to listen to him. We're not going anywhere. Right, Stella?"

Flori and Stella were sitting on the one bed, watching an old black and white movie on the movie channel.

"I'm sure he wouldn't mind if we took a walk along the beach. It's kind of sad to spend the last couple of hours here, glued to the television. I mean, we can do that in Parson's Cove, Flori. We might never see the Gulf of Mexico again."

"You heard what he said. And, Kyle, too. Kyle would be very disappointed if you left the room. You promised him you wouldn't, didn't you?" Flori looked at me and raised her eyebrows. The motherly look.

"I said that so he wouldn't worry, that's all. Just walking over to the beach isn't like leaving the premises."

"Going across the road is leaving the premises. Quit trying to wriggle out of your promise, Mabel."

"Okay, maybe that was stretching it a little. We could go to the pool. We haven't been there since we got here, Flori. It looks inviting and that's still in the hotel. Why don't we do that, girls?"

I was sure Flori would mention that we'd already packed
our bathing suits and that we couldn't get them wet but as it
so happened, neither one heard me because Humphrey
Bogart crushed Audrey Hepburn to his chest. Well, I don't
know if you could call it 'crushed'; after all, he wasn't very
young and if the truth were told, he didn't seem very
muscular either. Flori and Stella were wiping away the tears
and ready to watch it all over again. I slipped out the door.

I bypassed the pool and went out the rear exit door. I
needed one last look at Avenue P½. Before I headed down
the back lane, I took a quick peek around to the front of the
building and the parking lot. No sign of Kyle or any other
uniformed person. Maxymowich was probably in Parson's
Cove by now. I imagine he felt there was no point in
hanging around here if he couldn't even make any arrests. I
wondered what Reg and the boys were doing back home.

I checked my watch. This would have to be a fast run. I
had two hours, max. If I didn't show up when the shuttle
bus arrived, Flori would disown me. Or, worse.

One thing going for Yellow Rose was the back lanes. It
seemed that every street had them and some streets that were
really streets, looked like back lanes. In about ten minutes, I
was on P½. I went down the lane until I hit Thirty Sixth
Street. This was apparently Ben Williams' home. The
home of Ben, the cop, and Andrea, the tough one. How, on
earth, did they ever get together?

Everything looked quiet and normal. Hard to imagine
there'd been a shoot-out just hours before. I snuck in beside
the garage where we'd parked the Cadillac and checked out
the house. How long would I have to stand here and wait
for someone to come out? Ridiculous. I wasn't going to
waste the day doing that. Two hours go by very quickly.

I'd already used up too many minutes.

I walked up to the backdoor and banged on it.

The door swung open and there stood Andrea Williams. Not the black one or the dead one but the one who'd won the trip to Las Vegas. My mouth gaped open but no words came out. She had a wild animal look in her eye. Before I could swallow the saliva building up in the back of my throat, she'd grabbed my arm, pulled me inside, and slammed the door shut.

I had a feeling this wasn't going to be the friendly reunion I'd been hoping for. Her fingernails cut into my arm as she whisked me through the kitchen and shoved me into a chair in the living room.

No one had said anything to me yet. They didn't have to. Andrea had a gun in her hand and her friend, Mr. Hatcher was holding a gun. Andrea had hers pointed at me, and Mr. Hatcher had his pointed at Cecile Tucker.

Cecile looked me over and said, "Who the hell are you?" Before he could say anything more, Hatcher shoved the gun to his head and said, "Shut up. We'll tell you when you can talk."

This was the first time I could get a good look at Cecile. If he were a cop, he could've fooled me. He still looked like a slime ball and I doubt a shave, bath, and haircut would've helped.

I had no idea what Hatcher or Andrea knew about me. Cecile, the supposedly good guy, didn't know anything. Surely, the other two thought that I was Mabel, the innocent one, who truly believed she'd won a trip to Las Vegas. What else could they think? I decided to pretend that I hadn't noticed the guns.

"Andrea," I said, (my heart was beating at such a rate, I was sure everyone could see my shirt flopping up and down) "you never said how beautiful Yellow Rose was. To be truthful, I would prefer to visit here than Las Vegas any day. And, you, Mr. Hatcher?" I stretched my dry lips into a smile. "Why, on earth, are you here? Don't tell me someone else won a trip? That is awesome. I just came over to tell you, Andrea, how much I enjoyed sharing the experience with you. (At this point, I was starting to feel like a bobble head.) Is there going to be another one soon, Mr. Hatcher? I was wondering; can a person keep sending in coupons or do you have to wait for a while? You know, is there a time limit? Like, you can only send in every six months? I mean, I wouldn't want to be greedy, you know."

The last two words came out high-pitched. That happens when someone grabs the back of your hair and pulls.

"Shut up, you stupid old bag," Andrea said as she jerked my head back, using my hair.

Hatcher looked over at her. "Now, what are we going to do? I told you not to answer the door."

Cecile spoke up. "Let this woman go. She doesn't know anything. She's just here…" He turned his head to me. "Why exactly are you here?"

"I told you to keep quiet," Hatcher said. He slammed the side of the gun across the side of Cecile's head. It made a loud whack. He must've done it a few times before I arrived because I noticed several bright red scrapes along the side of Cecile's face.

"We'll have to get rid of both of them. We have no choice." Andrea once again grabbed my hair. If I didn't die, I would be bald. "Too bad you got so nosy, Mabel. You should've stayed back in that little hick town you came from."

"So," I said, trying to ignore the pain in my scalp.

"You're going to shoot me between the eyes like you did Grace?"

Andrea looked puzzled. "What are you talking about? I didn't shoot Grace between the eyes." She let go of my hair and put her face up to mine. "Or, are you telling me that that's what you want? A nice clean shot?" She laughed. "I can do that easy enough."

I looked up at Hatcher. "It was you then? You shot Grace?"

I'm not the best judge of character but I was sure the look on his face was blank. Cecile tried to say something but his jaw was swelling at an amazing rate and I couldn't understand him. He needed ice in a very bad way.

"In other words," I said, "neither one of you claims to have killed Andrea Williams?"

"Are you nuts? I'm Andrea Williams." Andrea pointed her gun at Cecile. "What's this woman talking about?" He shrugged.

"He can't talk," I said. "You've obviously broken his jaw, Hatcher. If you had any decency in you at all, you'd get some ice for it."

Hatcher shook his head. "I've had enough of this. Tie them up and gag them. We'll dump them in the Gulf tonight."

Andrea nodded and left the room. I assumed to hunt for rope.

"Hatcher," I said. "What's going on here? Why are you going to kill Mr. Tucker and me? What have we done to you?"

"Well, I'll tell you what Mr. Tucker has done to me, Mabel. He double-crossed me. Know what I mean? He pretended to be a friend."

I cringed as he pushed the butt of the gun into Cecile's

ear. "Didn't you, old buddy?" he said, and shoved it farther inside.

"Stop, Hatcher, there's no need to wreck his eardrum. He was only doing his job. Why should you kill someone for doing his job?"

He laughed but it wasn't a nice laugh. "Oh yes, he did a real good job. Didn't you, Cecile?" He removed the gun and jabbed Cecile's jaw with his fist. Cecile winced. "You've got me in big trouble and you know it. If you don't own up and tell me where that money is, my life is as good as over. And, so is yours, Cecile, don't forget that. You're going to die before I do." He waved the gun at Cecile's head. "Everything was running nice and smooth. Nice and smooth. Then, all of a sudden, something goes wrong. The money disappears. Grace disappears. Some stoolie comes up to me and says, don't trust Cecile Tucker."

"You trusted a stool pigeon?" I said. "I wouldn't trust one as far as I could spit. Maybe you're the one who made the mistake, Hatcher. Maybe you lost the money."

"I didn't make a mistake, lady."

"But what about me? Why are you going to kill me? I don't sell or buy drugs. I don't even gamble. Or," I said, "did you think I did? Is that why you wanted me on that trip? "

"I'm going to kill you, Mabel, because you have no business being here and already you know too much. Why are you in Yellow Rose anyway?"

"I came to find out who killed Grace Hobbs."

"What are you talking about? First, you say Andrea is dead and now you say Grace is dead?" He forgot about poking Cecile in the face for a moment and stared at me.

"Yes, Hatcher. Grace is dead. Shot right between the

eyes. You don't have to try to put that shocked look on your face. You don't fool me. I know you and your friend, Andrea here, had something to do with it."

"You're a crazy old woman talking nonsense. Why would we kill Grace? And, why did you say Grace and then change it to Andrea? You don't even know who you're talking about, do you?"

Andrea appeared in the doorway, her gun still pointing in my general direction. "I told you she was one weird old duck. Now we know for sure. I think she's losing her mind."

"No, I'm not." I looked at Andrea and then at Hatcher. "And, I'd appreciate if you would both stop calling me old and weird. At least, give me some dignity before you murder me. I'm telling you the truth - Grace's real name was Andrea Williams." I looked at her. "The same as yours. She was an undercover cop. She and Cecile here were working together."

They both stared at me. Cecile groaned.

"You're an undercover cop?" Andrea walked over to Cecile.

Through a mouth almost swollen shut, he said, "Don't listen to her. You said yourself, she's as crazy as a loon."

I then realized that I'd said too much.

"So, if they don't think you're a cop, why are they holding a gun to your head?" I asked.

"Because," Hatcher said, "he swindled all our money. That's why we've got a gun to his head."

"But," I said, "if Grace is dead, why don't you think she stole all the money?"

"I don't know, Mabel. You're so smart. Maybe it's because Cecile is the one who talked me into using her? So, if she really is dead, maybe the two were in it together and

Cecile killed Grace to get all the money for himself."

"Well," I said, "wouldn't it be pretty stupid to show up here then? Wouldn't Cecile be somewhere on a beach in the Bahamas now? Isn't that what all you big time crooks do?"

Hatcher and Andrea exchanged looks. It never ceases to amaze me how stupid these criminals can be.

"Quite a deduction. I guess if he didn't steal it and run, he *must* be a cop, Mabel. You were telling the truth, weren't you? Now, we have a better reason for sending him to the bottom of the Gulf."

"Just a minute," I said. "Whose house is this anyway? Isn't this where Ben Williams lives? And, isn't Andrea Williams, Ben Williams' wife?"

Andrea stuck out her neck and widened her eyes. "Oooh, Mabel. What are you? A detective? Or are you just snoopy? Well, guess what? You're right. I'm Andrea Williams and I'm Ben's wife." She laughed.

"But Ben is a cop." I turned to Cecile. "Isn't he?"

Cecile didn't say anything but by the expression on his badly bruised face, I knew I was right. Either that, or Cecile would've like to kill me himself.

Andrea laughed again. "Yeah, he's a real baaaad cop." She walked towards me with a rope in her hand. "I'm sure you've heard of them." She looked over at Cecile. "I guess it's kind of like a cop pretending to be a drug dealer. Right, Cecile?"

"Who do you think my contact in jail was?" Hatcher grinned as if he'd been nominated for a Nobel Prize.

Cecile shook his head.

"What's the matter, Tucker? You wanna say something?" Hatcher moved the gun away a few inches. "Go ahead. Make it good."

"Ben is a good cop," he mumbled through swollen lips. He looked over at Andrea. "You're the one who went bad, Andrea. Ben is our link to you and Hatcher."

"No way. You're a liar." She whipped across the room with her gun pointed straight at Cecile's heart. "Don't tell me you know Ben better than I do."

"Hold it," Hatcher yelled. He grabbed for her wrist. She screamed. The gun went off and the front window shattered into a million pieces. As soon as I heard Hatcher yell, I'd instinctively wrapped my arms around my ears and dropped my head. Shards of glass flew everywhere. I glanced up at Andrea; blood was running down her face and arms. There was a moment of total silence, except for a few leftover pieces of glass falling to the floor.

This, I knew, would be my only chance to make a run for it. Cecile, I decided, could look after himself. After all, he had a lot more experience in this sort of thing than I did. I could hear Andrea's screams as I raced through the kitchen and out the back door.

I'd barely made it off the back step when two police cars seemed to appear out of nowhere and pull up into the yard. Kyle and another cop jumped out. Two more emerged from the other car. All of them had their guns drawn.

"Mabel, get in that car," Kyle yelled, but it was too late. I was already past him and running for the hotel. There was no way I was going to spend the next who knows how many hours in a police station answering questions. Besides, I had no answers. Everyone who lived on P ½ was mentally deranged as far as I was concerned. Except for Stella, of course.

As I neared the hotel, I could hear someone yelling my name.

"Yoo hoo! Mabel, Mabel, where are you?" Then, with a

bit more volume, "Get here right this minute, wherever you are."

Just a wild guess but, I would say I was in trouble with Flori.

I dashed around the corner. Our shuttle bus was sitting in front of the door. All our suitcases were in a neat pile by Flori's feet. When she saw me, she screamed.

Screamed and then raced over and hugged me as if she'd thought I'd died or something.

"Where have you been?" She started sobbing. "You said you were just going to the pool. We've been searching and searching."

"You heard me tell you that I was going to the pool?"

"Of course, we heard you, didn't we Stella?"

Stella nodded. She looked very somber. Maybe she was going to miss us more than what I thought.

"It's okay, Flori. I'm here now so let's get going." I looked at the driver. "Are we going to be late for boarding?"

"Not if we leave this second." It was obvious that people showing up late wasn't something new to him. Perhaps, meeting someone like Flori might have been a new experience, however. Probably half the population of Yellow Rose had heard her screams.

"Good. I don't want to be here a second longer than I have to, either." I searched through the luggage until I found my purse. "Let's get moving. Stella," I said, "it's been great meeting you. Thanks for all your help. Flori and I will give you a call as soon as we get home." I started handing the driver our suitcases so he could store them. "Okay, Flori, let's go. We don't want to miss our plane." I walked over and hugged Stella. "Thanks again." I held eye contact. "Sorry to rush but we have to leave *immediately*, if you know what I mean."

Any minute now, I was expecting to hear sirens and cop cars screeching into the parking lot. Stella glanced around and nodded as if she might be expecting some herself.

Flori took longer to say her good-byes because of the tears and nose blowing until finally Stella almost pushed her inside the shuttle bus. Stella slammed the door shut and raced off to her own car. I glanced out the back window as we drove away and watched until the back end of the pink Cadillac was out of sight.

Somewhere in the distant background, I did hear sirens screaming. Flori turned to look at me but I pretended not to notice. If I never saw Yellow Rose, Texas again, it would be too soon for me.

Chapter Twenty Seven

It was almost one in the morning by the time we finally reached Parson's Cove. Because of our friend, Captain Maxymowich, we ended up changing planes and spending three hours in Chicago's O'Hare International Airport. Flori isn't cranky too often, but this night she definitely was. Of course, it could have had something to do with me. It didn't help that every time I wanted to explain why I'd left the hotel in pursuit of who knows what, she told me she didn't want to talk about it. Well, I can't say I didn't try.

Reg and Jake met us at the airport. It's hard to describe the atmosphere. If there were an antonym for Disney World fun, this was it. Jake is a weird person when he's happy and fuming simultaneously. In other words, he was happy to see Flori and fuming at me but he knew that if he were nasty to me, he'd make Flori miserable. Quite a no-win situation.

Reg was just plain fuming. Personally, I can't imagine why. Our trip had nothing to do with him. So what if we got into trouble with Maxymowich? It wasn't any skin off his derriere. He was annoyed because he had to give up watching some television show and drive all the way to the city to pick us up. That's why he was gnashing his teeth. The thing was he didn't have to come. Jim was now sheriff so if this was a police matter, why did he come anyway? His problem is 'letting go' - he still thinks he can do the job better than the young fellows.

Jake and Flori sat in the backseat of the patrol car and I sat in the front with Reg. I'd tried to sneak in with Flori but Jake, without saying a word, grabbed my arm and shoved me into the front. Under normal circumstances, I would've argued.

Everyone sat in silence until we got off the freeway and hit the highway to Parson's Cove. Not that there wasn't anything to say, we just held our breath and clung to our seat belts as Reg drove down the freeway, breaking the sound barrier. I now understood why he took the patrol car! Nobody ever stops a speeding cop car even when the flashing lights aren't on or the siren wailing.

Reg was the first to speak. "What in Sam's name were you thinking, Mabel?"

"About what, Reg?" My blood pressure was beginning to return to normal but my heart was still pounding out of control.

"You know exactly 'about what.'" I could feel his eyes boring into me but I kept mine on the road.

"You'd better watch where you're driving."

"Watch where I'm driving, you say?" Fortunately, he listened and turned his attention to the front. "How about keeping my eye on you? How many times have I told you to keep your nose out of other people's business? Do you ever listen?" He looked over, waiting for a reply. When there was obviously not a reply forthcoming, he answered himself, "Oh no, not you! You have your own set of rules. Not only that…" He looked around into the backseat. "You involve Flori. Flori, an innocent bystander has to get involved in illegal investigating, all because of you. What do you have to say to that?"

"Watch the road," I screamed. "You can't look at me,

look into the back seat, and still drive, Reg."

"Don't tell me what I can and cannot do, Mabel Wickles." He did, however, straighten the wheel and return to the pavement from the shoulder. I remained silent.

After about five minutes, he said, "So? That's enough time for you to think of a good excuse. Why did you do it, Mabel? Why did you get Flori to go to Yellow Rose, Texas, with you?"

"Because we wanted to see the Gulf of Mexico?"

He sucked in a deep breath and let it out slowly.

"Not good enough. What did you accomplish going there, besides getting into trouble with the Law?"

"The Law? We didn't get into any trouble with the Law. We didn't, did we, Flori?" I looked around at Flori but she was clinging to Jake and looking too terrified to talk. "In fact, the Law, as you put it, loved us. And, if you must know, Reg, we made new friends and helped solve some of the mystery."

A car went by and Reg put his lights on high beam again.

"I hate to think of what kinds of friends you made, Mabel. Should most of them be behind bars?"

"For your information, they were all good upright citizens. In case you were wondering and I'm sure you weren't - one of the men in my photos was Cecile Tucker. Cecile happens to be an undercover cop."

Now, Flori found her voice. Sometimes she does when she shouldn't.

"Of course, we didn't know that. He looked just like a gangster. Even Stella thought he was. So did you, didn't you, Mabel? Imagine Stella living next door all that time and thinking he was dealing drugs. Well, I guess he really was, wasn't he?" She giggled and carried on, "It was nice of

Kyle to fill us in on that, wasn't it? Such a nice deputy, wasn't he, Mabel?"

Jake thought he should get in on the conversation, I suppose.

"Who is this Stella?" he asked. "And, why would you think this guy was dealing drugs? What were you doing there anyway, Flori? When we talked on the phone all you talked about was how beautiful the water was and how good the restaurants were."

"Oh, Jake, we weren't really *doing* anything. And, it's true, the restaurants were awesome, weren't they, Mabel?" I nodded and she kept talking. "Reg is just upset, that's all. There was no way we got into any trouble with the Law. Well, at least, Stella and I didn't. All we did was follow Hatcher and when we saw him going into the jail, we went back to Stella's. Mabel is the one who took all the chances. She really should be a private investigator."

"Thanks so much," I said.

"Yes," Reg said. "Thanks so much, Flori. Now, Mabel, how about you fill us in on what you did while you were in Yellow Rose? It was enough to get Captain Maxymowich to leave town and go hunting for you." The car swerved as he turned to talk to me. "Well, what do you have to say? It's the taxpayers, like Jake here and me, who are paying for that plane ride back home, you know."

"You're kidding," I said. "You mean we can get our money refunded for the return ticket?"

Reg shrugged. "Check with the airlines. All I know is that Maxymowich arranged to have both of you brought back. Seems he doesn't worry where the money comes from."

Jake piped up. "That sounds good. You might be able to get your money back, Flori. Did you know that?"

"I really don't care, Jake. You can check it out if you want to. Mabel, you might as well tell them everything. We're going to have to eventually anyway."

I was kind of hoping it would be 'eventually' and by that time, there wouldn't be a mystery anymore and everyone would forget I was even involved.

"All right, Mabel. Come clean. What did you find out down there?" Reg said, in a very stern police officer's voice.

"You sound just like a cop, Reg. You do realize that legally, I don't have to answer any of your questions, right? I could insist on waiting to speak to the real sheriff."

There was dead silence in the car for several minutes. I knew I'd hit a sore spot and it was nasty of me.

"However, since you served our community for so many years and guarded us with your very life, I will answer your questions, Reg. I do respect you as my friend and for all that you have done."

The retired, but obviously not *completely* retired, sheriff did not respond. I took a deep breath.

"Where do you want me to start?"

"Anywhere. Just start, damn it, woman."

"You don't have to use foul language, Reg."

I looked at him and he glared back. The tires hit the gravel. I gasped and Reg swung back onto the road. If someone had been tailing us, they would've thought they were following a drunken cop.

"Okay, I'll start from the beginning. First, we found out that Grace Hobbs lived on Avenue P½. Who, we discovered afterwards, wasn't Grace Hobbs at all. Well, there was a Grace living there but it wasn't the Grace we thought it was. You know, the one who was murdered. The real Grace, Cecile's wife, is somewhere safe and I think she's called

Grace Tucker. I don't know where she's in hiding but I'm sure she's still alive. The cops would make sure of that. Actually, it wasn't until we met Stella who lives next door to Grace and Cecile, that we found out that there wasn't anyone named Hobbs living there anymore. Good thing the phone number and the name hadn't been changed in the phone book. It was still under G. Hobbs for Ginger Hobbs. Stella thought she died mysteriously but actually she was another undercover cop; at least, that's what Kyle told us and he said she'd been shot in the knee or something. Anyway, she's probably in another assignment or if she was really shot in the knee, I would think she's doing desk work somewhere."

Reg shook his head. "Could you get back to what you were doing there, Mabel and stop talking in circles?" Another glare - which I caught from the lights on the dashboard. "If you don't mind, that is."

"Not at all, Reg. Just keep your eyes on the road. Here's what we did. Stella, Flori, and I staked out Cecile's house. Since Stella lives next door, it really wasn't a problem. We shut the lights off and watched through the hurricane blinds. Of course, we didn't know at that point that it was Cecile, the cop's, house. We thought it was Grace's house and that she had a drug dealer husband named Cecile."

Jake interrupted. "Who did you say this Stella was?" He seemed to be fixated on her.

Flori answered, "Stella lives next door to Cecile Tucker. She's the most wonderful person. And, you know, Jake, she's as black as I am white. Never mind, you should've seen the meal she made for us. Wasn't it delicious, Mabel?"

"Yes, it was. Almost as good as your meals."

"Back to your story, Mabel," Reg said.

"Okay, okay. Well, the first night we watched the house.

After a couple of hours, we saw Hatcher go in. Who, you know, was in Las Vegas with me. At this point, he believed that Cecile was a nasty criminal like he was. It wasn't very long and another man arrived and went inside. As I listened under the window…"

"What did you say?" Reg looked over at me and the car swerved.

"Watch the road, Reg. I told you, you can't drive and look at me at the same time."

Wisely, he pulled over onto the shoulder. How he could have been a traffic cop for years before coming to Parson's Cove is a mystery to me.

He turned off the ignition. "Now, would you repeat that? You listened under the window?"

"I don't have to repeat it, Reg. You just did."

"Don't get smart with me. Why were you under the window?"

"To listen. I wanted to hear what was going on." I could make out every expression on Reg's face. In fact, I think the shadows made them even more pronounced. His expression wasn't too reassuring. I knew that if I didn't cooperate, we'd be sitting here when the sun came up.

"Do you want to know what I heard?"

"That would be nice."

"I heard the boss, who by the way, had a Mexican accent. At least, that's what I think. He was telling Hatcher that he wanted the money and he was very upset because Hatcher had trusted this woman, Grace Hobbs. Of course, we now know that it wasn't Grace at all. This woman was Andrea Williams and Andrea Williams was really dead.
Apparently, Hatcher didn't know this. Or, at least, that's what he claims. I have my suspicions though. He's a good

suspect for Grace's murder."

"You mean Andrea's," Flori spoke up.

"Right. Grace a.k.a Andrea."

"Skip over a lot, Mabel." Reg sighed. "Just tell me the highlights. I can't make sense of anything you're saying."

"Okay. Do you want to know how Andrea forced me into the house at gunpoint?"

"You said that Andrea was dead."

"You didn't tell me you were forced at gunpoint." Flori suddenly became alive again. "Why didn't you tell me, Mabel?"

"Okay, to answer both your questions - Flori, I didn't tell you because I knew you'd freak out. Reg, this was the *real* Andrea Williams. Well, the dead one was too, but this was the one who was on the trip. You know, the trip to Las Vegas. Of course, the other Andrea came on the trip with me too but I only knew her as Grace."

Reg looked confused. "How many Andrea Williams women are there?"

"Two."

"Actually," Flori spoke up, "there are three. Remember, Mabel? There's that other Andrea Williams too."

"Yes, I know but let's not make it any more complicated than it already is, Flori. We'll just stick with the two that are involved in the case."

"All right," Reg said. "Tell me what happened when you were forced into some house at gunpoint."

Flori came to life again. "It wasn't just some house, was it? I bet you went back to the house on P ½ where we did surveillance that night, didn't you? The one where there was a shootout and we almost spoiled it for the police?"

Reg's eyebrows shot up.

"Thanks for your input, Flori," I said. "How about you

let me tell it my way?"

"It better be the right way, that's all I can say," Reg said.

"Trust me, it will be right."

"It always scares me when you say, 'trust me.'"

"You know, Reg," I said, "if you promise not to look at me while you're driving, we could head for Parson's Cove and we wouldn't be so late getting home."

He grunted and started the car. I waited until he was up to the speed limit before resuming my story.

"It's true, I did go back to the house on P½."

Flori interrupted, "But, you should explain that there are two houses of interest on P½. Actually, three, counting Stella's but I know you wouldn't bother going back to her place. I really don't understand why you went back at all, especially since Kyle and the Captain gave you strict orders to stay in the hotel."

"Once again, thank you for revealing that, Flori."

Reg started to turn to me but I stopped him by saying, "Watch the road or I stop talking."

"All right, but you'd better do some explaining."

"First of all, it was our last two hours in Yellow Rose. Do you think anyone in her right mind would spend it sitting in a hotel room, watching television?"

"That's exactly what Stella and I did, Mabel, in case you forgot."

"I know and that's just fine for you. It wasn't for me. We really hadn't come any closer to solving Grace's murder than when we left home. I couldn't just leave. There had to be some connection to her."

"And was there?" Reg asked.

"Well, of course, there was. We found out who Grace Hobbs was and what she was."

"Did you find out who murdered her?"

I sighed. "No, that we didn't."

"So, in other words, your trip was for nothing. All the things you found out in Texas, the police already knew. In fact, I would say, you probably came close to blowing their whole operation. Am I right?"

"Well, I wouldn't go as far as that, Reg. Maybe the three of us even helped."

"Oh yeah? In what way?"

I turned to Flori. "In what way, Flori?"

Flori sputtered, "I'm sure in some way, Mabel."

"Oh, I know," I said. "When the bullet went through the window and shattered all that glass, those cops rushed in right away. If that hadn't happened, they might've been too late and either Cecile or I might have been killed."

"Mabel." Flori gasped. "You never told me about that."

I turned around. "That's because you said you didn't want to talk about it. Remember? All the way home, I wanted to explain and you kept saying that."

"Well, I would have talked about it if I'd known you almost got killed."

"Okay," Reg said. "I know when I'm beat. Let's ride the rest of the way in silence. Mabel, you can tell your tale to Maxymowich. Maybe he'll make some sense of it."

Therefore, that's what we did because in the end, we do what the old retired cop says.

Reg dropped me off first. As soon as I opened the door, all the cats raced outside. I knew then that I wouldn't be hopping right into bed because within ten minutes, they'd all want back in again. How did I ever manage when I had seven? Not one of them had even stopped to ask me how I was. This is supposed to be companionship?

While I waited for them, I slipped into my pajamas, went

down to the kitchen, filled a tumbler with ice and poured in a jigger of gin. I even splurged and cut a bit of lemon for it. As I settled into my chair in the living room, I came to one conclusion - never again would I traipse off half way across the country to solve a crime. If Reg was too old to be a cop, I was too old to be a detective. It had cost me time and money and I was no closer to finding Grace's killer than before I left. All I knew was Grace's body wasn't Grace's body, it was Andrea's body.

One thing for which I'm forever grateful is that I didn't see the red light blinking on my answering machine. I thought Maxymowich still had my phone so I didn't even look in that direction. I guess Reg must have returned it and plugged it in for me. How thoughtful. If I'd listened to it, I wouldn't have slept all night. Not even after the gin.

Chapter Twenty Eight

Once again Reg Smee sat at my kitchen table, listening to my answering machine. Déjà vu. It seemed like only yesterday that we'd been sitting, trying to figure out the other message - the life threatening one. This time, however, he wasn't quite so quick to dismiss it as a prank call. This one wasn't threatening; it was perplexing.

"I'm sure this is a different person, Reg. And, this time, I know for sure that it's a woman's voice. Listen again."

Without a word, Reg hit the replay button.

Sorry, I don't have time to explain. Don't want to make trouble for you. Just wanted some information. You could've helped. I don't know. I don't think I'll see you again.

"You can't think of anyone who might have left this?" Reg asked.

"Reg, I have no idea who it is or what it means. I mean, who would make trouble for me? I didn't get into any trouble, did I?"

"You're always in trouble, it seems." He hit 'play' again. "I know one thing; you need to get a new tape for this thing. It's too old and scratchy." We listened. "What do you think she meant when she said she wanted some information, that she needed your help?"

I shook my head. "I don't have a clue."

"We're thinking it has something to do with this murder but it doesn't have to. Could it be someone who happened to drop by to visit when you were gone?"

"I can't think of anyone. I don't really know many people outside of Parson's Cove, Reg." I stared at him. "Except for Esther."

"Well, it's obviously not Esther. You can't blame everything that happens to you on her. What about relatives?"

I shook my head again. There were no relatives. The Wickles' lineage ends with me.

"You know what haunts me, Reg? The voice. It's so depressed sounding. Don't you think?"

"Yeah. Whoever it is sounds like they just lost their best friend."

"Maybe that's it. Could it be someone who knew Grace Hobbs? Or, I should say Andrea Williams? Maybe it was someone who heard about the murder so came to see what had happened. What do you think?"

Reg thought for a moment. "Do you know any of Grace's friends or Andrea's friends, or whatever her name was?"

Now, it was my turn to think. "The only ones I knew connected to the murdered woman (I wasn't going to keep repeating her two names anymore) were the ones who were on the trip to Las Vegas. Out of all of us, there was just Hatcher and the other Andrea Williams who were friends with the deceased. There's no way it could be Andrea because she was in Yellow Rose when I was there. Besides, why would she leave a message like that for me?"

"What about the others on the trip? Who were they?"

"Well, there was Ralph and Sally but they were innocent

213

too. We had no idea this was a front for trafficking drugs or laundering money or whatever else they were doing."

"How do you know they were innocent?"

I had to admit that was something to think about. How really did I know? So far, I wasn't exactly too accurate in any of my judgments of characters.

"I'm sure they were. There are some things a person just knows."

"Like your knowing Cecile was an undercover cop?"

"Point taken. I guess I don't know for sure but don't you think Cecile would've known about the others? I mean, if they were involved in any way? After all, it was his operation. I'm sure Kyle would've told us if anyone else was mixed up in this."

He nodded, grunted, and stood up.

"Well," he said. "I don't know if this is relevant or not but I guess I'd better pass this information on to Maxymowich. Make sure you don't erase anything. He'll probably want to talk to you again, by the way."

"I'm sure looking forward to that." (Like a woman looks forward to pap smears. However, I didn't say that thought aloud.)

He grinned. "I thought you would be."

Chapter Twenty Nine

It took about three days to get back into routine. I had my little session with the Captain. It went quite well. He threatened to make me sign a paper saying I wouldn't leave Parson's Cove for the next three years. Of course, he was joking, but with him, it's hard to tell. I did get the point, however. His parting words to me were, "Mind your own business and stay out of the morgue." With that, he sauntered to the door but before leaving, he said, "You don't happen to have any muffins in your freezer, do you?"

"Oh Mabel," Flori said later when she came over to the shop for coffee. "I do believe that man has a crush on you."

"Don't be ridiculous. He could be married; not every man wears a wedding band, you know. Besides, I'm old enough to be his mother. The only crush he has is on my muffins."

"Oh well, you know what they say about the way to a man's heart? It's through his stomach."

"Just because that worked with Jake, it doesn't mean it will work on every man. Anyway, to quickly change the subject before it gets too weird, who do you think could have left that message for me? It doesn't make any sense, does it?"

Flori took on her look of wisdom. This comprises of holding her cup in midair, staring off into space and humming a mindless tune for several seconds. Finally, she said, "What I don't understand is, why didn't the person leave her name? For Pete's sake, you're not a mind reader."

"See, Flori? That's why I never wanted an answering machine. Look how it's got all of us so upset and worried. If I didn't have one, we'd be innocently ignorant and enjoying life."

"What a foolish thing to say. We would be still worried because a woman was murdered. That has nothing to do with your answering machine."

"What about the first message? That, my friend, was the beginning of everything. The beginning of the end. Did you forget about that?"

Flori didn't have an answer to that so she just sat in the wicker chair and drank her coffee. I started stocking some of the shelves, muttering a few cuss words under my breath.

"What are you doing, Mabel?"

"I'll tell you what I'm doing; I left Delores in charge and she rearranged half my store. I did not pay her to do this. Look." I pointed to the window facing Main Street. "She put all the English china teacups on this window shelf. Now, when someone comes in and slams the door, they'll hit the floor and break into a million pieces."

"That's actually too bad, isn't it? I like them there. They sort of brighten up the window, don't they?"

I gave her a dirty look. "No, they don't, Flori."

"Well," she said, getting up from the chair in a huff, "I don't think there's anything I can say to brighten up your mood today, is there?" She went into the back room and washed out her cup. When she came back, she continued, "If you keep up with this bad temper, you'll chase all your customers away. Is that what you want?" She raised her eyebrows at me until they were out of view.

That phone call was bugging me, the rearranged shelves were bugging me, and now Flori was starting to bug me too.

"I don't need you mothering me today, Flori."

"Heaven forbid," she said, and walked out the door.

I spent the next several hours putting everything back where it belonged, trying to be polite to customers and at the same time, playing that phone message repeatedly in my brain.

I closed up shop at four-thirty. The only customer who ever came after that was Esther Flynn if she happened to be in town and I was in no mood to be heckled by her. The fact that she hadn't really purchased anything worth more than five dollars in the past forty years was an irritant in itself. If Reg would let me put up a notice saying that I'd banned her from the store for life, I would be truly happy. Unfortunately, Reg doesn't approve of store bans.

My mood didn't improve after I got home. I'm usually not prone to moodiness but things were starting to get to me. It bothered me that no one knew who murdered Andrea Williams. What was Maxymowich up to anyway? It also bugged me that no one had connected her murder to Parson's Cove. There had to be a reason for someone to dump the body in Parson's Cove. Why? Why pick a small nondescript town to dump a dead body? (Oops, a light went off in my head.) Was that why the murderer *did* pick Parson's Cove? Because it was small and nondescript?

On the other hand, could it have had something to do with me, the only person on the trip from Parson's Cove? How else would the murderer know about this small nondescript town if he or she hadn't been on the trip with me? What about Hatcher? Perhaps, *now* he would like to try to connect me to a murder but certainly not before I went to Yellow Rose. I'm sure he's wishing it was my body out behind the nursing home. Andrea Williams? I don't think I meant much to her before she dragged me into her house and shoved a gun in my face. All I hoped for her was a very long jail term. It's true, Hatcher and Andrea talked tough but were they capable of murder? Would they have really dropped Cecile and me into the Gulf? The thought of salt water filling my mouth and then my lungs made me shudder.

I was deep in thought and sinking deeper into despair when the doorbell jolted me awake. Let me tell you something about Parson's Cove. Everyone has a doorbell but no one ever uses it. It is only for out of town visitors or strangers. When it rings, our guard goes up immediately. We tread warily to the door, usually on tiptoe, to sneak a look through some blind or out from behind a curtain. If it's a stranger (or relative) who doesn't meet up to our standards, we remain HBH (home but hiding).

I was in the process of tiptoeing to the kitchen window when I tripped over one of the cats that had decided, at the last minute, to make a wild dash for the door. As I grabbed a chair to keep from falling, it flipped over, and I ended up sprawled on the floor. This, in itself, wasn't loud enough to cause attention. My screaming as I flew up and landed smack on my sacroiliac caused the attention. I laid there for several seconds, first hoping I wouldn't be spending the rest of my life in a wheelchair, and then wondering if there was a dead cat under me.

As I was mulling all this through my mind, with my eyes closed, I heard the door open and someone call my name.

"Mabel, are you okay?" the voice asked. "Is anything broken?" Hands started to lift me.

"Is there a cat under me?" I whispered, without opening

my eyes.

"A cat?" The hands pulled me up to a sitting position. "No, there's no cat under you." There was a pause. "There are quite a few in the room though."

I opened my eyes.

"Ralph!" I said. "What, on earth, are you doing here?"

I struggled to get up. He helped me with one hand while he pulled the chair up with the other. I'm not big so it didn't take much effort to turn me and plunk me onto the seat.

"Ralph Murphy," I repeated. "What are you doing here in Parson's Cove?"

"Are you sure you're okay, Mabel? Is there anything I can get you?" He nervously scratched his head and a light smattering of dandruff fluttered down onto his shirt.

"I'm fine." By this time, I'd figured out for myself that there were no injuries. At least, not fractures; it was hard to say how long my tailbone would be sore.

"I'm so sorry, Mabel. I didn't mean to harm you."

"Ralph," I said, feeling the need to take hold of the conversation. "You didn't harm me. I tripped over one of my cats. I do it all the time."

"You do?" He looked somewhat bewildered.

"Well, not to this degree. But, no, look at me." I stood up and did several stretches. My tailbone *did* hurt. "Absolutely, one hundred percent, perfectly fine." I smiled at him. "Now, would you sit down and tell me what you are doing here in Parson's Cove? Surely, you didn't come just to pay me a visit."

"Actually, I did, Mabel. I remember you telling us when we were in Las Vegas, how you've helped the police solve several crimes, so I came seeking your help."

"Why don't you just go to the police?"

He blushed. "Because I'm not certain it really is a crime."

"So, you aren't talking about Grace?" I wasn't sure if he knew her real name or not.

"Well, sort of. In fact, I'm talking about all of them, except for you."

"All of them? What do you mean?"

"You know how we were all together on one plane until we got to Denver? Then, you had to transfer to another flight. Well, the rest of us were supposed to stay on that same plane. Except that's not what happened."

"What do you mean, that's not what happened?"

"I'm the only one who stayed on that flight. There was a two hour delay while they checked the plane engine or something and a few passengers got off, while several others came on."

"You're telling me that Grace, Sally, and Andrea got off the plane and never got back on?"

He nodded.

"What about Hatcher?"

He shook his head. "He didn't get back on either."

"Ralph, are you sure you aren't mistaken? Maybe they were all catching different flights too."

"No, we were all taking the same flight to Houston."

"You didn't notify the airline?"

"That's where I checked it out. I explained to them that all of us were supposed to be on the same flight."

"So, what did they say?"

"They did some checking and said that the four of them had changed their flight at the last minute."

"Really? Why do you think they did that?"

"That's what I'd like you to find out, Mabel. Could it have been my fault? I don't think I did anything to get them all upset. Sally maybe, but not the others. Do you think she turned them against me?"

"Isn't that reading too much into it? You must have a better reason than that."

He shrugged. "Something had happened, Mabel. I don't know what but I was beginning to worry about Sally. She was trying to get in with that Hatcher fellow but I didn't trust him. Whenever I tried to say something, she just said I was jealous. I know I'm not as good looking or have as much money but I didn't want her to get hurt." He pulled a piece of paper out of his shirt pocket. "When we were still friends, she gave me her phone number. I've tried and tried but there's no answer. I'm worried that something's happened to her."

"Ralph," I said. "There is good reason to worry. Did you know that Grace is dead?"

"Grace?" His eyes got big and filled with fear. "What happened? Was there an accident?"

"There was a murder."

"A murder? Grace was murdered?" His face lost its color and his hand shook as he reached for his scalp. It took all the willpower I had not to put my hand out to stop him. "But, why? Why was she killed and who killed her?"

I shook my head. "I've found out a lot about those people but I haven't found the killer. Nor have I found out why her body was dumped in the woods, right here in Parson's Cove."

"Right here in Parson's Cove?"

He might have said more but the pupils of his eyes suddenly rolled up out of view and Ralph Murphy collapsed in a heap on my floor. There were no cats under his body.

Chapter Thirty

There is one ambulance in Parson's Cove and when its siren screams, everyone and his dog rushes to the street to see what's happening. Or, as in my case, multiple cats. We're like everyone else in the world; we have a morbid curiosity in pain, suffering and unexpected death. This day was no different.

By the time, Hermann Lawson backed the ambulance into my driveway, people lined the sidewalk in front of my house. Since I live alone, I already knew what they were saying - I either fell and broke my hip but was able to painfully crawl to the phone, or had chest pains but was still conscious and able to crawl to the phone. Whichever it was, there would be crawling involved.   Or, there was a terrible odor emitting from my house and on checking it out, I was found to be dead. Since I'd been at work all day and quite alive, perhaps no one was saying the latter.

Although Ralph seemed to be all right now, I wasn't taking any chances. I'd thrown a pitcher of cold water in his face and that had brought him back to life but I certainly didn't want it happening again in my presence. Thus, the 911 call. Hermann wasn't taking any chances either. He doesn't get many customers (I don't like to use the term 'patients' because Hermann only took a first-aid course so his job is not to treat or diagnose; it's just to drive the four blocks or so to the hospital with his siren going). However, when he does get a call, he makes the most of it. About the only thing he didn't do was wrap Ralph in a body bag.

"Did you give him mouth-to-mouth resuscitation, Mabel?" he asked, with a depraved gleam in his eye.

I glared at him. "No, I did not. I told you, I threw a pitcher of water in his face. Perhaps, Hermann, you noticed that he's all wet." In fact, Ralph looked like he'd fallen into the lake, fully clothed.

"Oh, oh yes."

Ralph, by this time, was pulling himself up onto a chair and shaking some of the water from his hair and ears.

"Mabel," Hermann said, "Would you help me move this gentleman on to the gurney?"

"No, I won't," I said. "Why didn't you bring someone to help you? I've already fallen today; I'm not going to start lifting heavy men."

"I didn't bring anyone because I thought it was just you here. I certainly wouldn't need help lifting you up. How was I to know you were entertaining a gentleman friend?"

"I'll have you know, Hermann, I was not, as you put it, entertaining a gentleman friend. His name is Ralph Murphy, if you must know. All we did was go on a trip together, that's all."

If I thought Flori could raise her eyebrows, it was nothing compared to what Hermann could do with his. He reminded me of an owl with his bushy eyebrows poking over his round black rimmed glasses.

"Perhaps, I worded that wrong. We didn't go on a trip *alone* together as I can see your perverted little mind is thinking. It was the trip to Las Vegas. You heard about that. Ralph, here, was one of the winners too."

Ralph started nodding his head.

"That's all it was, sir," Ralph said, sounding very much like a school boy trying to explain to a girl's father why there was lipstick all over his face and his shirttails were hanging out. "And, now I'm perfectly all right. I really don't see any need for a gurney." He turned to me in desperation. "Don't you think so, Mabel?"

"I'm sure you don't need a gurney but maybe you should get Doc Fritz to check you out. A person shouldn't just pass out like that."

"No, it's okay. Just get me a drink of orange juice, if you have some. My blood sugar's off, that's all."

I went to get a glass and some juice. Hermann seemed disappointed as he started returning all his equipment into his backpack, especially when he packed up the little paddles used for jumpstarting the heart. I guess he felt he should say something medically related, however, so he said, "You should do something about that dandruff, Ralph. Could be caused by some serious medical problem." With that, he hoisted the front end of the folded gurney under his arm and dragged it out the door.

On his way to the ambulance, I heard him call out, "Don't worry. Wasn't Mabel at all. She's fit as a fiddle. Some gentleman friend she was entertaining passed out, that's all. "

I don't know what someone then asked but Hermann answered by saying, "Don't think it was gin. Can't say I smelled any liquor. Could've been vodka, I guess. They say there's no odor to it."

Chapter Thirty One

Ralph settled down at the table with his juice and I put on a pot of coffee.

"Have you eaten anything within the last couple of hours?" I asked.

He shook his head. "Guess I haven't in awhile. I was just concerned about getting here and hoping to talk to you."

"Did you get a room at the Hotel or what were you planning to do?" Not that I wanted to rush him out the door but I knew there would be people hiding behind trees and lampposts waiting to see what was going on.

"No, I didn't book a room. I didn't know if there was a hotel here or not. I could drive back to the city, if you think it would be better."

"Don't drive all the way back. The hotel here is all right, if you're staying one night. Obviously, it isn't what we've been used to. You'll probably get the third degree from someone but don't worry, they're all harmless."

He gave me a humorless smile. "Unless one of them is a murderer."

"Well, I guess there is always that."

Before I could say anything more, the phone rang and it was Flori.

"Mabel," she screamed. "What's going on at your place? Who's the stranger who had a heart attack and almost died?

And, when did you learn to do CRP?"

"First of all, no one almost died. Secondly, it wasn't a stranger; it was Ralph Murphy. Remember, he was on the Las Vegas trip with me. And, Flori, it isn't CRP, it's CPR and I have no idea how to do that. No one had a heart attack or stopped breathing. I wouldn't have even phoned for an ambulance if I'd known Ralph would come to after I dumped a pitcher of water on his head."

"But, Mabel," she screeched, "what's he doing at your house? Is it about the murder? Does he know anything? Is it okay if I come to your place?" She paused for a moment and whispered, "You have no idea how people are gossiping about this. I think it's better if I come over. See you in five." She hung up.

Flori would arrive in three.

"My friend, Flori, is coming over," I explained. "She says she's worried about my reputation but she really wants to meet you and find out what's going on."

"I sure didn't mean to make so much trouble for you, Mabel. All I wanted to do was find out what happened to our friends. It's so hard to believe that Grace was murdered. But, why? Why would someone kill her? She seemed like such a nice person, didn't she? It was the other one, that Andrea, who seemed kind of miserable to me."

The door opened. Flori walked in, panting. I looked at the clock. Two and a half minutes - a new record! That woman can really run when she wants to.

After the introductions, the three of us sat down at the kitchen table. Flori and Ralph talked about Las Vegas while I whipped up some ham and mustard sandwiches, opened a jar of homemade pickles, cut up some cheese, and dumped a bag of barbeque potato chips into a bowl. If this was supper, this was it. I filled everyone's cup with fresh coffee. Ralph didn't say anything because he was busy eating. Why, on earth, if you have a tendency to pass out from not eating, would you not eat? I'm perfectly healthy but never miss a meal.

We settled into the living room with our second cup of coffee. I did have some carrot muffins and a few orange and date muffins in the freezer but thought it best to keep them frozen and out of sight. There was no need to gamble with Ralph's blood sugar again.

"So," Flori finally said, "why did you come to Parson's Cove, Ralph? Did you just come to visit Mabel or was it about Grace's murder?" She turned to me. "It is really a coincidence, isn't it? You know, if he just *happened* to come here?"

"Flori, please don't talk to me as if Ralph can't hear you. He's sitting right in front of you." I smiled an apology. "Don't mind Flori. She's very upset about this murder. All of us are. Flori and I even flew down to Texas to try and find the killer."

Ralph's eyes got big. "You went down to Texas?" He put his empty cup down on the coffee table. "What did you find out?"

"Well, for one thing, I can tell you that two of the missing travelers aren't missing. Hatcher and Williams are both in Yellow Rose, Texas."

"You're just telling me that now?"

"Sorry, Ralph, but I thought it might be more upsetting. So, if those two aren't missing, I'm sure Sally isn't either. It's just a matter of hunting her down."

"So, where would I start?"

"Do you think she wants you to start? I mean, Ralph, if Sally isn't interested in you, maybe you should leave things as they are. And, be happy she wasn't with Hatcher in Yellow Rose."

"I don't know, Mabel, I was thinking maybe I'd try again with her. You know, our time together was so short; she never got to know me all that well. I think if she understood me, she'd come to care for me. I'm a lonely man and she's a lonely woman. We would be so good for each other."

I looked over at him. He was no prize. Not that I told him that. I didn't have to.

"You know, Ralph," Flori started out. "I know a bit about men and women. I've been married for almost fifty years. I'll tell you right now, you'll have to make quite a few changes before this woman will be interested in you. To begin with, your clothes are a bit out of date. I noticed too that your shirt collar is worn quite badly. Also, you need a haircut and a good dandruff shampoo."

I think if Flori's list would've been any longer, Ralph's eyes would have rolled up and I would've had to dowse him again.

"Okay," I said. "Let's not worry about this love thing right now. You have lots of time to work on your image. What I'd like to find out is, why did all those people get off the plane in Denver? It was right after that, that Grace turned up dead. First of all, what day was it that we landed there?"

"Well, surely, you remember," Flori said. "It was *your* vacation. You left here on Monday, July 18th and returned on Friday, the 22nd. On Friday, you arrived in Denver at one in the afternoon and immediately boarded the other plane. The limo brought you right to your door at three in the afternoon. It would've been sooner but it took awhile to find your luggage. Delores stayed at the shop on Saturday because as I told you, you needed to rest but you were back at work on Tuesday morning. If you could have gotten a direct flight from Las Vegas to the city here, you could've been home by one on Friday. I don't know why they have so many flights going all over the place. It's so confusing."

"Thank you, Flori. I didn't realize you looked after my welfare with such precision. That means Esther found Grace's body on the Wednesday because it was the day after I got back to work. So she was killed somewhere between here and Denver sometime between Friday and Tuesday which means that only three took that flight to Houston: Hatcher, Williams, and Sally." I put my cup down on the coffee table a bit too hard and a few drops slopped over the side. Flori quickly reached over and wiped them up with her napkin. "Thank you, Flori. Now, where would Grace have gone and who went with her? And, why didn't she take the flight to Houston? Who stopped her from leaving?"

"It must've had something to do with either the drugs or the money," Flori said.

Ralph looked confused. "Drugs?"

"Oh, I guess we didn't explain everything," I said. "The real reason why I hope Sally didn't get involved with Hatcher is that he's a gangster."

"He's a gangster? What kind of gangster?"

"He's in with some Mexican and who knows how many others, dealing drugs and doing some sort of illegal gambling. I don't understand that part. The thing I do know is that this whole 'Win a Trip to Vegas,' was a front. We were just a front for Andrea and Hatcher."

"What about Grace?"

"Grace was an undercover cop."

"Really? Someone murdered a cop? I didn't know she was a cop." Ralph's face turned chalky. His hand shook as he set his cup down. "So, that's pretty easy to figure out then; either Hatcher or Andrea murdered Grace."

I shook my head. "Not if they were on a flight to Houston that night. They couldn't kill her, move her body to Parson's Cove, and make the flight in time. Besides, neither one of them knew that Grace was dead. I'm quite sure of that. In fact, I was actually right inside Grace's house when Andrea phoned. She thought Grace was home but she wasn't, she was dead."

"Well, of course, she'd say that if you were there."

"No, Ralph, you don't understand. No one knew I was there. Andrea left the message on the machine and I heard it."

"Of course," Flori added, "at that point, Andrea Williams thought it was Grace Hobbs while it really was Andrea Williams."

"Pardon me?" Ralph said. I was even confused for a moment myself.

"Flori, let's not get into that. Just take my word for it, neither Williams nor Hatcher knew Grace was dead."

"You believe that?" Ralph was starting to get agitated. "You said Hatcher was a crook. It had to be him if he found out she was a cop. They would kill her for sure."

"I know it seems that's the way it must've gone but I was there when they found out that Cecile and Grace were undercover. Trust me, they didn't know."

"How come you were always there?"

I shrugged. "Pick of the draw, I guess. Somehow, I always manage to be in the wrong place at the wrong time. Just ask Flori."

Flori finished her coffee. "Trust me, Ralph, it's true."

"Well, no matter what you say, Mabel, I still think it had to be Mr. Hatcher or that Andrea. I didn't like her. It's the only thing that makes sense."

"It would appear that way. Well, I guess we'll find out. The cops were picking them up when we left Yellow Rose."

The clock on the wall behind Flori struck eight. I didn't want to be rude but I was exhausted and I was ready for everyone to go home.

"Would you like another cup of coffee?" Flori asked Ralph.

I felt like giving her a good kick but instead, I said, "Ralph has to go and get a room at the hotel, Flori. We don't want to keep him any longer. Besides, he had that fainting spell today and you're really supposed to rest afterwards."

I don't know if Ralph took the hint or just wanted to get out of my house and go to bed but anyway, I was relieved when he stood up and made his announcement.

"It's been a long day. Thanks for everything, Mabel. I'll drop by tomorrow before I leave town to say good-bye."

"You're leaving already?" Flori said.

He nodded. "As shocked as I was to hear about Grace, I can see that Mabel doesn't have any information about Sally. She's the one I was the most concerned about." He turned to me. "You're sure she isn't in Yellow Rose?"

I shrugged. "We didn't see her. I guess that doesn't mean she couldn't be there," I said. "Does she have your number?"

"Oh yes, she does."

"Then, Ralph, why don't you let *her* contact you? You wouldn't want Sally to think you were stalking her, would you?"

Ralph's face turned red. "I would never stalk her. Don't you ever accuse me of that, Mabel."

"No, I'm not. I'm just saying that you wouldn't want people to think that, that's all."

Without saying another word, a very red-faced Ralph Murphy turned and walked through the kitchen and out the back door. Perhaps, Miss Sally had accused him already.

For the record, I can say that no one has ever attempted to stalk Mabel Wickles. I'm not sure if I should feel relieved or disappointed about that.

Chapter Thirty Two

You know how sometimes in the middle of the night a thought comes into your subconscious mind and it wakes you up? You sit up in bed and wonder what, on earth, was I dreaming about? Well, maybe it hasn't happened to you. Usually, when it happens to me, I've found that the best thing to do is go down to the kitchen and get a drink of water. By the time I've had my water and made a trip to the biffy, I sometimes remember my dream.

This time, I decided to try the same ritual; however, before I was half finished my water, I knew what had forced me to wake up. I put the glass down on the counter and walked cautiously to the phone. This time, my eyes were watching for any quick-moving cats. I didn't want to land on the floor again. My tailbone was still bothering me. I hit the message button to listen to my two old messages. Reg told me not to erase them until Maxymowich solved the crime. He had a lot of faith in the Captain. Once he caught the killer, I would get rid of, not only the messages, but the whole telephone and answering machine. Unless, of course, I could prove the first one was Esther and if it was, I might keep the tape. Mind you, not for blackmailing purposes but I'm sure I could figure out some way to harass her with it.

"I knew it," I said to the closest cat after I'd listened to the second message for the third time. "It was Sally on the phone. That's why I couldn't understand her; she talks through her swollen lips." The cat gave me a questioning look and meowed. "You wouldn't understand," I said. "You, my dear cat, will never have to have rat poison shot into your lips with a big needle." I'm not sure if it was the word rat, poison, or needle, but the cat ran out of the room and I could hear her discussing it with the other cats, who all sounded quite dismayed.

I went back to bed but I couldn't sleep. The first thing I was going to do in the morning was contact Reg Smee. Also Ralph. I wondered how he would feel about knowing his beloved had been right here in Parson's Cove. Personally, I was wondering 'why?'

Chapter Thirty Three

"I don't think you had to get me out of bed at six, Mabel, no matter how important this information is."

Reg Smee sat across from me at my kitchen table.

"Be happy it was this morning. I almost called you in the middle of the night." I got up and refilled his cup of coffee. Reg muttered his thanks.

"By the way, Reg, not that I want to hurt your feelings or anything but you look terrible. Are you sick or what?"

Reg looked up at me with bloodshot eyes. What hair he has left on top was standing on end and it looked like he'd slept in his clothes. Before saying anything, he gulped down about a quarter of his coffee. My coffee is scalding. I would've been begging for a fire extinguisher for my throat if I'd done that.

"I'll tell you, Mabel, I hope this investigation wraps up soon. I'm trying to help Jim and Scully out as much as I can but I suddenly realize I'm not a young man anymore." He sighed and ran his hand through his hair, making most of it stand up more than it was before. "Maybe if Maxymowich would keep all of us informed, it wouldn't be so bad but this not knowing anything…"

"I have an idea, Reg. Why don't you and I work together? Maybe we could solve it and Sheriff Jim could get his police station back, along with his new chair, and we could get our lives back."

Reg stared at me for several seconds, then grinned. "Mabel, you say the damndest things. You and me, solve a murder? Are you serious? No, forget I said that; I know you're serious." He laughed, grunted, and said, "Hell, why not? At least, I'd feel like I was doing something. Who knows? Maybe we could find the killer."

"Of course, we can. You can't use cuss words around me though."

"What cuss words? You know very well I don't swear, Mabel."

"Okay." I reached over and shook his hand. "Let's get started."

"First," he said, "what's all this about the phone message? Let me hear it again. You said you recognized the voice?"

I sat down. "Yes, it came to me in the middle of the night. This sometimes happens to me. I'm either dreaming or you know, kind of half awake and half asleep…"

"Just a minute," Reg interrupted. "I won't cuss if you won't ramble on about things. Now, who phoned you and does it have something to do with the murdered woman?"

I leaned forward. "I don't know but I think it might be significant. It was from Sally Goodrich. Remember? She was on the trip with me to Las Vegas. Now, if she'd phoned and said, 'I'm in Parson's Cove for the day, sorry I missed you,' that wouldn't have been too mysterious, but it was what she said and how she said it, that worries me."

"What did she say again?"

I got up and took a paper out of my cupboard junk drawer.

"Here it is. I copied it down as best as I could."

Reg read it aloud.

Sorry, I don't have time to explain. Don't want to make trouble for you. Just wanted some information. You could've helped. I don't know. I don't think I'll see you again.

"See what I mean, Reg? Why did she say she never meant to make trouble? I don't think she made any trouble for anyone except Ralph and why would she think that involved me? But it's the part about needing my help that worries me. What did she mean when she said she might never see me again?"

"She probably thought she'd never be in Parson's Cove again."

"Or, someone was threatening her life. She might be dead now. In fact, I think that's exactly what she meant, Reg. She knew she didn't have much time left."

"Okay, Mabel, let's not start speculating too much. First, what about this Ralph character? I hear he was at your place. Why?"

"Oh dear, I almost forgot about Ralph. I guess I'd better phone and tell him to come over and listen to the tape. He'll know it's Sally's voice for sure."

"Phone him? You mean he's close by?"

"Of course. He stayed at Main Street Hotel last night. I'll give him a call." I looked up at the clock. "He'll probably be up already."

Millie Clark answered. She's Parson's Cove's answer to Minnie Pearl. The farthest south she's ever been is Hazelnut Junction, which is a half hour drive at the most, going top speed. Somehow, she returned with a southern accent.

"This here's Main Street Hotel," she said when she picked up. "How can I help y'all?"

"Millie," I said, "this here's Mabel. I wonder if you can get Mr. Murphy for me. It's quite important."

"Mr. Murphy? Are you pullin' my leg, Mabel? Is this here some kinda joke?"

"No. Why would you think I was joking?"

"Cause, honey, there ain't no Mr. Murphy here."

"One of your guests. He checked in last night. Probably, about 8:30."

"No, we ain't got no Mr. Murphy here."

"You're sure? Did you check the book?"

"What book?"

"Well, don't you have a book that all your guests have to sign or something? I believe it's called a register. Doesn't everyone have to sign their name when they check in?"

"Of course, they do. That's why I know we ain't got no Mr. Murphy. We didn't have anyone check in last night at all. This here hotel is plumb empty."

I hung up and went over to fill our cups with coffee.

"That's strange, Reg. Ralph didn't stay the night." I shrugged. "Oh well, I guess he figured that there was no need. He was only interested in finding Sally and when I couldn't help him, I guess he thought there was no point in hanging around."

"What did he tell you, Mabel?"

"The strangest thing. Did you know that when we got to Denver, I was the only one who was supposed to change planes? But, Ralph tells me that everyone else got off too, except him. They were all supposed to be taking the same flight to Houston but the four never got back on. Of course, we now know why Grace didn't get back on."

"So, where did he go?"

"Well, I imagine he went home."

"Where's that?"

"You know, Reg, if I knew at one time, I've forgotten now. I mean, we did all get together when we first got to

Vegas and each of us had to tell something about ourselves. Offhand, I can't remember where his home was. I should've asked him when he was here. I thought I'd be seeing him today anyway."

"Well, it's probably not important." He took his little black notepad out of his breast pocket and licked the end of his pencil. "Okay, so we know that four of them got off at Denver but only three got back on." He started scribbling. When he'd finished, he looked up. "I'd say that means Andrea Williams or Grace Hobbs was murdered during that time, right?"

I nodded. "The only thing is, Reg, I'm sure Hatcher didn't know about Andrea. When we were in that house on P ½, I swear he was totally shocked to find out she was dead. So, that leaves Sally and Andrea."

"You think Sally killed Andrea or Andrea killed Andrea?"

"You know what?" I said, "Let's call the deceased Andrea, Grace. That's how I knew her anyway. It's hard to imagine that Sally would kill Andrea, I mean, Grace, but there is the phone call. Maybe she needed help because she'd killed Grace and didn't know what to do."

"Why? She would need a motive."

I shook my head. "I can't see any reason at all. Besides, where would she get a gun? Unless, they got in a fight and Grace's gun went off. I'm sure she'd have a firearm of some sort."

"That doesn't make much sense, Mabel." He sat with the tip of his pencil in his mouth. "How much do you know about this Ralph guy?"

"Ralph? I know he's nuts over Sally. I would say even to the point of stalking her. Also, he's not all that healthy.

If he doesn't look after his sugar levels, he seems to faint."

"Faint? You mean, like a girl?"

I nodded. "Yes, like a girl, Reg. You know what I would do? I'd find out which flight Hatcher, Andrea, and Sally took."

He stood up. "We'll feel stupid if Maxymowich already knows this, Mabel, but I'm going to go ahead anyway."

"Who cares if he knows? This is our own private investigation. Did you tell him about my call from Sally?" I asked.

"Are you kidding? Trying to get in to see him is like trying to get through security at the airport. You know what that's like. Besides, they're more interested in breaking up a gambling ring than worrying about a murder. At least, that's my opinion."

Reg left and I got ready for work. Flori phoned and said she'd bring some fresh cinnamon buns over to the shop for our coffee break. I never argue with that.

It was a cold miserable day with on and off rain so there were very few customers. The weather governs people's lives in Parson's Cove. They smile when the sun shines and tend to spend money but they growl and hoard when it doesn't.

It was past four in the afternoon when Reg finally walked into the store. I'd almost given up hope but he looked like he'd gotten a new lease on life. At least, the furrow between his eyebrows wasn't quite as deep.

"Mabel," he said, after he'd looked around to make sure we were alone. "I found something very interesting out." He brought out his little black notebook. "Ralph Murphy never stayed on that plane either. He was lying. The only ones who boarded for Houston were Hatcher, Andrea Williams, and Sally Goodrich, and they were not on the flight they were supposed to be on either. "

"Really? How long were they in Denver then?"

"Long enough for one of them to kill Grace but not long enough to dump the body in Parson's Cove and get back in time."

"Unless, of course, they had someone do it for them. Don't forget, Reg, we're dealing with an organized crime group. I imagine they have 'friends' all over the country."

"You're right and that would definitely remove whoever did it, as a suspect."

"Okay, so if Hatcher *didn't* kill her, he would be really worried, wouldn't he? When he was talking to that Mexican in Cecile's house, he must've been almost out of his mind, wondering where the heck she was. After all, she'd disappeared with the money. Do you think they took a later flight because they couldn't find Grace?"

"That would depend if they were all together. I mean, Mabel, let's face it, Hatcher could've been off by himself and the two women could've been together. Maybe they decided they wanted to tour around Denver so decided to take another flight."

"Tour Denver? After being in Las Vegas? I don't think so. No, if Hatcher didn't kill Grace that means, it had to be either Sally or Andrea."

"I thought you said it couldn't be Sally because she wouldn't have a motive."

"So, that leaves Andrea. However, she's the one who made the phone call to Grace at Cecile's house when I was there. Grace obviously gave her that phone number and must have wanted to keep in touch. Unless, it was for the other Grace…" I shook my head. My brain felt full of cobwebs. "This is just my gut feeling, Reg, but I'd swear that when she was standing with the gun pointed at me, she looked shocked to hear that Grace was dead. I don't know but I'm beginning to think perhaps, I can't rely on my intuition every time."

"Mabel, I *never* rely on your intuition."

"Thanks, Reg."

"Do you think Ralph knew about this money?"

I shook my head. "I can't see it. But, maybe he found out somehow. He was never around Andrea or Grace much. I don't know, Reg, he's such a klutz. You know what I mean? I would think the only reason he wouldn't get on the plane would be if he thought Sally wasn't getting on. That man has only one thing on his mind."

"What if he found out about the money and thought if he stole it, this Sally would be more interested?"

"I suppose that could solve the lost money but it wouldn't explain the murder. I think if Ralph saw blood, he'd probably faint."

"Okay, I guess our next move is to talk to this character and find out why he lied to you."

I nodded. "And, why he didn't stay in Parson's Cove and come back to see me like he said he would. He's turning out to be quite the liar, isn't he?"

"I have a feeling he knows a lot more than he let on to you, Mabel. Any idea how I can track him down?"

"I know he has a son going to college. He might know where his dad is. Seems to me the college wasn't all that far from here either if I remember correctly. Let me think…" I closed my eyes and tried to dredge it back up. "Seems to me it started with an S. Sanford? Stanford? Something like that."

"The only college starting with an S that's not too far from here is Stelling College and that's about a five-hour drive away."

"That could be it. I wish my memory were better. You could phone and check though. I don't know his son's first name but how many Murphy's would there be there?"

Reg put his notepad back into his pocket, slapped his cap back on and said, "I'll get back to you. While I'm doing that, Mabel, why don't you sit down and write up a little profile on each person on that trip?"

"Why?"

"Do I have to say, because I said so?"

"Gottcha. I'm going to close up now so you can reach me at home."

I locked the front door and walked home in the rain. During the last windy rainstorm we'd had, my umbrella decided to turn itself inside out, so I wrapped my old windbreaker around me and let the rain fall where it may. Two delinquent cats were sitting on my back step when I rounded the corner. They resembled two large smelly wet rats and their moods were as foul as the weather.

"All right," I said. "You don't have to give me that look of disgust. I walked home in the rain and I'm wet too." I opened the door a crack and they burst through. Neither one talked to me for the whole evening. Of course, when you have a few scattered around the house, it's almost a blessing when a couple of them remain mute.

Chapter Thirty Four

"What's that awful smell in here?" Flori asked. She'd phoned to see if she could come over for the evening. Jake was entertaining some of his drinking buddies and she grew tired of reprimanding them every time they said a filthy word.

"Why didn't you get Jake to speak to them?" I asked.

"Hummph," she said. "He's worse than the rest." She put her nose in the air and sniffed. "What stinks, Mabel?"

"It's those two," I said, pointing to the two pouty cats, hiding under my mother's china cabinet. "They didn't come in this morning when I left for work so I left them out all day."

I'm sure Flori didn't approve of my disciplinary action but she didn't say anything. We have a rule: I don't complain about how she trains her children and she doesn't find fault with how I train my cats.

"You want a glass of wine, Flori?"

"If you still have some of Sadie's chokecherry."

"Believe it or not, I still have a few bottles. I don't know what I'll do when they're gone. Surely, some of my customers must make homemade wine. I'll have to start asking around." I went into the pantry and brought out a bottle. I almost enjoy the containers that Sadie used as much as the wine. Anything that had a cork in it, she filled with her chokecherry wine. This one was an old barbeque sauce bottle. The label read *Ye Olde Hotsauce.* That was such an accurate description of the contents. I might find another wine maker but none could ever replace Sadie MacIntosh. She always brought in jams and jellies to sell but sadly no one ever bought them. I didn't want to hurt the old gal's feelings so I would buy them all up myself and figured with all the free wine she gave me, I came out even.

Flori and I sat and drank our first glass without too much conversation. Definitely, a drink meant for savoring. And a moment to remember Sadie.

"So," Flori said, "how's the investigation going? Did Reg get back to you or was he just trying to appease you?"

"No, he got back to me. You won't believe this but good old Ralph was lying to us. He never got back on that plane. And, you know what else Reg found out? The others didn't get on when they were supposed to either. Can you believe that?"

"I'll believe anything. Especially, after I have another glass of wine."

"You're supposed to sip wine. Not guzzle." I reached over and filled her glass.

"Thank you, Mabel. Okay, what were you saying about the plane?"

"None of them got on the plane when they were supposed to and Ralph didn't get on at all. What do you make of that?"

She took a mouthful, swished it around, and swallowed. If she had any idea how it looked, she would never do it again.

"I'd say that means that any one of them could've killed that nice undercover police lady cop, Grace. Or, what was her other name? Andrea?"

"Don't ask for any more wine, Flori. You're starting to get tipsy."

"I am not." She cleared her throat. "Isn't that what it means? Any of them could have killed her?"

I nodded. "I guess so. But why? There has to be a motive."

"Of course, and even in my drunken state, I know what the motive was. It was money. Or, love. People kill for either love or money. There are no other reasons."

"Or self-defense."

"Well, yes, but that's not the case here."

"How do you know?"

"Because Grace was a cop. She wouldn't try to murder someone, would she? So, there would be no reason for someone to be defending herself against her."

"I guess you're right. Why did you say 'herself?'"

"What do you mean? Herself?"

"Why do you think a woman killed her?"

Flori took another mouthful, swished, swallowed, and thought.

"I guess because I can't see a man wanting to kill a woman. It just doesn't seem right."

"It doesn't seem right for anyone to kill anyone."

"Oh well, that goes without saying, but you know what I mean. I think it was another woman."

"You think Andrea could've killed her?"

"Without blinking an eye."

I refilled my glass. Somehow, I could see Andrea doing it without blinking an eye too.

"Did you tell Reg about the phone call? That you know who it was now?"

"Yes, I told him. There's another mystery. Where did

Sally disappear to after she came to Parson's Cove?"

"You know, Mabel, I was thinking. Who says she came to Parson's Cove? People do make long distant phone calls."

I sat and stared at her. Now, why hadn't I thought of that? Of course, she could have phoned from anywhere. It just sounded like she must be in Parson's Cove. She might have only wanted to speak to me; not see me in person. For all I knew, she could have phoned from Yellow Rose.

"Flori, that's brilliant. You should stay perpetually wasted."

"Oh, for Pete's sake, I'm not wasted," she roared and fell back into the chair, laughing. Her wine spilled all down the front of her blouse.

I went into the kitchen for a wet cloth to dab the wine stain, and to grab the box of tissues for her nose and eyes.

When things had calmed down a bit, I said, "There has to be a way to check that out, isn't there? The telephone company would know where your calls came from."

"Of course, they do, Mabel."

I poured the last of the wine into our glasses. Finally, we would be able to solve part of the mystery. Still, not the murder but, at least, the case of the missing person. This was information I would *not* share with Ralph. I was very upset with Mr. Murphy.

Chapter Thirty Five

I was barely out of my housecoat when Reg banged on my door the next morning. The cats raced to the back entrance with their tails standing straight up and squawking as if I'd been keeping them in servitude for years.

"You cats are worse than a pack of dogs," I said, as they clamored to reach their escape route before I did. The door opened three inches and they were gone.

"What's wrong with those felines of yours?" Reg asked as he stood on the step and watched them disappear into hedges and under fences.

"This," I said, "is what happens when we have one day of rain. I don't even want to think what they'd do if it rained for two weeks."

"They'd probably murder you." He walked into the kitchen, picked up a clean cup out of my dish rack, and poured himself a cup of coffee. After sniffing it and apparently, approving of it, he opened the fridge, took out the carton of half-and-half, and measured just the right amount into his coffee. He then reached into the cupboard, removed my sugar bowl, carefully filled the sugar spoon three times and proceeded to stir.

"Thanks for getting my sugar spoon all wet," I said.

"Speaking of murder," he said, as if he hadn't heard me at all, "I have some more news to share."

"Aw," said I. "I also have some news to share."

Reg sat down at the table, took a big swig of coffee, swallowed, and said, "Really? What could you have dug up overnight?"

"It was something Flori said. You know Sally's phone call? How we just took it for granted that she was here in Parson's Cove? Well, she might not have been. It could easily have been a long distance call. I'm going to check with the phone company to see if they can tell me where the call came from. I mean, the call was for me so I should be able to get that information. So, what's your news Reg?"

"I found Ralph's son."

"No way."

"Yep. You were right about the college. He's at Stelling College."

"So what did you find out? Does he know where his dad is?"

Reg stopped and took a drink.

"You don't have to stop to drink, Reg. Tell me what he said."

"Yes, I do have to stop. It's the perfect temperature right now."

He took another swallow just to irritate me.

"He gave me his dad's cell number and his home address. Other than that, Daniel has no idea where he might be. He said his dad has contacted him only once since he got back from the trip. From the sounds of it, I'd say he's not too close with his pa."

"So? What did Ralph have to say?"

"I've called several times but he's got his phone turned off."

"What about Captain Maxymowich? Did he already talk

to Ralph's son?"

"Nope. I asked the lad and he said nobody talked to him. He didn't know anything about the murder at all. He said he took it for granted that his dad was phoning from home but he couldn't say for sure."

"I guess he could be home then, couldn't he?"

Reg nodded. "I'll keep trying his cell. The last time I phoned, I left a message. Gave my number and your number and asked him to call."

"Did you say why you wanted to talk to him? You don't want to scare him off, Reg."

"I know that, Mabel. I said that you were worried because you didn't know where he was. That you were really nervous after the murder and wanted to know if he was okay."

I laughed. "I'm sure that will have him calling in right away." I took my coffee and sat across from Reg. "You want a rhubarb pecan muffin?"

"Sure took you long enough to ask."

The Sheriff was on his second muffin when Flori burst through the door.

"Did you find out where Sally is?" she asked. Her face was red and she was out of breath. At least, she was dressed. She had on her coral pink pantsuit with matching headband. In fact, she'd even taken the time to put on makeup.

"You must really want to know if you don't even say hello first, Flori. And, by the way, you look like a big spring flower today."

"Why thank you, Mabel. Although I don't know if I like the word 'big.'" She stood with her hands on her hips. "Well?"

"I haven't phoned yet. Sit down and I'll bring you some

coffee. Want a muffin?" I didn't wait for an answer. Flori says 'no' but always has one so I put two in the microwave. Reg was almost finished his second one. "Reg has news. He has Ralph's cell number and his home address." I plopped the muffin on a plate and poured coffee for her. "He left a message for Ralph to phone either him or me." I took a swallow of my tepid coffee and smiled. "So, don't you think we've made some progress?"

Flori shrugged. "I'll feel better when I know where those two are." Her eyes filled with tears. "I dreamt last night that Sally was dead." She reached down the front of her coral pink top and took a tissue out to wipe her eyes and nose.

"Flori," I said. "Do not put that soggy tissue back in your bra. My goodness, can't you buy clothes with pockets. Look how you're embarrassing Reg."

Reg, however, was carefully removing the mushroom shaped top off one of the extra muffins I'd left on the table and apparently hadn't heard or seen anything.

He looked up when he saw us watching him and said, "All right, if you want me to contact the telephone company, I will."

Easy to tell Reg is a married man.

Chapter Thirty Six

It was Monday morning and even though it wasn't eight yet, the sun was high over the horizon. Only one day of rain and what a difference - the grass had turned from dusty brown to emerald green and flowers, once drooping, were lifting their heads heavenward again. It was a wonderful day not to have to go to work.

It has been a few years since I made the announcement, I was going to take every Monday off. It was one of the better decisions that I've made in my life. It makes me feel like I have a long weekend every weekend. There was really no reason to stay open that day anyway. The only reason I always went was that I didn't know what else to do. If I were going to sit in the store all day and do nothing, I might as well sit at home and do nothing. Flori did find it upsetting at first because she was so used to coming and having her morning coffee with me or as a second thought, maybe there was something wrong with me. Of course, she as well as all the other folks in Parson's Cove grew used to the idea and before you knew it, other establishments were doing the same until eventually Monday was a day everything on Main Street remained closed except for the Post Office and Main Street Café.

This morning, I *was* being lazy. Since I didn't have anyone to bring breakfast in bed to me (although if I called

Flori, I knew she would rush over), I decided to bring breakfast to myself. I spent twenty minutes in the kitchen fixing my tray up with a ham and cheese omelet, two pieces of whole grain toast slathered with peanut butter and honey, a large cup of coffee and a small glass of juice. It wasn't as enjoyable as I'd anticipated. Next time, I'll put all the cats outside first.

I was almost finished with my coffee when the phone rang. Who would phone at eight on a Monday morning? If I would throw all the cats off the bed, stretch my arthritic knees and make my way down the stairs, whoever it was, would hang up. By the time I'd thought all that through, the phone had already stopped ringing so there was really no decision to make. I drained the last of my coffee and picked up a book I'd put on my end table months before.

I opened to Chapter One and the phone started up again. Since my situation hadn't changed since the previous call, I put it out of my mind, and started reading. I was on page three when someone started banging on my door.

This time, I jumped out of bed, grabbed my housecoat, and screamed at all the cats to get out of my way. No one ever comes to see me on a Monday morning unless it's Flori and she doesn't knock.

All of us reached the door at the same time. I flung it open.

"About time, Mabel."

"What are you doing here, Scully?"

"Reg's home with the flu so he asked me to come by. He said he talked to the Captain and thought you might be interested."

"Okay, I would be. So, what did he say?"

"Oh, here." He held out his hand. "He said to give you

his notes. And, he said you'd owe him big time because he also managed to get his hands on some pictures. He's in bed today. His throat's real sore so he can't talk. The doc gave him some antibiotics so he should be up soon but right now Beth won't let him out of the house."

I glanced down at the notepaper and the large brown envelope he'd handed me.

"Reg actually thinks that I can read his writing?"

He shrugged and grinned. "Well, don't ask me to help." Scully stepped down off the step. "Sorry to wake you up so early, Mabel. Reg asked me to bring this over last night but I forgot. Me and Jim are going fishing now. Might as well make good use of our time while all the other cops are here." He grinned again and disappeared round the side of the house.

Reg was sick and Sheriff Jim and Deputy Scully were going fishing. I'm sure every citizen of Parson's Cove could feel safe and protected.

Just before he disappeared from view, however, I called out, "Did you phone me this morning?"

"That was to warn you I was coming. Why don't you answer your phone?"

At least, I hadn't missed a call from Ralph.

I poured another cup of coffee and took it to the table. Just as I was about to start deciphering Reg's notes, the phone rang. I grabbed it before the second ring.

"Ralph?"

"Ralph? Mabel, it's me. You mean, Ralph hasn't called you yet? What about the phone company? Did you find out where Sally called from?"

"No, to everything, Flori. I thought you might be Ralph. Anyway, do you want to come for coffee? Scully brought over some of Reg's notes and I don't know if I can figure them out on my own. You know what Reg's writing is like." I turned over the envelope holding the pictures to see if it was sealed. It was. "He also sent some pictures for us to look at."

"Why would Scully give you notes and pictures? Can't Reg come over? Don't tell me Beth got him to do some yard work. That would be a miracle."

"He's sick, Flori. Sore throat or something. Are you coming over or not?"

"I'm on my way."

I spread the three pieces of paper on the table in front of me. This might prove to be as tricky as trying to solve the murder. Instead of starting without Flori, I decided to make a fresh pot of coffee. I threw out the old, along with what was in my cup, and brought out some fresh Sunshine Health muffins from the freezer. Flori arrived before the coffee was finished brewing.

We each filled our cup, put a muffin on a plate, (Flori first applied a layer of butter to hers. So much for 'Health') and sat down at the table.

"Where do we begin, Mabel?" Flori asked, before taking a bite.

"Your guess is as good as mine. Here, let's just start with the first one here."

His printing was large so there wasn't too much information on each page.

"This is what I read. See if you think this is right. *Gambling. Insiders collecting chips. Passing on. Insiders getting suspicious.* Is that what it looks like to you, Flori?"

Flori held up the paper, squinted, and scanned the page.

"I'm amazed you could read that. Look, some letters are large and others are so small." She looked at me with an accusing eye. "How come sometimes you can see things and other times you can't?"

"I told you, Flori. It all depends on the light. If the light is good, I can read anything. And, it isn't that his writing is small, it's illegible, that's all. Okay, next page."

"This isn't quite so easy to read, Mabel. It's smudged with something. Is that ketchup?"

I sniffed it. "Can't smell anything but I'm sure it isn't blood. See if you can make out what it says."

"Let's see. I think this says *Maxy*." She showed me the paper. "What on earth would that mean? Surely, not sanitary napkins."

"It means Maxymowich. Keep going."

"Oh, all right. *Maxy figures either Andrea or Hatcher*...what's that next word, Mabel?"

"*Much?* No, maybe *must? Have suspected*...the next word has to be Grace, even though it looks like *Grapes*."

"So, he's saying that Captain Maxymowich thinks either Andrea or Hatcher killed Grace?"

"No, I don't think he's saying that, Flori. He's saying that they must have been suspicious of Grace, that's all."

"Suspicious that she was a cop?"

"Maybe; although I don't think so. I think they were suspicious she'd steal the money. What's this about *insiders collecting chips*? What do you make of that?"

"I don't know anything about gambling, but you know Jake indulges in it once in awhile. I think it means that someone inside the casino was collecting chips. You know, slipping them under the table, stealing them, and then passing them on to others to cash in. That must be how they were getting money illegally, Mabel."

"There had to be someone inside helping because, I'll tell you, Flori, even though I didn't go inside and gamble, I could see cameras and security guards all over the place. They really guard that money."

"So, it must've been either Andrea or Hatcher who committed the murder. Who else would have a motive? And, you know, Mabel, there always has to be a motive."

"I don't know, Flori, I could've sworn both of them were shocked to hear that Grace was dead. Otherwise, they are two very good actors."

"All criminals have to be good actors. After all, they're pretending to be good citizens so no one will be suspicious."

"Come to think of it, Flori. Undercover cops have to be good actors too. Look at Cecile. It's still hard to imagine him being one of the good guys. Even now, I have my doubts."

"Let's see the last page. Can you figure that one out, Mabel?"

"I'll try. I think Reg should take a course in handwriting. He's worse than Fritz."

This page was worse than the others were, if that were possible. It didn't help that Reg had ripped a corner off.

"Here goes, Flori. I think this says *Sally*... spelled with one 'l,' of course. This word has to be '*called*'... *from Y.R. Address on P and something. House number*... Now, who can read these numbers? It does look like a three and six though, doesn't it? Or, is it a nine? Can you believe this? What kind of notes are these?"

"They're good notes. He's telling you that Sally phoned you from Yellow Rose, from a house on P ½. If the house number has a three and six in it, it could be Stella's, Cecile's or Ben and Andrea Williams' house. We'll have to check with Reg to get it, Mabel. "

"Holy Hanna, you're right. Where is my brain? Of

course, that's what he's saying. The Y.R. sort of threw me off for a second." I got up and filled our cups. "I'm beginning to think that Sally must've been kidnapped and was calling for help. I'll bet you anything she phoned from Andrea's house."

"How would you be able to help her if she was there and you were here?"

We sat for several seconds, each solving the mystery in our own minds and in our own way.

"I think," Flori said. "Sally went willingly because she was after that Hatcher fellow but her plans fell apart when she overheard him talking to someone about the murder. When he discovered that she knew he'd killed once, he killed again."

I warmed up two more muffins. Somehow, the sunshine didn't seem so bright anymore. It didn't matter which one of us was right, neither idea sounded promising. Sally, if she were still alive, would be in danger if she went to Yellow Rose.

"Flori," I said. "I wonder if we saw Sally in Yellow Rose."

"What? No, we didn't. Where would we have seen her?"

"Coming out of Andrea's house. Remember, we saw that man coming out at night and shoving a woman into a car. Flori, I'll bet you anything that was Sally."

Flori chewed and thought. A couple of tears ran down her cheek. She sniffed and wiped them away with her hand.

"Maybe you're right. What a terrible thing. She'll be dead then." Flori's face screwed up and I raced for another box of tissues.

"We'd better go and talk to Maxymowich, Flori. This is getting too complicated even for me. I can handle one murder at a time but not two."

"And, I can't handle any." Flori closed her eyes and groaned. "Why did you ever go over to the morgue, Mabel? If you'd stayed in your shop where you belonged, none of this would be happening." She blew her nose and glared at me.

"My going to the morgue had nothing to do with this. Grace was dead before I went over there and who knows? Maybe Sally was already kidnapped." I glared back. "Besides, we've done a lot of good detective work."

"Okay, if you say so. I don't think we've done too much. But, we won't argue about it." She blew her nose and hiccoughed. "Aren't you going to look at the pictures Reg gave you?"

"The pictures. I almost forgot." I opened the envelope as carefully as I could. Usually, I just rip but I didn't want to take a chance in case I tore whatever might be inside.

There were three 8X10 photos: two in color, one in black and white.

Flori took one glance and covered her eyes. "I can't look at that." She turned in her chair and faced the window.

They were all pictures of the deceased. One was of Grace in the woods. She wasn't in the fetal position that I'd pictured. She was lying on her back, gazing up at the treetops, except with unseeing eyes. To me, it looked as if someone had been carrying her down the path, perhaps heard something, and then tossed her body into the bush. I don't know exactly why but it didn't look like a planned drop. The photographer had taken the next picture in the morgue. The white cloth covered her and only her face was showing. Now, at least, someone had closed her eyes. I picked up the black and white. This shot was in the morgue also but without the cloth. She lay there, fully clothed, looking very peaceful. The quality of the picture was so well defined; I could see the pores in her skin.

"Flori," I said. "Look at this picture and tell me what you see here." I pointed to Grace's clothing.

"I will if you cover her face. I can't stand seeing her look at me like that."

"Her eyes are closed. Now, open yours and tell me what you see."

 She leaned over the table. "What? I don't see anything."

"There." I pointed.

"I really don't see anything and I don't see how you can. Your eyesight is worse than mine is, you know.

Maybe she was right. Maybe I was seeing things. I took the photo over to the window. No, I was not seeing things.

I had a good idea who killed Andrea Williams. a k a Grace Hobbs.

Chapter Thirty Seven

It was Tuesday morning and I hadn't slept much the night before, waiting to hear from Maxymowich. At eight, he called me and I went straight to the police station.

The Captain sat in Jim's chair, facing me. Files and official looking papers occupied most of Jim's desk, not the sports and fishing magazines that usually filled that space. There was a scowl on his face.

"Very interesting theory, Mabel," he said, after several seconds, which to me, seemed like several hours.

"Is there some way you can check it out?" I asked.

"Definitely," he said. "However, we do need DNA from the suspect."

He stood up.

"That might not be so easy to get," I said.

I stood up.

"Don't worry, we'll get it."

"Will you need me then?" I asked.

"No, we'll manage on our own, but thanks for coming in. I appreciate it and always enjoy your visits, Mabel." His lips didn't smile but his eyes did. "I'd also appreciate it if you left the rest to us. This is a complicated case and I don't want you getting hurt. You do understand I'm sure."

Who doesn't agree with the Captain?

"Of course, I understand."

"No more running off to Yellow Rose, Texas, then?"

"No, sir. I'm finished with my vacation for this year. Besides, I think we've as good as solved this case." I smiled. "Just my gut feeling, Captain."

This time his lips smiled too. "Well, let's hope your gut feeling is right, Mabel." With that, he pulled out his cell phone and sat down. I knew enough to exit.

"What did he say? What did he say?" Flori asked, the minute she burst into the shop.

"He said he'd look into it."

"That's it? He'd look into it?"

I nodded. "That's it."

"But didn't he think it was a brilliant deduction?"

"Flori, you don't know the Captain like I do. If he thought it was, he wouldn't say anything until the case was solved and then he'd come to thank me. That's just the way it works."

"Well, I hope we hear something soon. I still think you might just be seeing things." She poured her coffee and sat in the wicker chair.

"By the way, I phoned Beth to see how Reg is and she said he's better. Even if he's still sick, I think she's going to drug him up and send him out. She can't take much more of him, sitting around and feeling sorry for himself."

I smiled. "I phoned him this morning. He said that even if he's still sick, he's going to get out of the house because he can't stand Beth fussing over him all the time."

"So, no matter which way you look at it, Reg will be out spreading his germs, won't he?" Flori laughed until I had to hand her a handful of tissues.

At noon, I walked to the Post Office to pick up my mail. Charlie was sitting in his favorite spot so I sat down beside him.

"I took a trip to Texas. Did you hear about it?" I asked. Charlie nodded.

"They still haven't caught the person who murdered Grace but I think I might know who did. The police are checking into it now. Anything you can tell me that might help, Charlie?"

Charlie started rocking and humming. It was a warm day but he seemed to be quite cool in his flannel shirt and denim overalls.

"Just saw him running."

"You saw someone running? Who?"

"Don't know."

"Someone running away from the body?"

He nodded. "Saw Esther coming and then man running away."

"Did Esther see him?"

He shook his head.

"Did you ever see this man before?"

He shrugged. "He got into a car and drove away."

"If you saw a picture of him, would you know him?"

He shook his head. "Too dark."

"Was he tall or short?"

Charlie kept on rocking and humming.

"Can you tell me now who Esther was meeting?"

Charlie kept up his rocking and humming but there was a secretive smile on his face.

"You're too nosey, Mabel."

"Some friend you are, Charlie," I said.

I stood up and as I started to walk away, he said, "Looked like a man that sells houses."

"What?" I screeched and rushed back to the bench. "What are you saying, Charlie? Someone's moving back to

Parson's Cove? Not Esther, please. That's not what you mean, right?" Without realizing it, I'd grabbed Charlie's shirt and was shaking him.

"Ask Esther," he said.

"You better believe I will." I reached my arms around him and hugged. "Thanks, Charlie." He blushed and started rocking again.

I called Flori the moment I got into the shop, as you can well imagine. She was beside herself. First, she was horrified that Esther was returning to Parson's Cove and then started feeling sorry for the poor sucker who had married her. When she started getting all sentimental on me and started blubbering about broken hearts, I told her someone had just come in and I had to go.

At ten minutes before closing time, I looked out the window and saw Esther coming towards the shop. I can't even explain what I was feeling. Except to say murderous comes to mind.

"So," I said, trying to keep my voice calm, "anything new with you, Esther?"

"What do you care, Mabel?" She looked down pretending to be interested in buying the most expensive vase that I have.

"Oh, I care. By the way, that is my best vase. If you really like it, I could pass the word around. You know, it would make a great welcome back to Parson's Cove gift." I looked her right in the eye and winked.

She jerked her head up so quickly that her glasses almost slid off. Her skin turned white and then red.

"What are you talking about? Who's coming back to Parson's Cove?"

"Well, you should know, Esther. You're the one who's out there, sneaking back into Parson's Cove through the bush."

Oh, oh. Not exactly the right words to say when someone is holding an expensive gold plated vase. Her mouth gaped open, she gasped in horror and my beautiful vase fell to the floor.

As I watched Esther running across the street with her skirt flying, I thought how happy I was to have such good insurance and that this was something I wouldn't have missed for the world.

Chapter Thirty Eight

I went to bed early that evening, content in knowing I'd almost driven Esther insane. She deserved it if she was the one who left that phone message for me. And now that I knew she was leaving her husband and coming back here, I was sure she was the one who sent it. It seemed like a decade ago now. Flori told me to forget about it. Let bygones be bygones. Easy for her to say, she didn't have the nightmares.

I was trying to concentrate on my book when Phil raised her head and twitched an ear.

"What's the matter, old girl? Did you hear something?"

She stood up and meowed.

"What do you hear? A burglar?" I reached over and ran my hand down her back. This usually makes both of us relax. Phil views every little sound as a potential disaster and it's her mission to protect me. "Silly, old thing."

At this point, she usually starts to purr, entwines her body around my arm and lies down again. This time, however, she kept standing, watching the door, and meowing.

"Phil, come and lie down. You're making me nervous."

All Phil did was stare at the open door and keep talking. All of sudden, the other three cats who had been sleeping in various areas in my bedroom, stood up and dashed out the door.

"Who's out there?" I called out.

There was only silence - except for the faint sound of my hallway floor creaking.

"Who's out there?" I yelled. Phil jumped off the bed and ran under it.

The light in the hallway was not on so I could only see darkness beyond my bedroom door.

A figure appeared in the doorway. I was expecting it but when it happened, my heart almost jumped out of my chest.

What I wasn't expecting was the gun in his hand.

"Ralph," I said. "What are you doing here? Why do you have a gun pointed at me?"

"Don't you listen to the news, Mabel? Everyone in the country is looking for me. There's a warrant out for my arrest. For killing Grace. Can you believe it?" He grinned. "But, I didn't need to tell you that, did I? You knew all along. You're the one who went squealing to the cops."

"No, I didn't. I only told them what I suspected. What do you think, Ralph? That you should get away with murder? And you could've, you know. I never would've believed it was you. Not in a million years. It was only after I saw the dandruff on Grace's clothes that I thought it might be. That's the honest truth, Ralph."

"I didn't mean to kill anyone. Do you believe me?"

"Of course, I believe you. What do you expect me to say when you have a gun pointed at my head? I think you should tell me what really happened so I can talk to the Captain. He's a very understanding person. Tell me the truth - was it an accident?"

Ralph's eyes were red but not from crying. Probably from lack of sleep. His hand holding the gun was shaky.

"It was. You know, all I wanted was Sally. She's the

only one who meant something to me. Sally found out that
Grace had this money. I don't know where she got it but
there must've been a million dollars. Her brown bag was
full of it. That's what Sally told me. There was a gun in the
bag too so Sally stole it and gave it to me. She told me that
if I pointed the gun at Grace, she would hand over the
money and Sally would go away with me. She promised
me, Mabel. We made our plans before the plane landed in
Denver. When the plane landed, I didn't get back on like I
told you. I told Grace that I needed to talk to her in private.
I told her it was about some stolen money. She had the bag
with her then but when she met me and I pointed the gun at
her, she didn't have the bag. I made a fool out of myself for
nothing. She grabbed for the gun and I pulled the trigger. I
don't know why. It was just a reflex, that's all. You
understand, don't you, Mabel?"

"I can't say I do. What happened then?"

"Then? I stood there and watched her die, that's what
happened. She slid to the ground."

 "No one heard the gun go off?"

"No. Sally told me about this secluded underpass close
to the airport. There was traffic going over and planes at the
same time. There was a car rental office close by so I
waited until it was dark and then put her in the car."

"You sat with the dead body until it got dark?"

He nodded. "Well, it was almost dark when I killed her.
But, I covered her up. There was an old tarp under the
bridge. I put that on her so I wouldn't have to look at her.
She kept staring at me, Mabel. Everywhere I looked, she
was looking at me."

"Dead bodies tend to do that, Ralph, especially if you've
just murdered them. So, what was your plan after the
murder?"

"Please, don't call it a murder."

"But that's what it was. You *murdered* Grace Hobbs. That's what you did. Why did you stay there? Why didn't you run? You might've gotten away with it if you'd left and got onto the plane home. No one would've connected you to her if you hadn't carried her and got dandruff all over her clothes. You do realize that, don't you?"

"I couldn't leave. I was waiting for Sally. She said she'd come to meet me there."

"What if Sally already had the money? If she had the money, she wouldn't need you for anything."

"No, she didn't have the money. I know she didn't. Besides, she wouldn't have done that to me."

"Don't count on it. You aren't too swift when it comes to Sally."

The gun was now pointing at the floor but I didn't want to spook him. After all, if he lifted it and fired, I wouldn't have a chance.

"So, you came here to kill me? What good is that going to do, Ralph? The police know you killed Grace so if you kill me, it's not going to change that. All it's going to change is how long you stay in prison or if you get the death penalty. That's all that's going to do."

Ralph looked down at the gun and then let it drop to the floor.

"You're right. I don't know what's wrong with me." He looked at me, pleadingly. "That Sally. She's made me crazy, Mabel. I was never like this before. I have a son, for god's sake. What's he going to think of me?"

Before I could tell him that his son was sure to think his father was a jerk, Ralph Murphy was on the floor, in a dead faint.

I stepped over him and made my way downstairs to the phone. This time I wasn't going to be concerned about throwing water on him until after the call.

Within five minutes, my house was overflowing with cops. And, Flori, of course. She'd seen the flashing lights and followed.

"I knew it had something to do with you, Mabel," she said, and hugged me until I thought she'd wring the life out of me.

Ralph was sitting on a kitchen chair. Water was still dripping down from his hair onto his shoulders and there was a puddle around the chair.

"Why is he all wet like that?" Flori whispered.

"Because he fainted," I said.

Maxymowich read him his rights, cuffed him, and hustled him out.

Reg hung back. He still didn't look too good. His eyes were puffy and his nose was red from blowing. He obviously should have been in bed.

"Thanks, Mabel. Sorry I couldn't do much these past couple of days. Maxy told me about the dandruff theory. So all you saw were a few white spots on that black and white picture and you figured it was dandruff? Why would you think it was dandruff when it was around her waist?"

"Because he had to hoist her over his shoulder to carry her when he dumped the body so that's why the dandruff would be there."

"Huh! Not bad, Mabel. Actually, quite brilliant if I do say so myself." He stopped to sneeze. When I saw it coming, I shoved his arm into his face so his sleeve would get the full force and I wouldn't.

"Sorry." He pulled out a large red rumpled handkerchief and blew. Afterwards, he shoved it back into this pocket.

"I'm not quite over this thing I've got. By the way, did he say where this Sally is? Do you think he killed her too?"

"He apparently doesn't know where Sally is, or so he says. I wish I could've asked him more but you know Ralph – he fainted. By the way, does Maxymowich know why Ralph brought the body here to Parson's Cove?"

Reg's face turned red. At least now his nose didn't stand out too much.

"I'll forgive you for this one, Mabel, but don't let it ever happen again. When you were getting dressed a few minutes ago and Ralph was confessing, he confessed that he brought the body here because of something you said."

"Something *I* said? What did I say?"

"That you'd had to help solve several murders in Parson's Cove because the police force here was inadequate. Or, did you say, 'a very young sheriff, an incompetent deputy, and an old retired sheriff?' I believe that's how you described the Parson's Cove law enforcement."

"You're kidding? I said that?" Sometimes words can really come back to bite you, can't they? "You know I didn't really mean that, Reg. You did say you were forgiving me, right?"

He nodded and grinned. "I probably wouldn't if I wasn't running a fever."

"By the way, Reg, we're pretty sure we might have seen Sally at Andrea's house when we were in Yellow Rose."

"You read over my notes, didn't you? I told you that the phone call came from there. Do you know who lives at 3800 P ½ ?"

Flori and I stared at each other.

"That's Stella's house. How can that be? That can't be right. Why would Sally be phoning from Stella's house?"

Flori said.

"Never mind, Flori, do you realize *when* she made that call? She made it when we were right there in Yellow Rose. How could she have phoned from Stella's house when we were right there? There has to be some mistake."

Chapter Thirty Nine

"What are you telling me, Flori? Stella's phone is disconnected?"

"Just says she's not available. That's what the recording said."

We stared at each other over my kitchen table. It was Monday again and I couldn't believe how fast time was flying by.

"Oh, Mabel," she said. "I'm so glad you have Mondays off. It's too bad you didn't think of it years ago. Imagine all the things we missed out on all those years."

Offhand, I couldn't think of too much.

"Like what?" I said.

"Like berry picking," she said.

Well, I guess that would have taken care of the Mondays in June.

I'd phoned Reg after Flori gave me the news and he said he was on his way over. I made an extra big pot of coffee, took out the last bag of Sunshine Health muffins and popped them into the microwave oven. He still sounded congested so I thought I'd give him something a bit healthier than his usual strawberry or blueberry muffin. I'm sure Beth would be pleased. Being an ex-cop's wife was stressful enough; she didn't need to worry about his health issues too.

A few minutes later, he arrived. The moment he got

through the door, he sneezed and sent my cats scurrying for cover.

"Please, come in and share your germs with us," I said. Flori had wisely grabbed a tea towel, which she now draped over her face. "Flori," I said. "You can't spend the rest of your life with a towel over your face. If you're going to catch it, you're going to catch it. And I'll let you take that one and put it in the laundry basket."

"So, what's this, Mabel?" Reg asked in a nasal voice. "This friend of yours in Yellow Rose … Stella … doesn't have a phone anymore? You're sure this is where this Sally person phoned from?"

By this time, Reg had already poured his coffee and was placing a muffin on a plate.

"That's the address you gave me, Reg. Did you tell Maxymowich?"

He nodded. His mouth was full so he couldn't talk. It isn't a pleasant experience watching Reg eat, so Flori and I bit into our muffins too.

"Wish I could taste these," Reg said, as he was tearing his second one in half and adding butter. He looked up at me with feverish eyes. "Lost all sense of taste with this cold."

"Well, you could've fooled me," I said. "Are you taking your medication?"

"Most of the time." He plopped the last bit into his mouth, chewed, swallowed, and said, "Maxy is sending someone in Yellow Rose over to check this Stella's house out." He stood up. "I'll let you know what he finds out. Thanks for the muffin and coffee. Good, as usual."

"He could've told me all that over the phone," I said, after the door closed.

"He just wanted coffee and something to eat. Poor man

is feeling so terrible. I think I'll make some chicken soup and take it over for him."

"Flori, I'm sure Beth can make soup. He isn't taking his antibiotics so it's his fault he's so miserable."

I filled our cups up and we ate in silence for a few minutes.

"Can you figure this out, Mabel? Where would Stella be? She didn't say anything about leaving Yellow Rose. Do you think someone killed her too?"

I shook my head. "Of course not. Ralph killed Grace. That had nothing to do with anyone else. What I don't understand is why would Sally be at Stella's house and if we were right there in Yellow Rose, why didn't she tell us that Sally was at her place?"

Flori held her cup in midair and stared into space. Then, she turned to me and said, "Maybe she didn't know that we knew Sally. Did we ever talk to her about Sally? Do you think someone kidnapped Sally; she escaped, and then just happened to run into Stella's place to phone? Perhaps, someone was after her?"

All I could manage was a groan.

"And Stella just happened to forget to mention it to us? I don't think so. Personally, I'm beginning to think that everyone who lives on Avenue P ½ is weird. Maybe all Texans are crazy. I don't know."

"Oh well, at least, the murderer is caught and that's all that matters. You should be proud, Mabel. You were the one who figured it all out. Imagine, seeing dandruff on Grace's clothes. I would never have connected that with the murder." She raised her empty cup to me. "You, my friend, are a good detective."

"Well, thanks, Flori, but you know it isn't over. We still

have to figure out what happened to Sally and I have to force a confession out of Esther."

"Force a confession? For what? Surely, you're over that school thing. I mean, Mabel, that happened over forty years ago. I told you, you had to come to grips with that. If you let things fester, they just get worse and worse."

"This has absolutely nothing to do with things that Esther did to me years and years ago. This is the phone call she made and scared the wits out of me, that's what this is about."

"You have no proof that Esther even left that message."

"Well, who did then?"

She shrugged. "I don't know; maybe it was Sally."

"No. The second message was definitely from Sally but not that first one. I'll have to listen to it again."

"My advice to you is to forget about it. No one has harmed you so it was either a prank call or you didn't hear it right."

Ping! A light went off in my brain.

"Maybe we *do* know Sally was at Stella's, Flori. "

"What do you mean? Sally was at Stella's? We definitely did not see Sally at Stella's."

"No, but we could've heard her. Remember the music? I thought it was strange that she had the music playing so loud. Then, when I went back to wait for you and Stella, I turned the volume down and I did hear something coming from below but I thought it was the water pipes or something. I bet you anything she was tied up in the shed under the house."

"I was in the garage, Mabel, and I didn't see or hear anything."

"What was under there?"

"Her washer and dryer. The car, of course, and some

kind of shed. Probably for tools and things like that."

"That's it then. She was tied up in the tool shed under the house."

Flori shook her head. "I don't know. That seems kind of farfetched."

I ran over to the phone and called Reg on his cell phone. He agreed with Flori, that it was farfetched but he did what I asked anyway. He called Maxymowich.

Chapter Forty

"You were right, Mabel. And, I'm not going to say *again*." Reg was back in my shop the following morning. No one comes in to buy anything until after eleven even on my busiest days. That's not good for sales but, at least, we were able to speak and not worry about anyone eavesdropping. "They found Sally, locked up in the shed under Stella's house."

"Was she alive?"

"Barely. She'd run out of food and she was in bad shape. They found Stella too."

"You're kidding. Where?"

"Galveston. She'd just returned from a Caribbean cruise."

"What? She didn't tell us she was going on a cruise. Honest, Reg. She didn't say a word. Did she know about Sally? Please, don't tell me that she was in on all of this too. It will break Flori's heart if she was."

"Okay, I won't tell you." He walked over to the coffee maker. "The coffee isn't ready yet, Mabel."

"Of course, it isn't. I just walked in the door. Who do you think I am anyway? Superwoman? And, what did you mean when you said, I won't tell you?"

"I thought that's what you wanted."

"No. I mean, that's what I was hoping; that Stella wasn't

mixed up in this. But, you have to tell me if she was, Reg."

He sighed and sat down in the wicker chair. His eyes were clearer now so the fever was gone but he still sounded stuffed up when he talked.

"She was implicated in a very innocent way."

"Implicated? What the heck does that mean?"

"It means that when lovely couple came to her and offered her a lot of money plus a free cruise, she didn't ask a lot of questions. That's what that means." He took out his red and white handkerchief and blew his nose. "When will the coffee be ready?"

"When I get all of my questions answered, that's when."

"So, what more do you want to know?"

"What more do I want to know? First of all, who was this nice couple? Why would they need Stella's shed? Aren't there other places to hide someone? Plus, I want to know if Stella knew what they were storing in her shed and I want to know if she knew who Sally really was. And, I want to know if she was leading us on so I know what to tell Flori. That woman is not going to hurt Flori, if I can help it."

"Well, let's face it, Mabel, Stella doesn't have much money to her name. If it weren't for her son, she would be living in government housing so when some nice guy and a woman show up at her house and tell her that they will pay good money just to store something in her shed for three or four days, she didn't think twice. You have to remember, this is Yellow Rose, Texas. Folks do things differently down there. If they think they're helping someone out, they do it and don't ask questions. That's the way it is."

"They offered lots of money? Who's they?"

He nodded. "Quite a bit of money. More than Stella was

used to seeing, that's for sure."

"How much?"

"A couple thousand, plus a five-day cruise out of Galveston."

"So whomever it was wanted to make sure the house was empty for awhile so they could lock Sally up in the shed?"

"Well, it wasn't originally meant for Sally. It was meant to store ill begotten gains."

"Was Stella back home when they arrested her?"

"I don't think they arrested her. They did find her at a hotel in Galveston. She'd just come off the cruise and her son was going to pick her up after he was finished work."

"So her son knew what was going on?"

"I think he thought she'd rented the house to some vacationers for a few says. That's what it sounded like to him."

"Seriously? People just rent out their houses to strangers?"

"Yes, they do. I told you; it's Texas."

"Stella had all this going on and she didn't breathe a word to us?"

"The couple who called on her said it was a surprise and not to tell anyone."

"I still don't understand. Who's this couple who went to her?"

"Ralph and Sally ."

"*What*? What on earth are you talking about?"

"Ralph Murphy was in Yellow Rose too. Sally went down on a hunt for Hatcher and Ralph followed. He found Sally before you and Flori even got there. He found her, showed her all the money, and asked her to go away with him. I guess she still had her eyes set on Hatcher but she played along with it, thinking she'd trick him into giving her the money."

"That means that when Ralph met Grace under the bridge, she did have the money with her. I didn't think she'd let that stolen money out of her sight. Another lie he told me. Did he tell Sally that he'd killed Grace?"

"Not at first. She told him they should hide the money for awhile until the whole thing blew over because they didn't want the cops looking for them. He agreed and that's when he thought about Stella's place."

I sat down on the Coke box. "I can't get this straight, Reg. Ralph was right there in Yellow Rose when we were?"

He nodded. "Yep."

"How did he happen to find Stella? I mean you don't pick a house on a street and say, I'm going to leave a bag filled with stolen money in that shed under that house. Right?"

"Of course, not. He knew he'd killed someone named Grace Hobbs who lived in Yellow Rose. He thought she must be Cecile's wife so he went to his house."

"How could he find that out?"

"I guess just the same way you did, Mabel. Doesn't take a rocket scientist to look up numbers and addresses in a phone book. That's when he saw you and Flori going in and out of Stella's house. He also knew about the other house on P ½ where Andrea lived. As far as I can figure out, he thought by involving Stella, it might point a finger at you."

"Me? How could I be involved?"

"Well, let's see, Mabel. A dead body turns up in your town. You end up in Yellow Rose, visiting the woman who lives next door to Grace Hobbs, the murder victim. Some people might make a connection. Of course, he had no idea what a law abiding citizen you were."

"I can't believe Ralph would think that way, Reg. We were friends. I liked him better than any of the others."

"Mabel, Mabel, didn't you get the hint? He really didn't like you. Maxymowich told me Ralph said he should've killed you the first time he went to your house."

"Really? He's just saying that because I'm the one who fingered him."

"Fingered him?"

"Yeah. You know, I pointed him out as the murderer. That's cop talk, Reg."

"If you say so. Well, with some friends, who needs enemies, right?"

"You got that right. I just can't believe that all along he had that stolen money. No wonder he couldn't get back on the plane! Boy, did he have the wool pulled over my eyes."

"I think we're quite sure you can't believe a word Ralph Murphy says."

"So, is it all figured out now? Are all the criminals in jail? But, what about that phone call, Reg? Why would Sally phone my place and how did she manage it if she was locked up below the house?"

"Don't forget Ralph and Sally were together at first. Stella thought they were a couple. At this point, Sally had no idea what the future might hold. She always thought she had Ralph twisted around her little finger so when he went out to get the money for Stella, Sally asked if she could make a phone call. She wasn't quite sure if Ralph was telling the truth about Grace so she was going to ask you about it. Stella, of course, had no idea what was going on; she thought they were renting her shed to store something but she didn't know that it would be Sally. She said she thought it might be things they bought while in town and had no place to keep them. Sally thought Ralph was going to hide the money there so her plan was after getting rid of him, she'd collect it herself. When Sally asked if she could use the phone, Stella told her she could. If you had been home and told Sally that Grace was dead, she would have known Ralph had killed her."

"I wonder what she would've done then?"

"Probably left an anonymous message with the police about Ralph and then taken off with the money."

"Did Stella ever know it was Sally who was in her shed?"

Reg shook his head. "Well, I'm sure not at first but she must have wondered when she heard bumps and bangs coming from there."

"So, what was she thinking? Why didn't she go and look for herself?"

"Ralph assured her not to worry about it and that everything was fine."

"Wasn't she concerned?"

"I don't think she thought there would be a person there, Mabel. Maybe she just thought there was some hanky-panky going on so she turned up the music."

"And, Ralph left Sally there to die."

"He went to check on her several times, trying to get her to go away with him but when he realized that she just wanted the money; he left and didn't go back."

"How long was she there all alone?"

"Quite a few days. Ralph did try convincing her to go with him by offering food and wine but it finally got through to him that by this time, she hated him."

"I don't blame her. I'd hate him too, the jerk. And Stella never went down there to feed her or check on her?"

He shook his head. "Well, when you and Flori were there, she was always on the go and probably thought the couple who rented it were coming and going. She never thought of anything being criminal about it and then as soon as you left, she went on her cruise. I'm sure if she knew there was a woman down there, she would have gone for help."

"Will Stella go to jail?"

He shook his head. "She's never been in trouble, so probably not. She's pretty shook up about it. Or, maybe the best word is ashamed. Her son's with her now and he's not too happy with his mama. At least, that's what Maxymowich tells me."

We sat in silence for a few minutes.

"Do you think you could make the coffee now, Mabel? I haven't had a cup all morning."

"Is that why you look so terrible? Where's Beth?"

"I let her sleep in. Guess I've been keeping her awake all night with my coughing and snoring."

I made the coffee, all the time wondering how I would go about telling Flori about Stella. How could she have been so foolish? Because of her, a woman could have died. Well, I guess I couldn't say that. Because of Ralph, another woman could've died. Some way to treat the woman you love.

We were half way through our first cup when she walked in. Somehow, I could tell by looking at her that she already knew.

"Flori, you've heard the news? They found Sally and she's alive."

"I heard. I also heard that Stella was keeping her in that shed below the house. You were right all along, Mabel. I'm never trusting another person as long as I live."

"Don't say that, Flori. There are lots of people you can trust; it's just that most of them live in Parson's Cove. And, even then, you can't trust most of them."

"I made such a fool of myself."

Flori started to sniff so I got up and forced her to sit in my chair. I retrieved the box of tissues. She wiped her eyes even though no tears had formulated yet; then, she wiped her cheeks and blew her nose. This was all in preparation for the downpour. Reg and I sat quietly and started our second cup of coffee, waiting for the cloudburst to finish.

"How did you hear about it, Flori?" I asked.

She made one last hiccough and said, "Jake told me. He went down to the restaurant this morning. Everyone is talking about it. Well, not that they knew Sally; they're just saying that a friend of *ours* – yours and mine, Mabel, hid this woman in a shed and left her to die. I never even met Sally."

I turned to Reg. "I think you should stop sharing information with Scully, Reg. He's such an old gossip."

"Speaking of sharing information," Reg said, "Scully is coming in this morning to see you. He has something to share with you."

"With me? What?"

"Oh, you'll see." He heaved himself up. "Well, I better get over and say my farewells to all those city cops."

He went out the door, singing, "*So long, it's been good to know you...*"

I filled Flori's cup. She hadn't looked this sad since her whole batch of dill pickles turned bad.

"Sorry about Stella but Flori, she was really innocent in the whole thing. She had no idea what Ralph was up to. He fooled her like he fooled me."

"Oh, that's okay, Mabel. Stella might have had me under her spell but I never did like that Ralph character. It doesn't matter; you're my only one true friend anyway. I sort of got carried away with Stella." She cradled her cup against her breast. "We seemed so much alike, didn't we?"

I smiled. "Only on the scale, Flori. Only on the scale."

Scully came in just before noon. I'd almost forgotten about him. Esther had entered about two minutes before he had. I decided that it was time to settle things with her and what better time than when there's a deputy in the room.

"So, Esther," I said. "I guess you've heard we solved the murder case."

"Oh, right. I like how you say *we*, Mabel. Like you're the great detective here." She sniffed and pushed her glasses back up her nose.

"Maybe I am. Did you know it was my idea to check the dandruff on Andrea's clothing and that proved Ralph was the killer?"

"Mabel, everyone knows you're a busybody, causing more trouble for the officers than what you're worth. I'm sure they could have figured it out without your little input."

"I don't think they feel that way, Esther. Right, Scully?"

Scully was standing behind a counter and looking like he wished he could be anywhere else in the world. He blushed, cleared his throat and said, "Whatever you say, Mabel."

"Thank you, Deputy. And while the Law has a representative here, I'd like to question you about something, Esther."

"What? I don't have time to fiddle diddle around here. I have things to do this morning. Not everyone is like you, Mabel, able to sit around, drink coffee, and do nothing all day."

"In that case, I'll get right to the point - what about that threatening phone call you made to me?"

"Threatening phone call? What nonsense are you talking about? I haven't called you in years and I don't plan on ever phoning you in the future."

"Come off it. You know very well you phoned me right after I got home from my trip."

"And why, pray tell, would I do that?"

"Because you were jealous, Esther. You were jealous because you never get to go anywhere. And don't deny it, I'd recognize your voice any day. And besides that, you wanted to rub it in my face that you were moving back to Parson's Cove."

Esther's eyes bulged and her glasses slid down her nose.

"I'll have you know," she said. "I did *not* make any phone calls to you. If I had, I would admit it. In fact, I would brag about it. And for your information, I have no intention of *ever* moving back to Parson's Cove."

"Well, if you're so innocent and so smart, *who* did phone and threaten me?"

Scully coughed and stepped out from behind the counter.

"Uh, the reason I came over, Mabel, has a bit to do with that phone call."

I stared at him.

"What do you mean? A bit to do with it?"

"Well, it's like I know who made the call."

"You know who made the call and it wasn't Esther? How long have you known this little secret?"

His face had now changed from red to crimson red. He looked down at his feet and started tapping the bottom of the counter with his toe.

"I guess you could say I knew from the beginning."

"From the beginning? Are you telling me that you knew who left that horrid message and you haven't come forward? That I've been having all these nightmares about Esther and it wasn't even her?"

Scully's face turned even redder, which I never would've believed possible, and he hung his head.

"Sorry, Mabel, but it was me."

"Pardon me? You're mumbling."

He raised his head. He didn't need to say a thing.

"You? *You* made that horrible threatening phone call, Scully? A member of our own police force? How could you?"

"It wasn't a threatening call. I can tell you what I said. You just didn't hear it properly."

"Why didn't you come forward and say something? Everyone in the police station heard it."

"Yeah? Well, that's why I didn't say anything. I was hoping you'd let it blow over. You think I was going to admit it with all those cops there? They would've laughed their heads off. And, what do you think Maxymowich would've thought? He would've been humiliated. I'm sorry, Mabel, I was too ashamed to say anything."

"So, what was the message, Scully? Where do you come off thinking that it wasn't a threat to my life? I distinctly heard you say that I should go away and that everyone in Parson's Cove thought I was wicked and should go to jail. I remember it like I heard it yesterday."

I ignored Esther's cackling.

"I didn't say that at all. I said how nice it was for you to get away to Las Vegas and that everyone in Parson's Cove wished they could get away like that. Then, I asked you to bring your pictures over to the jail, that we were dying to see your life in the big city and that we'd better watch out or you'd leave again. That's all I said. Maybe in different words but that's what I meant."

"But, you said 'wicked.' I heard it."

"Yeah. So? Don't you know what that means, Mabel?

It means 'awesome.'"

"Wicked means awesome? Now, that's a new one. How long has Reg known this?"

"Since this morning. He made me promise to come over right away and apologize."

I walked over and hugged him.

"You're forgiven."

"Just like that?"

"Just like that."

I turned to Esther, who was leaning up against the wall, wiping the tears from her eyes.

"You can stop laughing now. It was an honest mistake. If it makes you feel any better, Esther, I'm almost sorry it wasn't you. You have no idea what punishment I had all lined up."

"I expect an apology, Mabel. I'm sure you've told everyone in town that I was the one who did this, didn't you?"

"No, I don't think I told everyone. Most people just assumed it was you. However, to show there's no hard feelings, I'll make sure to tell a few people that it was Scully. Will that make you happy?"

"No. I'll see that you pay for this until I breathe my last breath."

With that, she opened the door and walked out.

Before she reached the end of the sidewalk, I managed to reach the door and call out, "I'm sure everyone will be interested in knowing who you were meeting when you happened to almost trip over that dead body, Esther."

Too bad she didn't see the little rise in the cement. Before I turned my attention back to Scully, I saw her skirts go up and her body hit the pavement.

It was then that I remembered her saying that she would never move back to Parson's Cove.

It wasn't until about a week later that Charlie finally came out with some information that I wished he'd told me sooner. It seems she was meeting a realtor so they could check out one of the cabins along the lake for a friend. A friend? Maybe the old gal had made a few friends in her new town. Wait until they discovered the real Esther.

Chapter Forty One

Captain Maxymowich dropped by the house a few days later.

"I take it all the loose ends are tied up and you're on your way home," I said.

The Captain smiled. "It's been a pleasure working with you again, Mabel."

I almost said, 'the pleasure was all mine,' but somehow, that sounded a little tacky. Instead, I said, "Don't mention it. If you ever need help solving a case, you know I'm ready and willing."

(Later, when I told Flori what I'd said, she felt that I sounded very presumptuous.)

It was almost nine. If it were any weekday but Monday, I'd have been late for work. However, because it *was* Monday, I was still in my housecoat and pajamas. My housecoat isn't a thing of beauty. It's faded cotton and only comes down to the tops of my knees. Knees, in case you didn't know, are not pretty when they're old..

Maxymowich, standing outside on my step and looking slightly uncomfortable, said, "If you'd like to get dressed, Mabel, I can wait. Perhaps, you have a few questions about the case you'd like answered. I know I'd sure appreciate a cup of your coffee."

"Of course, Captain." I ushered him into my kitchen, sat

him down at my table, and I rushed upstairs to dress. Three cats had snuck out the door while we were talking but I was sure the others could entertain him.

About ten minutes later, we sat at the table together. I'd pulled on my jeans and a clean white cotton shirt, brushed my teeth, and rinsed my mouth. The only socks I could find were animal print, black and white.

"I don't suppose," he said, "that you have any homemade muffins to go?"

"I think I might find a few in my freezer. I can pack some up to take with you if you like. Reg has been over quite often the past few days. I guess I don't have to say anything more, do I?"

He laughed. "No, I guess not."

We sat in silence for a few minutes, drinking our coffee. The Captain didn't seem to be concerned. We were almost finished our first cup and I wondered if this was it; would he finish his coffee, take his muffins, leave, and not say another word?

"Captain," I said, "what's going to happen to Ralph?"

He placed his cup on the table and slouched a little more in his chair.

"I would think he'll be behind bars for quite a few years."

"Sally?"

"Not much we can do with Sally. She'll testify at the court case and then she'll be on her way. There isn't any proof that she told Ralph to kill Andrea Williams and she didn't steal the money."

"On to find another sucker, I guess."

"We can't do anything about that, Mabel."

"No, I guess not. Reg didn't think Stella would be in too much trouble."

He smiled lazily. "I think her embarrassment is enough punishment for her."

"You think it will bother her conscience?"

"Oh yes, I think so."

"What did Ralph and Sally say about Stella?"

"Sally claimed that Stella was innocent and Ralph says that he didn't have anything to do with it at all, that it was a conspiracy between Stella and Sally to frame him."

"You're kidding, right?"

"I was never more serious."

"Will he get away with that?"

"Only if the jury is psychiatrically disordered."

I wasn't quite sure if he was serious when he said that but since he didn't smile, I decided not to laugh. Let's face it; half the world's population is psychiatrically disordered.

"What about Andrea Williams? Do you know what happened after I left the house on P ½?"

Now, there was a definite twinkle in his eye.

"Oh yes, the house on P ½. That seemed to be a very busy street, didn't it?"

"Probably the busiest in Yellow Rose!"

He shoved his cup towards me. "Since I'm taking my muffins to go, I'll settle for another cup of coffee."

While I was pouring it, Flori burst through the door.

"Mabel, you'll never believe this…" She paused when she saw the Captain. "Oh, Captain Maxymowich, I didn't even notice you." Her hand went instinctively up to her hair and she gave it a fluff.

"Flori," I said. "I'm sure you noticed the police car in my driveway."

She should've turned slightly pink but she didn't. Instead, she giggled and said, "The driveway? Oh, I guess I did notice a car there." With that, she walked over to the Captain, shook his hand, and told him how nice it was to see him again. Then, she settled into the chair across from him and asked me to bring her a cup of coffee.

This was definitely not my humble friend but afterwards she told me that she was trying to be extra courteous, in case I was in trouble for leaving the hotel after he'd told me not to leave. Flori is always thinking of others.

It's a good thing she told me this afterwards because I couldn't believe what I was hearing when she said, "So, Captain Maxymowich, I'm sure everyone on the Force is grateful to Mabel for solving this murder case."

If the Captain reacted in any way, I missed it.

"Yes, Mrs. Flanders, we're very grateful to Mabel. She's a natural crime-solver. We wish more on the police force had her instincts."

"Really?" I said. I was standing behind Flori with the coffee pot in my hand. He looked up at me and winked. Now, I would never be sure, would I?

"By the way, Mabel," he said, "you were wondering about Andrea Williams?"

"I was. And her husband. What's with that? Is he a real cop or not?"

He bent over to pour cream into this cup and stirred. Flori waited until he was finished and then she fixed her coffee: as much cream as she could put in without spilling it on the table, and three teaspoons of sugar. We both waited and watched while she leaned over and slurped some up.

"Well," he said, "Andrea is now incarcerated. She and Hatcher were arrested for smuggling drugs and stealing money from the casino."

"How did they steal that money?" I wanted to know. "I was there, Captain, and there were so many security guards around, I don't see how anyone could steal anything."

"The cops arrested two people who were working the tables too. They were stealing chips and passing them on to Andrea and Grace. Apparently, it was quite a complex setup. Grace was on that case for almost two years."

"I told you, Mabel," Flori said. "I knew that's what they were doing." She looked at Maxymowich. "Not that I gamble but my husband used to. Once in awhile. He hasn't lately at all."

"It's okay, Flori. I'm sure Captain Maxymowich isn't too concerned about Jake's involvement in the gambling ring. I was wondering about Ben though, Andrea's husband."

"He was collecting evidence. He's a good cop."

"But what about his wife? I mean, how can he be good and his wife be a crook?"

He shrugged. "I guess that's what happens sometimes. The money was too hard for her to resist. Police officers don't make that much, you know. Especially in small places like Yellow Rose. She thought she could make some on the side. Besides, she could get information from her husband and use it. Apparently, that was her downfall. Ben started to get suspicious. She was asking too many questions." He absentmindedly stirred his coffee.

I knew Flori would find this upsetting. She has definite viewpoints about the sanctity of marriage.

"So," she said, "what will become of their marriage?"

"I think Ben has already filed for divorce."

"That is so sad," Flori said.

"Flori," I said, "don't worry about them." I turned my attention back to the Captain. "There's a couple of things that still bother me."

"Ask away, Mabel. Maybe I'll know the answers."

"Well, when we were parked behind Ben and Andrea's house, someone pushed a woman out of the house and into a car. We thought it must've been Sally but now I realize Sally was locked up at Stella's place. Do you know what was happening there?"

"As far as I know, it was a woman coming for drugs. Andrea made sure no one ever came to the house but I guess this one was desperate. You do have a connection with her though, Mabel."

"I do?"

"She works at the Gulf Motel and told Andrea that someone had been around asking questions. Guess she thought she'd be rewarded with a few freebies for telling her."

"You're kidding! Somehow, I knew there was something familiar about her but I never would've guessed who it was."

"And the other question?"

"Where's the money?"

He smiled a lazy smile. "Always comes down to the money, doesn't it? Most of it was retrieved from the trunk of Ralph's rental car. The only amount missing was what he'd given to Stella and she gladly returned it. She hadn't spent any of the cash. That's it? No more questions?"

"I have to say I'm kind of curious, wondering who that Mexican man was; you know, the big boss."

"I imagine there are a few bigger bosses over him but he was the kingpin in Yellow Rose. His cover was a restaurant. In fact, he was a highly respected businessman."

"Don't tell me he owned a Chinese restaurant."

"Now, how would you know that?"

"Because the best Chinese restaurants in Yellow Rose are

run by Mexicans, that why."

"You learned a lot while you were there, Mabel."

"But, what about Cecile? Is he *really* an undercover cop?"

Maxymowich burst out laughing. It was the first time I'd ever seen him laugh so hard.

"Mabel," he said. "Cecile Tucker is the best undercover cop in America. After all, he had you fooled, didn't he?"

I had to admit that he had. But then, so had Ralph.

"Mabel," Flori said, "let's stop talking about this case. It's so depressing. Surely, there are other things to talk about."

"You're right. Captain Maxymowich asked for muffins and you know what, Flori? All I have are a few frozen bags in the freezer. I can't believe I've gone through almost all the muffins. I'm going to go right down to Macy's and get some flour and bake some more. From now on, I'll make Mondays my baking day."

"You forgot," Flori said. "You can't go to Macy's and get flour today."

"Why?"

"You know very well; you're the one who started it. All the stores are closed on Monday."

Good grief!

The End.

Mabel's Muffins

Mabel's secrets to fantastic muffins:
Proper mixing is the key. Do not over-mix!
Begin by thoroughly mixing the dry ingredients – flour, sugar, baking powder, and salt. Make a well in the center. Mix liquid ingredients – egg, milk, melted fat or oil, and other seasonings or spices – until well combined. Add fruit, chocolate chips, etc.
Pour the liquid ingredients into the well in the dry ingredients and stir just enough to moisten. The batter should be lumpy but not have any areas with dry flour.

BANANA MUFFINS

1 cup white sugar
½ cup margarine
1 beaten egg
1 cup mashed bananas
1 tsp. baking soda dissolved in 1 tbsp. hot water
½ tsp vanilla
1 ½ cups flour
Bake @350* for 20-30 min

CARROT MUFFINS

3 eggs
2 tsp. vanilla
14 oz. tin crushed pineapple (juice & all)
1 cup coconut
2 cups grated carrot
1 cup white sugar
½ cup oil
1 cup raisins
2 ¼ cup flour
2 tsp. baking soda
1 tsp. cinnamon
1 tsp. salt
Mix all in bowl
Bake @350* 25 minutes

ORANGE AND DATE MUFFINS

1 whole orange, <u>unpeeled</u>, cut in chunks with seeds removed
½ cup orange juice
½ cup chopped dates
1 egg
½ cup margarine
1 ½ cups flour
1 tsp. baking soda
1 tsp. baking powder
¾ cup sugar
Dash salt
Blend orange, juice, dates, eggs & margarine in blender
Put dry ingredients in large bowl and add blender ingredients; mix until moistened
Bake @400* for 15 minutes

haron Mierke

RHUBARB PECAN MUFFINS

2 cups flour
¾ cup sugar
1 ½ tsp. baking powder
½ tsp baking soda
1 tsp. salt
¾ cup pecans or walnuts
1 egg
¼ cup veg. oil
2 tsp. grated orange rind
¾ cup orange juice
1 ½ cups finely chopped rhubarb
Combine dry ingredients
Beat egg, oil, juice and rind and add to flour mixture; Add rhubarb.
Bake @350* for 25-30 min

SUNSHINE HEALTH MUFFINS
1 cup buttermilk OR 1 cup milk with 1 tbsp. vinegar added
$\frac{1}{4}$ cup veg. oil
1 beaten egg
1 tsp. vanilla
1 $\frac{1}{2}$ cups flour
$\frac{1}{2}$ cup whole wheat flour
1 cup brown sugar
1 tsp. soda
1 tsp. baking powder
$\frac{1}{2}$ tsp. salt
$\frac{1}{2}$ cup chopped nuts
3 tbsp. wheat germ
3 tbsp. sesame seeds
2 tbsp. poppy seeds
1/3 cup coconut
Combine wet and dry ingredients until moistened
Bake @375* for 20 minutes or until golden

CRUNCHY TOP CRANBERRY MUFFINS

2 cups flour

$\frac{3}{4}$ cup sugar

1 Tbsp. baking powder

1 tsp. baking soda

$\frac{1}{2}$ tsp. salt

$\frac{1}{2}$ tsp. ground cardamom or cinnamon

$\frac{1}{2}$ cup plain yogurt

$\frac{1}{4}$ cup orange juice

$\frac{1}{4}$ cup veg. oil

2 eggs

1 $\frac{1}{2}$ cups whole cranberries

TOPPING: $\frac{1}{4}$ cup sugar

1 Tbsp. grated orange rind

In large bowl whisk together dry ingredients

In separate bowl whisk together yogurt, juice, oil & eggs

Pour over flour mixture

Sprinkle with cranberries and stir until moistened

Spoon into muffin cups.

Combine sugar with orange rind and sprinkle 1 tsp. over batter in each cup

Bake @400* for 25-30 minutes or until tops are firm to the touch